BOOTY HUNTER

HAREM STATION

NEW YORK TIMES BESTSELLING AUTHOR, JA HUSS, WRITING AS

KC CROSS

BOOTY HUNTER

NEW YORK TIMES BESTSELLING AUTHOR, JA HUSS WRITING AS

KC CROSS

ISBN: 978-1-944475-86-4

Edited by RJ Locksley
Cover Design by JA Huss
Cover photo: Sara Eirew

Kay Cross is the not-so-secret naughty pen name of New York Times bestselling author, JA Huss (who normally writes filthy romantic suspense).

Welcome to Harem Station where every perversion is for sale and pleasure is the only objective.

Bounty hunter, Serpint, has just returned to Harem Station with a prize addition to his brother's elite collection of Cygnian princesses. But Serpint sacrificed a lot to bring this little gift home and now all he wants is some no-strings sex with a simple, obedient girl and a bottle of whiskey.

Enter Princess Lyra. She's any filthy-minded rebel's one-night-stand erotic dream. If you don't mind her bad attitude and lack of… luster.

Not quite the obedient girl Serpint was craving. But Cygnian princesses are hard to pass up. Even one with dark secrets. Because they have a very special, very specific, sexual talent.

They glow when they climax.

Lyra thinks she's one of the strong ones. If anyone can resist an overzealous alpha like Serpint, it's her. But his touch makes her light up like the sun. And she has never been with an Akeelian before…

They have two—yes two—super big, super thick, super long… *****

How long can she resist that?

Booty Hunter is the first book in Harem Station standalone series bursting with outlaw alien alphas with extra appendages, runaway princesses with erotic surprises, and a whole new world of secrets, mystery, and sex. Each book is about 80,000 words and *comes* with a glowing HEA.

CHAPTER ONE

As soon as we exit the gate there is nothing to see but the unimaginable beauty of Harem Station. Backlit by a reddish-purple nebula when entering from gate one and the Seven Sisters from gate two, it looks like a piece of Heaven no matter how you get here.

Hundreds of spacecraft orbit, waiting for clearance to dock on the lowest levels of the spinning ring. Thousands of outlaws, assassins, and hunters inside losing and winning money in the casinos, or fucking girls in one of the many harems, or drinking themselves stupid as they forget their recent losses or celebrate their wins.

But it wasn't always that way.

When we first found the place it was an abandoned mystery left over from some long-ago golden age of people who have since all disappeared. We weren't the first to come along and take notice of the empty station. The gates were already here. But everyone knew better than to try and travel through them.

It was owned and operated by a single artificial intelligence that claimed to be tens of thousands of years old. The discovery team who first noticed the AI's station hundreds of years ago were able to send back a single report warning others to stay away before they disappeared, never to be heard from again.

When we first arrived it was nothing but servo bots whirring about in eerie, dark silence. No sound except the continuous clicking and humming of the cleaning bots as they polished and re-polished the gleaming obsidian floors.

In other words… it was creepy as fuck.

It wasn't that we were particularly brave when we arrived, we were just desperate. And just kids. Crux was the oldest at sixteen and Draden and I were the youngest at twelve. The rest were somewhere in between.

We'd done something horrible. Something unforgivable. We had to go somewhere because we couldn't go home to the Akeelian System ever again. From what I remember of that trip, we had an invitation of sorts. Some code that would get us through the aggressive security system on the far side of the gate and allow us to dock.

The AI was charismatic and cordial. But we'd read the report of the first contact team and were expecting that.

We weren't expecting what came next.

Apparently even an AI can get bored after a few millennia. He—ALCOR is his name—had been alone for too long and was craving interaction, so we made a deal. We could stay if we connected him to the galactic web and let him rejoin civilization.

We didn't ask anyone if it was a good idea, we just said yes. Tray—resident evil genius of our depraved gang of seven—happily obliged and several hundred spins later the AI was content and happy and we had a new home.

He was the one who really built this place, but we were the ones who benefitted.

Call it luck, call it fate, call it whatever the fuck you want.

Point is, it's ours now.

And it's magnificent.

There are millions of people on the station at any given time. Most live here full-time, working in the service industry or as AI enforcers. But we get tourists. Not families with kids looking for a beach. No. We get the outlaws. Gunslingers passing through, femme fatales who need a little break, ownerless bots and cyborgs who maybe can't go home anymore because they had an accident with their defense systems… people like that. In fact, the Draco Assassin Association had its headquarters here.

So yeah. We're *that* kind of place.

But it's a helluva nice city with ALCOR in charge. A mile-wide city center along the entire perimeter of the ring filled with parks, and buildings, and there's even several rollercoasters.

And every time I come out one of those gates and see this place… well, my heart just fills with happiness. We all feel that way.

Except for today.

Because there is no *we* on my ship as I pilot towards my private lower-level docking bay and ease the *Booty Hunter* inside.

Draden is dead. Our bot, Ceres, blown up. Even my ship is damaged. So damaged that there is no autopilot right now and I have to concentrate so I don't kill any of the dock workers floating around inside my bay as I bring the *Booty* to rest.

And even though my cargo on ice is none other than the Cygnian princess Corla herself, a princess Crux has been desperate to get his hands all over for the better part of two Akeelian decades, I just can't make myself care.

Draden is dead. Ceres, blown up. *Booty* is damaged.

I will join the many who drink themselves stupid over recent losses tonight.

Crux and Tray wait for me on the other side of the airlock. I stare at them through *Booty*'s side window as I pull on my helmet, pressurize it, and wait for the door to open and the stairs to unfold.

Booty says, "Sa-*a-a-a*-fe to exit-*t-t-t*," in a damaged, stuttering female voice that just… hurts me inside.

"Don't worry, *Boots*. Crux has a team to fix you up good as new. I'll stop by in a few hours and make sure they're treating you right."

"Th-*a-a*-ank you, Serpint-*t-t-t*," she replies.

"It's the least I can do," I say into the helmet mic. The very least I can do.

I descend, limping from the damage I took back in Cetus System, and enter the first of two airlocks, then take off my helmet once it's pressurized. I smell like sweat and battle. Dried blood caked on my head, plastering my dark blond hair to my skull.

Crux immediately brings me in for one of those brotherly half-hugs that remind me of our early days when he handed them out too often in the wake of our many losses.

He says nothing and neither do I.

Tray just stares at me. Frowning.

He doesn't say anything either.

There is nothing to say. The seven of us made it all these years—hundreds of thousands of spins around this station for two decades—intact. And now one of us is gone.

And it's my fault.

Crux claps me on the shoulder as we leave the airlock and take the elevator up to his residential floor at the top of the station. He's murmuring orders under his breath, sub-vocalizing for people to extract the princess from the medical cell inside *Booty* and bring her up to the princess harem.

We exit the elevator and a few bots float up next to me, pulling on the tabs and seals that hold my suit together. One of them takes my helmet. Less than a minute later I'm out of the suit, standing shirtless and bruised inside the medical scanner.

"Two broken ribs, hairline fracture in your left femur, and a concussion," ALCOR states in his matter-of-fact omnipresent voice. "You need a recovery pod."

"Fuck that," I say, stepping out of the scanner. "I need a fucking shower, a bottle of whiskey, and a girl."

"I do not recommend—"

"I don't give a flying fuck what you recommend, *AL*." He hates it when I call him AL. "Draden is dead. Ceres was blown up. And *Booty* can barely talk. I don't even deserve a sun-damned medical pod."

"OK," Crux says to a bot floating by his shoulder. "Stay with him, 749. Make sure he doesn't die on us."

The bot bleeps out a litany of chirps and whistles, a reply that I don't understand, and then dutifully follows me past the training session going on in the harem room.

Crux keeps about a dozen Cygnian princesses here at any one time. Reserved for those who pass through Harem Station on a high note. Most of the rebels who stop here will never be able to afford one hour with these girls, let alone a full night. But for those who can—for those who pull off that big job and come back drowning in credits—they're here. Ready and waiting like perfect little dolls dressed up like queens.

Each one has a brilliant tiara on her head. Sparkling with jewels that match her skimpy lingerie. Each one reclines on velvet pillows and bots hover around them offering bubbly drinks and exotic fruit that comes from distant planets in far-away systems.

There are about half a dozen men here now. Plus one woman, who seems to have found a good match in the princess in blue with sapphires sparkling on her neck, and the cyborg harem master, ready to show these potential customers just what these Cygnian girls can do and why they're worth the price.

I recognize most of the girls but there are some new faces. Every now and then a trillionaire comes through and makes a purchase. Which is why we have me and the *Booty Hunter*. Got to replace those princesses somehow.

But there's a new girl bound to the punishment wall on the far side of the harem room. She is naked, filthy, and gleaming with sweat. Bright pink welts criss-cross her thighs from the cyborg master's whip.

She's been a bad, bad girl.

Some take to their new lives easily. Some are even happy. Let's face it, if you're a Cygnian princess and you end up at Harem Station it's because you were thrown out of your castle back home. There is no possible way for anyone to get past the security in the Cygnian system. They are outcasts.

Bad, bad girls and this is just the place for them.

But this one doesn't seem to feel that way.

She glares at me as I pass by, then tugs on her bindings. I lock eyes with her and she spits in my direction.

I almost laugh, but look over my shoulder instead. Just to make sure the master has seen this.

He has. And he's coming this way, his cyborg face blank. The only indication he's upset is his single vision sensor—just a slash of red light across his forehead—quickly scanning back and forth. And his fingers are transforming into a whip.

I stop and wait, hating myself for the pleasure I'll get watching her be punished, but then again, who gives a fuck about this reluctant princess?

Draden is dead. Ceres, blown up. *Booty,* damaged.

And she tried to spit on me.

I didn't do a single goddamned thing to this girl and she wanted to spit on me.

So you know what? Fuck her.

She asked for this.

CHAPTER TWO

The infamous bounty hunter, Serpint.

I've heard of him. Hell, every Cygnian princess has heard of him. His is the one face we never want to see.

I haven't. Until now.

So ironic that I'm here, captive in the penthouse of Harem Station, and Serpint wasn't the bounty hunter who brought me in.

It was a nobody. Not even an Akeelian. Just some dirty old hunter who was long past his day.

How did things go so wrong?

Forget that, Lyra. The only question needing an answer is… How will you get out of here?

I really fucked up. I really, really, *really* fucked things up.

I don't even know if my sister, Nyleena, is still alive. She has no clue I've been taken. She's stuck back on Bull Station, which, I have come to realize, is far, *far* worse than anything Harem Station will hand me.

This is luxury. Cygnian princesses are treated like the royalty we are.

Were. Since anyone outside Cygnian System is an outcast, Nyleena and I included.

Still. I could do worse than this place.

When we arrived on Bull I had a specific directive. *Just one fucking task, Lyra, and you had to go all rogue.* Now Nyleena is stuck there and I'm here. I knew I should not have trusted that old pirate. I knew it, but I did it anyway. And somehow I was stuck inside a cryogenic pod, transported here, and I woke up with the cyborg harem master standing over me, frowning.

"You don't *look* like a Cygnian princess," he'd said. Which is true. I don't look anything like a Cygnian princess. But there's a reason for that.

My eyes rolled up in disgust at the cyborg master as he made his doubts clear. As if this machine-man had any right to judge me.

So then I was hauled out of the capsule and dragged to the medical station where they poked and prodded me and did the "royal test."

I'm so humiliated. So, so, *so* fucking humiliated.

He did it in front of the whole harem. And the customers!

Bastard.

I put up a good fight, of course. I am bound to the wall now because I have a bad attitude and a filthy mouth. I've already struck a curious customer who'd never seen the "royal test" in person, kicked the cyborg master in his groin as he came at me with his vibrating fingers, and spit on the infamous Serpint after all that degradation was over.

What the hell was I thinking?

I could play along. I *should* play along. Just be one of those pampered girls sitting on velvet cushions being fed bubbly wine and pink tushfruit.

But I am not the kind of former princess who just gives up and goes along. I am bound to this wall without clothing because I simply cannot allow myself to forget that my little sister is stuck back on Bull and I must get out of here at all costs and save her!

I don't think anyone here gives a shit that me saving her is the only thing that matters in this whole galaxy right now, but it's true.

So I must be strong for her. I must be smart. I must… oh, for sun's sake. Why did I resist and be incorrigible? Why did I have to open my mouth and spit on Serpint?

Why did I let this happen to us?

We are both now doomed.

Serpint stops and stares at me for a moment. My spit didn't actually touch him. Just fell on the floor a good foot's length away from his well-worn leather boots. The cleaning bots whir into motion immediately, erasing the evidence.

He looks at me with his dark violet eyes and almost cracks a smile.

Almost. He doesn't quite make it.

He just looks over at the harem master, who makes a face of disgust—one I'm already far too familiar with for being here less than half a spin—and starts walking this way. His fingers already transforming into the whip that has struck my skin several times already.

"I told you to be still and quiet while we figure out if you're up to our standards, Lyra."

I hate the way he says my name, his voice emotionless and hard.

There is no good reply to his statement so I say nothing, my eyes stuck on the whip growing out of his fingers. It's longer now. And thinner. Which means it will sting worse than the last time.

"Hold up," Serpint says, putting an arm out in front of the master as he approaches me. "This is no Cygnian princess."

"She is." The master sighs. The first hint of emotion he's shown since I've been here and it's… resignation. "We did the test."

"I don't believe it," Serpint protests. Then he looks at me, his violet eyes glowing with mischief, and says, "I think you should do it again. Just to make sure."

"No," I say, growling at the master. "*No.* You did the test. In front of everyone." I'm gonna lose it. My voice is trembling as I writhe against my bindings. "You don't need to do it again! You already *know* I'm a princess."

But the cyborg master doesn't agree. And yes, he does have emotions. Because the corners of his mouth lift up in a sly grin. "I think you're right, Serpint. We should do it again. Just to make sure. We wouldn't want trash getting past our screening process. That's not fair to the other girls." His whip fingers retract until they are just normal fingers again. But now they start vibrating.

"No!" I shout. "Get the fuck away from me!"

"I'm sorry, princess," Serpint says, grinning now, just like the master. "*If* you are a princess. But I just don't think it's true." Then his grin falls. His mouth hardens into a straight line as he narrows his eyes at me. "So prove it. Or we'll toss you down into the lower levels and give you over to a less desirable harem."

Lyra, why can't you ever just be good?

Why must you always be such a bad girl?

This is what happens when you don't shut your mouth and do your job. You get captured by pirates, hauled off to Harem, and bound to a wall. While your sister is still on Bull Station waiting for you to save her.

Good job.

You deserve this humiliation.

I do. I deserve it.

Bots hover around me, recording the test the same way they did last time. If I thought I had a prayer, I'd tell them to just watch the footage.

But this isn't about proof. They already know what I am.

This is about Serpint's revenge.

The cyborg master steps close, a little bit to the side to give Serpint, and all the other people in the harem room, a good view. His fingers vibrate like a sex toy.

Because they *are* a sex toy.

He slips them between my legs.

I fight it. I do. I fight it hard.

I will myself not to feel. I force myself to think about Nyleena. The horror she's been through. So much, *much* worse than this.

But I am wet the moment he touches me, the vibrations from his fingers finding my secret spot like he's got a tracking device on my clit.

I hold my breath. I clench my teeth. I stiffen my whole body.

But that just makes it worse. Makes the vibrator between my legs press against my pussy even harder.

Serpint can tell I'm resisting because he steps closer too. Angling his body against the opposite hip from the cyborg master. Making sure the whole room can get a good, long look at me as he reaches up, squeezes my breast, and begins to kiss my neck, just under my ear.

"Give in," he says, nipping my earlobe. "You know you want to."

I lose it.

There is no way to stop this. No way I *cannot* climax.

I come even faster than the last time and a part of me is horrified when I realize… it's him. Serpint. He is the one who made my release bubble up to the surface and…

Glow.

My whole body glows gold.

Because that's how you know you've got yourself a bonafide Cygnian princess.

We glow when we come.

CHAPTER THREE

Fun fact about Cygnian princesses.

They are extra-special horny little minxes and they light up like a sun going supernova when they come.

That's the whole reason Crux keeps a whole flock of sexy swans up here in his private penthouse.

I've seen it before. Maybe hundreds of times. It's hard not to get a glimpse when every time I'm home on the station I have to be up here doing business with Crux.

But this one's glow is… I mean, I'm not trying to be disparaging, but it's… *dull.*

Barely worth watching.

When I glance over my shoulder everyone in the room has lost interest.

A half-breed, maybe? Is that a thing?

I direct my gaze to the cyborg master, who has withdrawn his vibrating fingers from between her legs, and find him cocking one eyebrow at her. Probably thinking the same thing. Probably calculating how much Crux paid for her, adding in the fact that she's unruly and belligerent, and deciding they should probably just send her down to the lower levels and cut their losses.

I let her finish moaning and writhing in her bindings. The best Cygnian princesses can go on for several minutes. Hell, I've seen one who took a full hour to finally calm down. But this one only lasts about thirty seconds.

Still, she's exhausted. It must take a lot of energy to produce color like that, so I give her an extra moment.

She takes it. Drops her chin to her ample breasts and lets out a long exhale.

Then she lifts her eyes to meet mine from behind a curtain of unusually dark hair. Most of these princesses have bright-colored hair. Bellatrix blue, Demon Star orange, nebula green, and even some Arcturus red.

The dark color is a disguise, I realize. And now that I look close I can see that her dye job is fading at random places all over her head.

What is up with this girl?

She seems recovered now. So I say, "That all you got?"

"Fuck you," she breathes, still panting. "Just… go away."

I allow myself a chuckle, but then I remember why I'm home in this condition and it fades like the daylight from three setting suns back on the home planet.

Draden is dead. Ceres, blown up. *Booty* damaged.

I turn away and call out to ALCOR, "Send me a bottle of good whiskey and a girl. I'll be down in my quarters."

"Very well, Serpint," ALCOR says with a sigh. It bothers me when he adds humanoid emotions to his typically flat speech patterns and normally I'd tell him to knock it off, he's fooling no one with that bullshit. But today I can't be bothered.

I'm too fucking sad.

To my dismay the stupid bot Crux ordered to stay with me actually stays with me. Hovering at shoulder height and just a little too close, so I have an urge to swat him away.

But I don't. ALCOR is protective of his stupid bots. Treats them like family—which I can respect. I'd be pissed as hell if ALCOR went off on one of my brothers. Shoot his server beds up with laser fire if he ever pulled that shit.

So fuck it. I let the thing hover.

We descend in a private elevator that opens up right to my quarters. The bot and I move forward at the same time, bumping against each other, and the urge to flatten the annoying piece of junk against the wall almost overtakes me.

But ALCOR must sense this. Because his disembodied voice from nowhere and everywhere says, "Your shower is ready, Serpint. High-heat and lightly scented. Just the way you like it. I've even laced the steam with a mild analgesic. For your… injuries."

I appreciate the gesture. I can't remember the last time ALCOR has bothered to make me comfortable. We tolerate each other, but that's about it.

This makes me sadder for some reason.

"Thanks," I mumble under my breath.

"You're welcome."

"And stop being so nice to me," I growl. "It's making it worse."

"Very well."

I brush him off and walk down the hallway to my bedroom. The lights come on as I approach—a sure sign that ALCOR isn't taking my orders today, because I usually have to give voice commands for lights—and the bot hovers just behind me. I step into the room and press the button on the door to shut and lock it before the pesky thing can follow.

Feeling a little triumphant that I managed to acquire some privacy, I turn to take in my room.

It's big by station standards. Hell, most of the rooms in this place are no bigger than the bed. And more than half of them are just pods.

But mine is extraordinarily large. There's a bed fit for a king. Quite literally. Draped in silver-blue nyla-silk straight from a planet I can't remember at the moment, and more pillows than I can count. I could fuck seven girls at once in this bed. I might even have done that. Once. Back in the old days when I spent more time here.

There's a data station on the far end with a direct link to *Booty* and the docking bay, but the flashing red letters spell out OFFLINE on the screen. Telling me that she's not fixed yet.

I try not to think about that and let my gaze wander to the metal binding wall where I like to secure girls with magnetic bracelets. I have another one just like it out in the living room. Just thinking about the energy it takes to sexually punish a girl right now…

No. That's not the kind of sex I'm looking for today. Just a simple girl who likes to fuck is about all I can handle at the moment.

So I look at the bathroom instead. Which is another perk. Bigger than I need, filled with more gadgets than I'll ever use, it's what I miss most when I'm on ship because we have no water rationing here. This neighborhood has more floating chunks of ice than we could use in a million years.

Tiled in black obsidian from floor to ceiling and a shower that practically makes love to me, it's the epitome of luxury.

All of us brothers have quarters like this because even though Crux *runs* the station, he doesn't *own* the station. We all have equal shares in Harem. It was part of the deal with ALCOR from the beginning.

My home.

It hasn't changed since I left it several months ago. No reason it should, it's just…

I sigh and sit on the bed, my ribs screaming as I bend over to unfasten the tabs on my boots.

It's just… constantly being alone on the ship, hunting down runaway princesses, making trouble and getting into fights… it's starting to get old.

Plus, I think, kicking off the first boot, I wasn't really alone before and now I am.

I kick off the second boot and fall back onto the bed. Stare up at the ceiling.

The lights dim into something atmospheric, and I curse ALCOR under my breath. But I don't tell him to get the fuck out. Because then I really would be alone and I don't know if I could handle that right now. So I say, "Thanks, man. But I'm fine. Really."

ALCOR says nothing in reply. Perhaps respecting my wishes, perhaps he's at a loss for words. Draden was his favorite from the start. His wise-cracking and good-natured personality made him easy to like. Plus, he was so young. I was young too, just a handful of months older than Draden, but a handful of months has more meaning to Akeelians.

I chuckle a little, thinking about how childish Draden and I were when we got here. Playing war with anything that even remotely look like a weapon. Running all over the station with no one to reign us in but our little army of servo bot minions. Oblivious to why we were here or how we'd never go home again. But we didn't care. This station was a little kid's playground back then. All this space and only the seven of us to use it.

It was great, I realize. *He* was great.

And now he's gone.

Forever.

If ALCOR has emotions—and that's certainly debatable—then he's as sad as I am right now.

Wincing from the broken ribs as I force myself to sit up, then stand, and wince again, I realize I will have to get fixed up in a medical pod eventually. The ribs I can take. They will heal on their own no matter what. But the hairline fracture in my leg will just get worse the longer I leave it.

Still, it can wait another day at least.

I just need a shower right now.

I strip off my pants, kicking them into a corner that will be piled with dirty clothes before I leave again on the next job, and wander into the bathroom naked.

It's filled with steam. A slight medicinal scent in the air. I breathe it in deep, thankful that ALCOR is an asshole who doesn't listen because this is some fast-acting good shit and the pain in my ribs begins to ease with just a few breaths.

I limp into the shower stall and ease myself down onto the bench. There's a setting on the control panel that will eject little disposable scrubbing bots and normally, if I was myself, I wouldn't use that in a million years… but I'm not myself today.

So I reach over and press the stupid button.

A flurry of fluffy washing bots emerge from a side panel and the minute they hit the water they erupt with suds that smell like air, and wind, and other things you find on habitable planets but never on space stations.

They descend on me, whirring and pressing against my skin in a massaging way that feels much better than I remember.

I scoot forward a little, then lean back. Slightly reclined as I open my legs and… yeah. Like I said, this shower can practically make love to me.

Maybe I don't need a girl. I should tell ALCOR to nix that request. Why bother when I can just jerk off alone?

Alone.

I close my eyes and sigh. Reaching down to fist the shaft of my growing cock.

There is no particular girl in mind because there is no particular girl.

Never has been.

I really am alone.

"Serpint." ALCOR's voice comes from the ether. "Your girl and drink are here."

"Great," I say, still jerking off. "Just leave her in the living room. I'll be out when I'm done."

I'm not in the mood to explain that I've changed my mind. Both about the booze and the girl. I think all I want to do is go down to the medical bay and sit with *Booty* while they fix her. Be there when they bring her back online. Tell her we're OK. Everything's gonna be OK, even though it's not.

She's all I have left and unlike ALCOR or the cyborg master, she *does* have feelings. Real, humanoid emotions. *Booty* is a true super-sentient AI. She has hopes and dreams and she's experiencing the same loss as I am.

The four of us have been a team for almost a decade and now we are down to two.

I come uneventfully, squirting semen onto the obsidian floor, and then decide not to continue. I force myself to stand and let the scrubbers wash my back. They gently massage their way up and down my spine, descend down to my thighs and scrub my cock as it continues to swell and harden.

I have to pull my shit together for *Booty's* sake. She will pick up on my feelings and amplify them. I could send her into a depression and that's the last thing either of us needs right now.

Man up, Serpint. You're the fucking captain. There's no room for emotions today.

Right.

I tap the END icon on the control panel and all the little scrubber bots disappear into a recycle bin so they can be broken down and printed into new scrubber bots. Or whatever the fuck they'll get made into next.

The steam and water cuts off too, then hot air floods the shower room. I stand there, arms open, legs spread, still very hard—and I will be for a while because that's the natural consequences of only coming once—and try to enjoy the next thirty seconds of relaxing calm.

But like all good things, it ends. The hot air cuts off and the shower door slides open, ALCOR's not-so-subtle signal that I have to deal with reality.

I step out, warm, dry, and a little more relaxed than I was a few minutes ago. Then hate myself for that.

"Serpint," ALCOR says. "May I offer some advice?"

"No," I growl, stepping out of the bathroom. "And I really fucking mean that," I add. Because he's not an obedient personality. At all. "Get the fuck out of my quarters."

"Very well."

I don't know if I just imagine that I can feel his absence when he disappears, but I think I can. Because the whole place becomes just a little more empty.

Good job, Serpint. Got just what you wanted.

I open the door to find the stupid bot waiting for me, chirping a greeting I don't understand. Why couldn't Crux assign me a bot that spoke a real language?

Ignoring it, I walk down the hallway, hand automatically reaching down for the hardness between my legs out of habit, thinking I'll get myself a drink to enjoy as I get dressed and come face to face with…

The half-breed princess.

Bound to my punishment wall with magnetic bracelets. A giant pink bow wrapped around her waist and an electronic note hovering across her ample tits that reads: *She's all yours. Enjoy.* In bright green letters.

"What the fuck are you doing here?"

CHAPTER FOUR

Fun fact about Akeelian males.

They have two extra-long, extra-hard, extra-thick cocks.

But the only time you know they have two cocks is right after they come. Because one requires the other to emerge. Which means fucking an Akeelian is never quick or easy.

"I was brought here," I snarl at him, trying to pull off an attitude. But my eyes are stuck on his body. And even though I've already seen him shirtless, he was sweaty and dirty and now he's clean, and smells like a fucking planet.

For sun's sake. Why? Why did I mouth off up in the harem room? Surely, if I had just kept my trap shut I'd have ended up somewhere better than here. With *him.*

He slides his jaw to the side, gritting his teeth, clearly as irritated at my presence in his quarters as I am at being here. "*Why* were you brought *here*?"

"I dunno. Maybe the note floating in front of my tits explains the situation. I'm a fucking slave, remember? And I'm magnetically bound to this… this stupid *wall.* Obviously I didn't put myself here."

He and his little hovering bot walk towards me. Naked. Because of course he is. His two cocks swinging between his legs like… like a fucking alpha Akeelian who obviously just jerked off in his shower because that's the only way both his stupid, super-long, super-hard, super-thick cocks would be visible.

Gross.

His hand swipes through the glowing green letters emblazoned in front of my breasts, dismissing it. Then he snatches the note from the ribbon and opens up what is not really a note, but more like a thick packet of printed papers.

Paper. Who the hell uses paper?

"Oh, for fuck's sake," he says, rubbing two fingers alongside his temple.

He didn't bother to shave, I notice, then internally chastise myself for noticing. But also because now that he's had a shower and washed the blood off, the stubble is mostly… attractive.

"What?" I ask. "What do they say?" I lean forward as far as I can, but a sharp sting shoots through my body, forcing me to recoil back. "Shock bracelets?" I say, so pissed off. "You've bound me in shock bracelets?"

It's not just bracelets, either. They are on my ankles and my legs are spread—not quite wide open, but near enough. So a second shock slides up my legs too.

"Stop shocking me!"

"You're shocking yourself, princess." Then he tilts his head a little and adds. "If you really are a princess."

"You have some nerve," I say, then regret it. Maybe if I wasn't a princess I could get out if here? Gain my freedom and go save Nyleena?

I know for a fact that Harem Station only keeps Cygnian princesses as captive slaves. All the other harem rooms are filled with girls who get paid.

There is no paycheck in my future, and no saving my sister, if I continue to tell the truth about what I am.

"I was stolen," I say, literally thinking on my feet. "Right from my bed. For no good reason."

He lifts his eyebrow at me, tilting his chin down, so he's looking at me with one of those condescending expressions that say, *You're full of shit.* "You glowed downstairs, princess. Not well, I admit."

Fuck him.

"But a glow is a glow. You're a half-breed at the very least."

Half-breed. As if there was such a thing.

There is no way to be a half-breed Cygnian princess. You either are one, or you're not. And I am one. But maybe I don't have to be?

I still have my disguise. And it's still partially working. If I could just get another dose of palladium antagonist I could recharge it. I could make the glow disappear long enough to get the hell out of here.

Palladium can be found in lots of things. Circuits, mostly. It's all over ships. In the wires and just a little scrape off the outer coating of a hull could get me enough to make another dose of antagonist.

In fact, what if… *what if* I could convince this moron that I've been pretending to *be* a Cygnian princess instead of the other way around?

Oh, Lyra. Sometimes you're a genius.

So I say, "There's no such thing as a half-breed princess."

He squints his eyes at me, understanding that this declaration comes with a 'but.'

"But one can... *pretend* to be a princess. If they have the right concoction. In fact," I say, becoming braver as my lie fully forms in my head, "I bet half of those 'Cygnian princesses' up in that special harem room are fakes." I do air quotes with my fingers as I say this. Even though my arms are spread wide so it's kinda pointless.

His eyes dart to each of my hands in quick succession, noting my futile attempt at air quotes, then he laughs. Loud. And says, "You're full of shit. We do DNA tests, *princess.* And you can't fake a glow."

He's right. There is no way to fake a glow. You either have luminous flux or you don't. DNA tests are easy. Everyone fakes those these days. Which is why they have that humiliating glow test in the first place.

But lies are cool like that. Once you have a good one it's easy to build on. "You *can* fake a glow. I know, because I did it. You noticed it, right? How dull it was? How... lackluster it was? How no one in that room paid any attention to me."

Except him, I don't add.

"I was trying to get into the Cygnian System and I thought it would be the perfect disguise."

He laughs again. Even louder. "Why the hell would you do that? Bunch of bloodthirsty, antisocial motherfuckers, they are."

Like he has any room to talk. Akeelians are known for their murderous ways. Not to mention their desire for sexual dominance. Bunch of alpha-assholes is what they are. So he's got no room for his high-and-mighty attitude.

"Because they stole my sister. That's why."

It's… a little bit of truth. Kinda.

He huffs. And even though I don't want to, I can't help myself. I look down at his two cocks. Still very erect, still very ready. Because they are doing that tremble thing. That shaking thing they are known to do. Like they can sense a female and they are eager to be inside her.

This makes him laugh. "See something you like, princess?"

"I told you," I say, forcing myself to look into his eyes. Deep, purple-violet eyes. I don't understand why Akeelians have to be so damn attractive. Why do they get neon eyes in brilliant colors? Eyes that can transfix a girl in seconds and have her begging to be fucked by their two cocks?

My gaze redirects over his shoulder so I don't give him the satisfaction of catching me in a moment of weakness, and I continue. "I'm not a princess. I made a concoction out of palladium and took it. It doesn't work very well, as you saw upstairs. But it works well enough to trick dumbasses like you Akeelians. Obviously."

"You're lying."

"Am I? Then how do you explain my glow, or lack thereof? Hmmm?"

"What is it made of, this concoction? Exactly?"

"Wouldn't you like to know."

He raises his eyebrows again. "You're going to try to extort me?" He holds up the thick stack of papers. "When I'm holding your life in my hands?"

"What do you mean?"

"I mean…" He stops to laugh. "I mean I own you now, *Lyra*. Crux and ALCOR signed you over to me. I quite literally hold your life in my hands."

"Ridiculous! You cannot own a person!"

"And yet… it appears that I do." He tosses the papers onto a nearby table and turns his back, flashing a set of perfectly sculpted shoulder muscles as he walks down the hallway. "Bot," he calls. "Get her ready for me. And bring me that bottle of whiskey. I don't need a glass."

The bot says, "Very well. Mr. Serpint. I will do that. Right away, sir!"

But then the little bot hesitates, hovering. Turning its front side to me, then towards the hallway, like it has a question.

"What?" I ask it.

"Which do you think would make him happier? Fully restraining you first? Or delivering the bottle?"

I roll my eyes. These 700 series bots aren't the most clever. "Whiskey," I say. "It's always whiskey."

Which is another lie. It's always sex with an Akeelian male. But I'm not in any hurry to add more restraints.

I'm already bound by my feet and wrists.

Where else could restraints go?

CHAPTER FIVE

The bot delivers the whiskey and I drink it straight from the bottle as I wait for my hard-on to ease up enough to pull on a pair of pants.

Fucking curse of the Akeelian cocks. Always so goddamned demanding.

Once that's sorted I take the bottle over to my data station and pull on my boots, staring at the screen as I absently fasten them.

"Come online, come online, *come online*, for fuck's sake!"

But the word OFFLINE just flashes at me in bright red letters.

I hear the girl protesting as the bot gets her ready. Gasping and swearing once she realized what all that entails.

I smile a little. Can't help it. She's a very bad princess.

Is she a princess? Is she telling the truth about some crazy palladium concoction she whipped up to make herself glow?

I tap the screen and pull up the galactic web, doing a search called: *What makes Cygnian princesses glow?*

Several million responses pop up—must be a popular search—and I tap the first one and begin to read.

Cygnian princesses require a constant supplement of palladium xenide in their system at all times in order to glow. Palladium xenide can be found in tushberries, passion limes, youthfruit, and sparkling wines made from these fruits.

Huh. No wonder Crux is always shoving fruit and champagne down their throats. They need it.

I should probably know this already since I'm a fucking shareholder in the only Cygnian princess harem in the galaxy outside their home system, but I've never been into them. They are all so… girly. So bright and beautiful. And honestly, who cares if they glow when they come? Ya know? So they get off for a long time. Doesn't do anything for me.

I like girls with a little spirit in them. Tough ones. Mouthy ones. Ones who can drink, and swear, and don't need to eat passion limes all day long. I like a girl who can take care of herself and maybe, if I find myself in an uneven fight, help out a little.

Like this one, I reluctantly admit. Maybe she's not a real princess? Maybe she does have some secret concoction? And maybe there is some covert plan cooked up by women who think they can fool us?

Crux will want to know about this. Our whole business could be at stake.

Lyra is right about one thing. You can't really *own* a person. And we don't really own them up in the penthouse harem. We just… indenture them for five hundred spins once they get here.

Yes, it's shady on all kinds of levels, but the law is the law. If you find yourself on Harem Station without entry papers you must pay your way in through servitude. And since all these princesses came to us through unscrupulous bounty hunters—like myself—they all find themselves here under those conditions.

We give them a choice, of course.

They are welcome to go serve their sentences down on the lower levels. Harems, or restaurants, or whatever the hell job they want. But they won't find conditions like this down *there.*

There's a very good reason outlaws come here for rest and respite. It's because nobody fucks with us. The Prime Navy doesn't even patrol here. Not even when they should. ALCOR might be annoying as hell, but he's built himself a formidable security force over the past several thousand years. They patrol both sides of our gates and their motto is, "Shoot everyone unless they have the proper entrance signal."

We are probably better protected than the stupid Cygnians.

Besides, we practice equal-opportunity entrapment. We indenture anyone who enters without permission, not just princesses and women. Hell, ALCOR even indentures the sentient ships. That's how I ended up with *Booty.* And look, she's happy.

Isn't she?

I stare at the blinking OFFLINE message and sigh.

But my point is… these princesses aren't really slaves and they're not really owned, either. It's just the best deal they're ever gonna get so why not make the most of it?

Plus, Crux sweetens his pot to the point where they can't refuse. Hell, they don't want to refuse. The princess harem is pure luxury. And we don't force them to have sex with the customers. We just encourage them to find one suitable to their tastes and have a good time while their every need is taken care of. Then, when their five hundred spins are up and they've paid their entrance fee, we let them indenture themselves to a new host. We take half the dowry, of course. But they still make out with millions of credits.

Or they could stay with us. Take fifty percent of each customer and call this place home.

And if they just want to walk away penniless, we let them do that too.

None of them even consider that.

It's a good deal if you're an outcast princess who can't go home. There are far worse people in this galaxy than us.

It's wrong. I get it. But who cares? We're a bunch of fucking outlaws, what do they expect?

Besides, almost no one can afford these girls. It's not like they have to deal with the riff-raff down on the lower levels. They only meet the best people. The richest outlaws. The smartest, most ruthless ones. And if any of those assholes—because they are *all* assholes—lays one meaty finger on them or hurts them in any way, ALCOR just blips them out of existence.

Even after they leave us.

ALCOR might be a dick but he's one hell of a protector when it comes to these Cygnian girls. They are all fitted with neural devices with a direct link to the ultimate alpha male. He might not be able to personally leave the station but he can upload a copy of himself into any ship he wants and take care of business.

And he has done that for them. Many times.

So yeah, I'm not gonna feel guilty about what we do here. Not for one second.

The bot appears in my bedroom doorway, bleeping out beeps and chirps that make no sense. But I get the feeling he's saying something along the lines of, *She's ready.*

So I push away from the data center and stand up, my ribs still aching, my leg still weaker than it should be, but mostly feeling… better.

I don't deserve to feel better. Not when Draden is dead, Ceres was blown up, and fucking *Booty*, the only female in this entire galaxy who has never let me down, is down.

And it's all my fault.

The bot chirps again, this time with more enthusiasm.

"I'm coming," I growl, pulling on a shirt. Because I am. I need to get up to the docking bay and take care of my ship.

She's the only thing I have left.

CHAPTER SIX

OK. Note to self. Never presume that wrists and ankles are the only anatomical parts that can be restrained by an Akeelian alpha-asshole.

"Ow! Ow!"

"So sorry," the little bot chirps. "It's just a very tender spot."

"Which means," I hiss through clenched teeth, "they're not supposed to have magnetic bars clamped to them. This is—ow!—barbaric!"

My poor nipples. Oh, they will never be the same. You wouldn't think that two teeny-tiny magnetic bars could apply so much pressure, but holy mother of suns, these fucking things have some power behind them!

"It'll be over soon, don't worry. It goes fast."

"What?" I blink three times. "What goes fast? This is it, right? This is the restraint?"

"Oh, no." The bot laughs in its little bleeping language. "This is just to prevent the blood."

"Blood?" I cringe.

Look. I am one of those tough girls, ya know? I can shoot a target with a plasma pistol like a pro. I can kick, and I can flip, and I can punch. Hell, I even have better than basic knowledge of how to kill six different humanoid species with a single knife thrust.

But… "Blood coming out of my nipples? What the fuck, bot?"

"No, no, no," he beeps. "The magnetic bars will prevent the blood."

"That's not any better! What are you doing that you need to control the amount of blood that might gush out of my tits?"

"Just…" He whirrs over to a chest of thin drawers on the far side of the living room and a little appendage emerges from his hovering spherical body to open one. He whirrs back to me, dangling pieces of metal in his little grippy hand. "These. A simple piercing, that's all."

"Oh, hell no! Hell. The fuck. No. He is not piercing my nipples!"

"I'm afraid he is, princess. It's his standard procedure. I've taken all the classes the master cyborg has on Master Serpint and in no syllabus was there ever a scenario that didn't involve piercing all the lady parts."

"All the lady parts?" I look down between my legs. "Surely he does not plan on—"

"I'm afraid so. But don't worry. I'm very good at this now. I completed my certification course a few dozen spins ago—"

"What?"

"—and I was top of the class."

"This isn't happening!"

But then he turns into a whirling blur and the next thing I know… "Holy. Mother. Fucking. Suns!"

"There, there. The first one's done. That went well, don't you think?"

I am crying. Like real fucking Cygnian princess tears. Which aren't easy to produce under the inhibitor I'm taking, that's how bad that shit hurt.

He's done the second one and I think I even faint for a moment. Because when I open my eyes, he's hovering between my legs with yet another little piece of metal.

"No! No, no, no, no, no… pleeeeeeease, no!"

But it's done. And this time I do pass out. Because I wake to the sound of a metal collar clamping around my neck.

I wilt, my body exhausted. My head falls to my chest and I practically dangle from the wall.

This place is not better than Bull Station. It's just dressed in pretty clothes and fancy fruit drinks.

When I look up I swear to the sun the bot is chuckling at me. "What the hell are you laughing about?"

"I'm pretty sure you're not going to like that."

"Like what? What now?"

His little grippy-hand appendage points to the collar and then I think he shakes his head and make a chirp that sounds a little too much like a tsk-ing tongue. If he had a head and a tongue and wasn't just a floating blob, that is.

I look down, trying to get a glimpse of what I'm not gonna like. But all I see is a faint green glow emanating up from my neck. "What is that? Are those letters? Does this collar say something? What's it say?"

"It says," the commanding voice of Serpint booms from the hallway, "'Serving Serpint.'"

"Serving… you mother-sunning bastard. What the hell is wrong with you? You had him pierce my pussy!"

"Oh." Serpint laughs.

"That's not funny! It fucking hurt!"

"Well, it kinda is, princess. Because I really…" He laughs again. "I didn't tell him to do that."

"What?" I look at the bot.

It chirps out protests. Something about syllabi, and scenarios, and standard Serpint procedures.

"You little shit! I don't want to hear your excuses! I told you not to touch me!"

"Well, that's interesting," Serpint says. "You can understand that thing?"

I scoff at his insult. "The 700 Series was built to entertain three-year-olds, you arrogant prick. Of course I can understand him!"

Which makes Serpint tilt his head. "Not where I come from."

Ooops. Ha. I forgot. Most children outside the Cygnian System don't grow up with a palace filled with nanny bots.

"I'm just saying it's an easy language."

"Hmmm," he says, rubbing the stubble on his chin.

Shit. Change of subject time, Lyra. Before he starts to put two and two together and realize what you're really up to here. So I say, "I see you decided to put on clothes while I was being *tortured*. Might I have some as well?"

He stalks forward towards me. Deep violet eyes blazing. He stops just centimeters from my face and looks down at me from his superior height.

I don't want to look up. I do not want to meet his gaze and get lost in those stupid violet eyes.

But I can't help myself.

I sigh and get lost. That's how galactically beautiful these Akeelians are. "Don't look at me that way."

He just stares. And growls. God, I've heard of those growls. I've heard all kinds of stories about Akeelians growing up. But I thought they were mostly myths. Not until I arrived here at Harem Station this morning did I even consider that all the rumors might be true.

But they are.

Akeelians are an all-male race. There is no female in their species. They mate with other races and then the girl babies take on the race of the mother and the boy babies take on the race of the father. Which is Akeelian. Hence, all Akeelians are male. With those crazy-beautiful eyes, and two extra-long, extra-hard, extra-thick cocks. And a deep growl that has been known to send women into a sexually-induced trance state.

They are like something out of an erotic fairy tale.

If I ever get out of here and manage to find a way to save Nyleena and go through with my plan to get us where we're going, I will be famous. And once they hear about me back home, all my hundreds of princess cousins will die of jealousy over my adventures on Harem Station.

But right now none of that is looking likely because I'm pretty sure this asshole knows I'm lying about something.

"What?" I snap. "Why are you looking at me that way?"

Serpint reaches up, brushing his fingers down my cheek. He looks at his fingertips, rubbing them together. "What the hell is this?"

"What's what?" I ask, feigning ignorance. Because I just remembered… I was crying.

"Something pink."

"It's makeup, you simpleton." I add in an exaggerated eye roll for good measure, praying to the sun gods he buys my lie.

He growls again.

"Stop doing that!"

But he just continues and for sun's sake, I think the rumors are true. Because a deep-rooted throbbing begins in my lower belly and pulses out… "Ow. Oh, shit! That hurts!"

Never mind. Erotic excitement over. I double over a little, as far as I can with the bindings, and try to force my upper thighs together because the throbbing is really pain from my newly pierced pussy.

He sighs. "I have something for that."

"For what?"

"The pain. I really didn't tell him to do that."

The bot protests again but I spin my head to look at him and say, "You shut up about the stupid standard procedures! He just said he didn't, OK? You fucked up. Be a big bot and just own it, for sun's sake!"

When I look back at Serpint he's fishing through one of those skinny drawers that produced my newly acquired sexual jewelry and I catch him smirking.

"It's not funny. I've been mutilated."

"Oh, come on. It's not that bad. And this'll help." He turns around and walks towards me holding up a little metallic tube. "If you don't mind."

"If I don't mind what?"

"Well, you don't seem to have the use of your hands right now, *princess*." He exaggerates that word, like he's not sure which part of my lie is a lie and he wants me to know that. "So I'll have to apply it for you."

And then he grins.

"Or," I say, thoroughly disgusted at his innuendo, "you could just release me and let me apply it myself."

"Where's the fun in that?"

"In my hands," I say with fake sweetness. "Instead of yours."

"Exactly." He squirts a bead of purple goo out onto his fingertip and smiles. "So… do you want the pain relief or not?" I open my mouth to speak but he says, "Shhh. Before you answer, just know that I *will* be touching you later. So think hard about this before you make a decision. There'll be consequences."

"Pervert."

"Oh, I won't touch you with my hands, princess. Unless you beg me to."

"Asshole."

"Allow me to demonstrate." And then he pinches the air with his thumb and forefinger and spreads them wide. A display appears, lit up with a control panel. "Which one should I try first? Hmmm?"

"What are you talking about?"

But he must make up his mind because he taps the display and my nipples begin to vibrate. And while I might admit this could be pleasurable had my nipples not just been pierced by a deranged nanny bot, it is not pleasurable *now*.

"Ow!"

"See," he says, the vibration fading. "And believe me, that was the low setting. It only gets better from there."

"Better?" I snap. "You're insane. You're an insane, barbaric, two-cocked jerk!"

"One drop of this on those tender spots, princess, and it heals like magic. By tonight all the discomfort will be forgotten. The pleasure from the nipple rings will blow. Your. Mind." He bobs his eyebrows up and down at me as he grins. "So decide. Pain? Or pleasure?"

I hesitate. Because if he touches me I will probably glow again. And I don't want to give him that privilege. I don't want him to think I'm… into this. Because I'm not. I'm *so* not. Not to mention my inhibitor is already beginning to fail. If I don't recharge it soon it will stop working completely. And then he'll know I'm real. He'll start asking questions. Or do a galactic facial recognition search using my real identifying features.

And once that little secret is out, there's no hope of saving Nyleena and completing our mission. Well, not really completing it. We had no intention of completing it. But the other mission, the one where we get where we're really going—there'll be no hope for that.

But if he is going to keep me here, and do these things… wouldn't it be better if it felt good instead of terrible?

God. I'm rationalizing! Why am I trying to rationalize this? I'm the insane one! I've lost my mind. I've been blinded by the erotic myths. And the two cocks. And the… the… "Stop staring at me with those stupid eyes of yours!"

"Last chance. I've got shit to do. And I don't care either way."

"What… what shit to do?"

"Yes or no?" he says. "My ship came in with damage and I need to go see her and make sure she's OK."

"Her?" I laugh. "Your ship is a woman?"

"All ships are women, don't you know anything?"

I almost say, *Well, our ships are not female.* But I catch myself just in time. Because I think I've heard that before. That male ships are dangerous, or something. And no one gives a ship a male personality except us. Cygnians.

"And this one," Serpint continues, "is much more than just a woman or a ship. She's sentient and she's my partner." He sighs, looks away for a moment, then adds, "The only one I have left. So make up your fucking mind. I need to go."

There is an abrupt change in his demeanor with the mention of this woman-ship. Something sad, or maybe even worse than sad. Something gravely serious is happening in the moment and I get caught up in it. Start to wonder about it.

He reads that hesitation as a no and caps the tube, shoves it in his pocket, and walks away.

"Hey!" I call. "Wait!"

"Too late," he calls as he enters the elevator.

"But—"

"Bye, princess. Enjoy what's coming. And just know… I'll be watching you the whole time."

"What's that mean?"

But the elevator door begins to close.

"Hey! Stop! Wait! Can I come too?"

I could totally scrape some palladium off the hull of his ship!

But the last thing I hear from Serpint is the sound of a sad laugh echoing though the closing doors as he disappears.

A data screen flows out from my collar. Wavy lines and images materialize and resolve in front of my face.

"What in the name of two-cocked assholes is this?"

"Your tasks for today, princess," the bot says.

"What? What tasks? I'm bound to a fucking—" And just as the last word leaves my mouth, I fall to the floor. Magnetic bindings released.

I lie there in a lump of exhaustion for a few seconds, then turn over and find the bot hovering above me on the other side of the new data screen.

"You better get started," he says. "Serpint is known for his extensive task lists."

"Like you'd know." I snort. "Have you even worked for him before?"

"Princess, please. I'm deeply sorry for the misunderstanding—"

"Misunderstanding?" I snarl. "You pierced me! Three times!" But that's when I notice what's happening on the data screen. "Oh, hey. What's that countdown for?"

There's an icon of a bedroom. Which makes me roll my eyes. If that alpha-jerk thinks I'll be waiting for him in his bedroom when he gets back, he's sadly mistaken. But next to the bedroom icon is a little clock counting down from ten.

"Hurry up," the bot says. "You're running out of time!"

"Time for—"

And that's when the vibrations start. Deep down in my belly, like before, but not only there. The bracelets and anklets are pulsating too. It's not the same as the last time. It's still painful, but that's mostly because of the piercings, not the output settings.

In fact, if I wasn't so sore it would be undeniably pleasurable.

Damn. I wish I had that analgesic cream. Then I might get some satisfaction out of this whole miserable experience.

I try to block out the pain as the vibrating builds, both in oscillations and intensity, thinking maybe… maybe I can handle this. Maybe I can still enjoy it a little. Because I can feel the glow building inside me. Eager to escape after all these months of being locked inside. Eager for a real release after so many dull disappointments.

There's a noise now. Kinda low and thrummy. But it begins to build, the tone getting higher and higher with each passing second. It's something familiar. Like a charge… like something charging…

Oh. Shit.

And then the counter ends at zero and the data display flashes a bright red right in my face.

I realize—too late—what he's doing.

And in that same moment the charge finds its final level of intensity and releases.

The shock hits my entire body. The bracelets and anklets send signals up to the collar, which sends signals down to my nipples and pussy rings, which reverberate back up to the collar, and back out to my wrists and ankles.

My entire body bucks up in a spasm of erotic climax.

And this time when I glow… it is *spectacular.*

CHAPTER SEVEN

I close up the data display, Lyra's list of tasks complete, just as the elevator doors open onto my docking bay level.

And what is the first thing I see?

Booty.

Still tethered in the vacuum of hard space outside the motherfucking airlock.

"What the hell is this?" I snarl at the closest attendant. "Why the hell isn't she in a medical bay?"

"Oh, I'm sorry, sir," the woman says. "We're waiting on one to become available."

"Available?" I ask with mocking disbelief. "There is no waiting for *my ship*. Get her hauled into medical or I'll have your fucking job and you'll spend the rest of your servitude here scrubbing the decaying interior of old bots!"

Her collar tells me who she is, who she works for—Crux—and how long she has left on her sentence. Which is a lot of spins. Either she's a brainless fuck-up and has had spins added as punishment… or she's new here.

I try to calm down. Give her the benefit of the doubt and be a little understanding of her new situation. But I'm not sure I accomplish that because the next thing out of my mouth is…

"What are you fucking waiting for? Find her a sun-damned medical bay!"

She opens her mouth, squeaks out, "Ye-ye-yes, sir. Right away, sir," then stops and sputters again. "Buuut… but which ship should I kick out of a bay, sir?"

"Oh, for fuck's sake. I'll handle it myself."

I turn back to the elevator, get back in, and go up to the penthouse to find Crux. I could, theoretically, kick out any ship I want to get *Booty* the attention she deserves. But I've been gone for a long time and I have no clue what Crux is doing that has things so backed up.

Better to err on the side of respect and caution than fuck up his plans.

He'd do the same for me. And if there's one thing the seven of us—six of us, now—realize, it's that we have to stick together at all costs.

Alone we are nothing. We all know that. But together we are this. We are a team. We are Harem Station.

The elevator doors open to the harem room. I step out and look around, searching for Crux.

"ALCOR," I say.

"Welcome back, Serpint. You look… better."

"Liar," I mutter. "Where's Crux? I need to talk to him about *Booty*."

"He's in the cryogenic lab. I was actually just going to intrude on you for help about that."

"About what?"

"He's refusing to thaw out the new princess."

"Corla?" I ask. "The one we brought in?"

The one who caused Draden's death, is what I really mean. Crux has had a thing for this princess for ages. I cannot remember a time when he wasn't talking about her, or looking for her, or cursing her name.

But it was always while we were drunk. So no one cared, really. The ramblings of a man on whiskey.

So when I was passing through Cetus on my way back from a too-long trip to Hydra—that ended up being a bust and the biggest waste of time in my life—and heard that the mythical Princess Corla was on the station where we stopped, already neatly packed up in a cryo-capsule... well. You don't just pass up that kind of booty.

We took her.

And Draden died in the process. A stream of plasma coming from a dark hallway. Slicing across his neck and cutting through his guts. Ceres took the next hit. Blown into millions of pieces.

I was already maneuvering the princess's cryo-capsule into the storage slot when I looked out *Booty's* side window and saw the whole thing in real time.

Booty took over, closing the hatch. Less than a picosecond to determine there was no sense in delaying our departure since our two partners were undoubtedly damaged beyond repair.

Then she took the brunt of the battle. A fucking SEAR cannon wiping out most of her personality systems and a few other backup circuits—like auto-pilot—as we flew out of range and entered the nearby gate.

How the hell did that pitiful little station in Cetus get a hold of a goddamned SEAR cannon?

I was too busy piloting a dying ship to think of the princess again until I had to contact Harem to let them know I was coming home with losses.

And even through the audible grief in Crux's voice and the sadness on his face as he stared back at me from the high-res communication monitor, I could feel his excitement.

Princess Corla was real. And I not only had her, I was bringing her to him.

I think I hate that bitch.

Turning the corner I spot Crux inside the cryogenic bay, staring down at the capsule.

What the fuck?

I palm my hand past the biometric security, and enter when the door opens.

"She's still frozen?" I ask, a little too much residual anger in my voice. "For sun-fuck's sake. Why haven't you thawed her out? You've been pining over this dumb bitch for as long as I can remember."

He doesn't lift his head, just slides his eyes in my direction. Staring at me from underneath a curl of dark hair. Shoots me a look of…

"What?" I snarl. "She's the whole fucking reason—"

"No one told you to steal her for me, Serpint. That was all you."

"Yeah, well." I huff out a laugh. "Maybe I got sick of your fucking whining all these years? Maybe I just wanted to shut you up for once. Maybe I just wanted to bring home the one thing…"

But I don't have in me to keep going. So I just stop talking.

He redirects his eyes down at his princess and then leans over, placing both hands flat on the glass, and hangs his head. "It's not right," he says. "I can't fucking do it."

I take a few steps closer. Looking down at the princess's face. She's older than the one I have up in my quarters. Older than most of them out in the harem room too. More like a queen than a princess. She's one of the silvers. You don't see many of them. Most of the girls we see pass through here are golden-haired. That's the default color, I guess. We get a few blues, a few more greens, and every now and then a red or an orange. But we've never had a silver before. Or a pink, for that matter.

They are the top of the Cygnian food chain, so to speak.

I mean there are literally hundreds of thousands of princesses. Hell, every pure-bred female in Cygnian System is technically a princess. Those are the golden ones. The nobodies. The kind who get kicked out for being rebellious and angsty.

The other colors are higher up in the spectrum. True royalty. And I've heard, though this is nothing but rumor—because pretty much everything you read or hear about the Cygnians is just that, rumor. They are super isolationists—but I've heard that the pinks and the silvers are all in line for an actual *throne*.

They don't rule outlying territories, or random moon bases, or floating stations like the golds. They rule planets. And one of them rules the system with the king.

"Who is she?" I finally ask. Probably a question I should've posed to him a decade ago. Definitely one I should've had the answer to before I decided to fucking *steal* her.

Crux shakes his head with defeated sadness.

"Please," I say. "Do not tell me this one is the actual fucking *queen*."

Crux sighs. "I wish I could, brother. But it'd be a lie."

"I stole the fucking queen?" I blink my eyes three times quickly.

"You did, Serp."

And despite the fact that I lost two partners in this... I cannot help but be just a little bit proud of myself.

I stole the motherfucking Cygnian queen.

And I'm still alive.

How?

Booty, I realize. And Draden. And Ceres.

There is a long stretch of silence after that revelation. Long stretch.

Then Crux straightens up and turns to me. "We can't thaw her out, Serp. The moment we do they can track her. And I don't care what ALCOR says, if the Royal Cygnian Navy comes after us, there's no way we can win."

"I didn't say we'd win," ALCOR interrupts. "I said we'd give them a helluva fight."

"We'd lose everything," Crux says.

"So wait a minute," I say, holding up a hand. "I did all this for a fucking woman we can't even wake up?"

Crux looks me straight in the eyes, which are a lighter violet than mine, something almost neon swirling around inside his irises, and he nods. "That's the fucking situation."

He walks out of the cryogenic bay, leaving me alone to stew in that final thought.

ALCOR says, "Did you need something, Serpint?"

Which makes me remember why I'm here. "Yeah… *Booty* is still in the vacuum. She needs to be moved into a bay. Like *now.*"

"I'm rearranging the schedule as we speak. Sending orders to move her to Bay 201 now. Anything else?"

"Um…" Because there was something else I wanted to talk to Crux about. "Oh, yeah. You ever heard of a fake Cygnian princess, ALCOR? Because this one you gave me, she's claiming she's not a princess. That she cooked up some magic potion that allows her to glow."

"No," ALCOR says. "I can't say there's anything in any of the galactic databases on that one."

"Hmmm. Well, what do ya make of it?"

"Lies," he says simply. "Just lies. We did the DNA test and it wasn't faked. We can tell. And even though her glow is dim, it's real. So she's nobody special, that's for certain, but she's legitimate."

"You're sure?" I ask. Because something is definitely off about this girl.

"One hundred percent."

"Hmmm."

"You could feed her some passion limes. See if that brings her luminous flux up a few levels. That would provide the peace of mind you're looking for."

"Do we have any of those?" I ask, kinda wondering if he's become telepathic since I was last home. How does he know I'm having doubts?

"I'll send some up to your chambers."

"Thanks," I say.

"You're welcome, Serpint. Do you want me to come with you? Keep an eye on her?"

"You mean you're not already?" I say, kinda smiling. But not really.

"You told me to stay away. So I've stayed away."

"Since when do you listen to me?"

"Since you came back without Draden," he deadpans, his voice suddenly very mechanical. Like he needed to turn off his emergent feelings to speak that sentence.

"Right," I say, then exit the cryo bay and make my way back to the elevator.

I want to go drink myself stupid. I want to lose myself in drugs. Or fuck some random woman who is not obligated to serve me because she's here illegally. I want to forget what happened. And that it's all my fault.

But I don't do any of that.

I go to Bay 201 and wait for *Booty* to be brought in out of the cold darkness of vacuum so I can be there when they spin her back online.

Be there to say, *Welcome back.*

Or, *You're gonna be fine.*

Or, *I'm sorry.*

CHAPTER EIGHT

So apparently my job today was to clean Serpint's quarters. Like I'm the fucking bot in this place. He had fifteen tasks and each one came with a countdown. If I didn't start the task within ten seconds I got a shock. If I completed the task in the allotted time frame, I got a gold star.

A gold. Fucking. Star.

And… wait for it.

The bot got to assess me when I was finished.

On a scale of one to ten, how well did Lyra complete the task?

Was her attitude:

A. Positive and upbeat

B. Apathetic and neutral

C. She complained the whole time

Shit like that.

I looked the tin can pile of junk in his optical sensors and told him, "Look, you little nanny bot prick. If you give me anything other than a ten, and I get a shock, which sends me into exhaustive convulsions because of the *fucking piercings* you forced me to endure, I will kick your little ball ass out an airlock."

I don't think he's used to dealing with anyone older than a toddler because I have completed every single task with a perfect score and my attitude was the mirror image of positive and upbeat.

It's not like there was anything to really do. It's very clear that Serpint hasn't been home in ages. There was a small pile of charred, smelly clothes in his bedroom and his bed covering was slightly wrinkled, but other than that it was just going through the motions. Dusting. Running maintenance protocols on the auto-cook, and the shower, and the recycle systems. Which was basically just pushing a few buttons while the bot fed me instructions from the manual. And ordering ingredients for his favorite meal. As if this barbaric bounty hunter can cook.

No one *cooks.*

But I did it and it's like… fate or something. Because when the organic ingredients arrived for some weird meal called Mossian fowl with herb pasta, it came with passion limes.

I laughed out loud when I saw them. So loud the bot asked me if everything was OK.

Why, yes, you dumb little ball of metal. Everything is just perfect.

Because passion limes are the third ingredient needed to make a new princess inhibitor. The citric acid reacts with the powdered palladium and when you add xenon the magic happens. Poof. Palladium antagonist is born.

I have a feeling I can get the palladium off the hull of his ship. I'll just feign interest in her and ask Serpint to show me around. I'm gonna change my whole demeanor. Be a good little outlaw princess and bat my eyelashes at him. Then he'll take me to the ship, I'll figure out a way to get the bot to distract him, and presto. Done.

The last thing I need is the xenon. Which can be found in most lamps on my home planet, but I can't even reach the lights in this place. The ceiling is like six meters high and try as I might, the bot refused to float up and extract a bulb for me.

However… xenon can also be found in medical lasers. So I have a plan for that too.

Nope. I didn't get any more shocks today, but I do have an honest-to-god problem with the… uh… piercing *down there*. How do I put this? All this walking around the apartment caused a little… chafing.

And it fucking hurts. It fucking hurts like a mothersunner. My poor pussy. It hasn't seen any action in so long and now it has more than it can handle. Plus, my inhibitor is totally wearing off. I am sweating little pink beads. It's a good thing this bot is so stupid, because otherwise my jig would be up.

So the plan is wait for Serpint to come home, complain—loudly—about how my new mutilation is probably infected, and make him take me to medical. Then… I don't know. I'll need another distraction so I can steal the little xenon capsule from the closest laser.

I'll figure it out when I get there.

It seems like a long shot, but I am nothing if not a schemer. I wasn't chosen for this little mission I'm on for being demure and obedient.

Besides. I'm desperate.

Desperate people do desperate things and lots of times they work out.

Most times, anyway.

Well, maybe half the time, if I'm being honest.

But I'll take fifty-fifty odds. Because my only other choice is to tell these asshole Akeelians the truth and hope they decide to help a girl out.

Not likely.

So scraping palladium off hulls and stealing xenon capsules from medical lasers it is.

Then… maybe I can drug him? Yeah. I'll drug him. I'll put something in his whiskey. He has pain goo lying around. Chances are he's got something in capsule form I can slip into his nightcap, right? Worst-case scenario I'll sweet talk the bot into giving me access to the bathroom auto-pharmacy. I snooped while I was in there and Serpint's got a whole list of recreational drugs on his approved list.

He's such a catch, isn't he?

I snort.

Then I'll do my little chemistry experiment and *boom*. I'm not a princess anymore.

I'm sure this is all gonna work out.

Pretty sure, anyway.

I sit on the couch and fold my hands in my lap, trying to be casual, then cross my legs and swing my foot, satisfied I've got it all figured out.

In other business, I did find some clothes, so I'm not naked anymore. I stole a pair of boxer shorts—who wears those anymore?—and a t-shirt from his closet. Which, by the way, was one of the tasks I had to complete on the list.

Organize Serpint's closet by color.

As if that took more than ten seconds. He owns black t-shirts, white t-shirts, black military pants, two leather jackets, and one pair of boots.

But he does have nice hangers. They're made of the same soft silver material as his bed cover.

He gets a gold star for that.

I sigh and look around his living room. It's a big space. "Is he coming home soon?" I ask the bot. "I'm so bored."

"Master Serpint has been in the medical bay all day waiting for *Booty* to wake up."

"Who the hell is Booty?" Does this asshole have a girlfriend? I huff a little. Not possible.

"The ship."

"Ohhh." I laugh. "I should've guessed that one."

I've heard about bounty hunters getting overly attached to their sentient ships. He's definitely one of those freaks. The way he acted after mentioning she was hurt. Yeah, pretty sure this guy has a thing for his *girl.*

I yawn and reposition myself on the couch so I can put my feet up. It's been an exhausting day and it's not even half-spin yet. He could be gone for hours.

"So… maybe I could like… use that magical shower he's got in the bedroom?" I ask the bot.

"I don't think so, princess."

"But I'm dirty. All this manual labor has worked up a sweat. Don't you think Serpint would appreciate you taking initiative to clean me up so when he gets home I'll be pretty and smell like flowers?"

The bot considers this.

"Please. I've been good."

He makes a beep that is definitely the bot version of a snort.

"I have. And I'm sore from being manhandled. I'm sure Serpint—"

But just as I'm about to finish begging, the door slides open and the man of the hour walks in.

"How is *Booty*?" the bot asks.

Serpint looks at him and growls. And it's not the sexy kind like he was doing earlier, either. It's the don't-fuck-with-me kind.

Well. That sucks. He's in a bad mood. But I need to slip into my first scheme immediately if I have any hope of pulling this off.

So I groan. "Oh… ohhhhh… ohhh."

"What the hell is wrong with you?" Serpint asks, grabbing the bottle of whiskey that came with the food and pouring it into a glass.

"She's experiencing discomfort," the bot chirps.

"Something up, princess?" Serpint asks, turning his back to me to open the door to the fridge. He reaches in, grabs something and then turns, holding it in his hand so I can't see what he has.

I squint my eyes at him because he's squinting his eyes at me.

"Ohhhh… ohhh—"

"Cut the shit. I know what you're doing."

"What?" I ask, sitting up. Then for real, I squeak out a little gasp of pain because seriously, that pussy ring might be infected and it really does hurt like hell.

"Where did you get those clothes?" he asks.

I look down at his t-shirt and boxers, then back up at him. "Surely you didn't expect me to stay naked all day."

He takes a sip of his whiskey, then tosses a passion lime up in the air and catches it with the same hand.

I squint my eyes again and he grins. "Fancy a little passion lime, *princess*?"

"Uh… no. But thank you."

"Why not?" he asks, stalking towards me. "Afraid it'll bring your luminous flux levels up enough to make you glow the way you're supposed to? Hmm?"

"What?" I put my hand over my heart. A spectacular attempt at indignation.

Which he does not buy. Because he pulls a folding knife out of his pocket and cuts the lime in half.

Good god. Just the smell of the little green fruit is enough to degrade my inhibitor.

I stand up and walk away. But the rapid motion makes the folds of my pussy rub against the new ring and I have to squeeze my legs together to put pressure on the shooting pain between my legs.

"Oh, shit," I say. Then I turn on my best, demure, sad, I'm-a-damsel-in-distress face and say, "Really. There's something wrong with me, Serpint. I think I need to go to medical."

"Need a little passion lime boost, maybe?"

"Enough with the jokes, OK? I've been mutilated by that rogue bot and now my most cherished lady parts are infected."

He glares at me. "Eat this first. Then after I check you and find you're telling the truth, I'll send a medical bot up to take care of it."

"A bot?" I shout. "A bot is what did this to me! I want to see a real medical professional. And I can't eat that," I say, pointing to the fruit.

"Because it will blow your cover and out you as a princess?"

"No, because you can't eat raw passion limes, you caveman." So much for the good princess act. "They're poisonous unless they're fermented."

"ALCOR," Serpint says.

"Yes, Serpint."

"Is she telling the truth?"

"About what?"

"What do you mean about what? You hear everything, *AL*. Stop pretending that you're not spying on every living and non-living thing on this station every second of the spin."

"I was busy elsewhere and did not hear the conversation. Please repeat it."

"She said," Serpint growls through gritted teeth, "that passion limes are poisonous unless they're fermented. Is that true?"

I get the feeling Serpint isn't on good terms with the station AI. But I *am* lying. And this ALCOR, he will know that.

I start to come up with another reason when the AI says, "Yes, that's true."

"Well, why the hell did you tell me to feed her passion limes?"

Ooooo. Shit. They've been talking about me. That can't be good.

"I didn't, Serpint. I said tushberries."

"You did not. Play the conversation back."

"That conversation has been deleted."

Oh. Man. These two… if the AI was humanoid I get the feeling Serpint would knock his ass out right about now.

"Can I please go to the doctor now?" I whine. "I was mutilated by the bot and now it's infected. I need medical attention."

"Would you like me to make you an appointment?" ALCOR asks.

Holy suns! The AI is on my side! I smile sweetly at Serpint and say, "Why, yes. Thank you. Today, if possible." Then quickly frown to make sure they all get that I'm not feeling well.

"You have an appointment with the harem medical office in twenty minutes. See you then, Lyra."

"Thank you, ALCOR. I appreciate it."

"No problem, princess."

I have to turn away from Serpint so he doesn't see my smile

Because it's big. Very, very wide, and huge, and just...

"He's lying. You're lying. And don't think I won't make you pay for this. Bot," Serpint says. "Order me a tray of harem fruit and champagne. We're going to eat dessert first when we get back from medical."

I sigh. As quietly as possible. And mentally pat myself on the back as the bot chirps out his reply. Because my plan is still in motion. All I have to do is talk him into a pit stop at the ship to scrape the hull and I'm golden.

Quite literally.

This man will never see my true color if I can help it.

CHAPTER NINE

"Let's go then."

Lyra snorts. "I need clothes. I'm not going anywhere in your underwear. Which is not fashionable, by the way."

I give her a slow blink. "You organized my closet, correct?"

"So?"

"So you saw what I own. If you'd like to help yourself to a pair of my tactical pants, go for it."

"What I'd like to do is help myself to your auto-shopper and pick out something that fits."

I can't even manage a laugh. It just comes out as a half huff of contempt. "No, princess, that's not in your future. You're a giant pain in my ass and you're lying. Servants don't get rewarded with auto-shoppers when they lie."

"The AI said—"

"The AI lied and we both know that. And the second you get back you're going to eat that fruit and I'm gonna—"

"You're gonna *what*?" She takes a step towards me. "Make me glow?" She manages the laugh I couldn't and then whispers, "I don't think so."

"Well. Then I guess you go as you are. Ready? Because if we miss this appointment I won't allow another one."

She purses her plump lips at me. Were they always that plump? And are her eyes lighter?

"Let's go," she says. "My barbarically tortured lady parts won't heal themselves."

I wave her forward into the elevator, feeling a little bit of satisfaction that she's barefoot, wearing my t-shirt with no bra, and sporting my underwear. Which *is* in fashion here on Harem Station. Everyone knows Akeelian males wear boxers. Our two magnificent cocks require spacious undergarments.

The door slides closed and we ascend up to the harem room in silence. She's got her arms crossed over her chest. Probably trying to hide the fact that she's braless and this elevator is chilly.

But the ride is short and a few seconds later the door slides open again and she steps out first, her bare feet padding on the cold, dark obsidian floors.

She stops to look around for a moment. There are at least two dozen girls lounging about on couches, chairs, and in the laps of customers. Everyone turns to look at us, their eyes squinting as they focus in on her, and then the girls without partners begin to whisper behind cupped hands.

Lyra lifts her chin, looks over to the left where the medical scanner is, and then walks towards it like she's the one in charge.

I will say this. She definitely *acts* like a princess. She might not look like one at the moment, but there's no way to hide her innate haughtiness. She is used to being in control. She is used to getting her way. She is used to having… power.

And she's not giving it up easy.

"Over here," I say, guiding her with a hand on the small of her back when she continues to head towards the scanner. "There are private rooms this way."

"Imagine that," she says. "Good to know you have some respect for the girls you imprison here."

I just suck in a deep breath and hold in my response.

The door to the check-in area slides open as we approach and ALCOR says, "Go with the bot, Lyra. Serpint, wait here."

"Gladly," I say, sinking into a plush chair in the corner.

I need to check on *Booty* anyway. I stayed there all afternoon but they told me she probably wouldn't be back online until tonight.

My thumb and forefinger pinch the air, then spread a data screen open into the space in front of my eyes. Sure enough, the red letters are still blinking OFFLINE.

Something must really be wrong. Something bad. Something that can't be fixed with a software update or the usual decontamination procedures. She's never been offline for more than a couple hours before. And that was when we upgraded her into the current ship. That's the biggest procedure she's ever had. So this… this is not good.

Loud crashing sounds come from down the hallway where the exam rooms are. Then cursing. Which gets louder when a door opens.

"Oh, hell no. Oh, hell the fuck no." Lyra appears in the waiting room, shaking her head. "He's the doctor?"

I swipe my data screen closed and glance over her shoulder to find the cyborg master rolling his eye. Which is not easy to do since it's just a red light across his forehead. But he manages it.

Which kinda makes me smile and ask, "What's the problem now, princess?" in a fake, condescending voice.

Which she doesn't even bother to notice. That's how angry she is.

"He's not touching me! He is not a doctor. He's a… he's a sexual predator, that's what he is."

"Lyra," the cyborg master says in his calm, I'm-a-doctor-voice. "Not only am I wearing a doctor's coat, but I'm also certified in three thousand, two hundred and seventy-one surgical procedures on seventeen humanoid species. I *think* I know what I'm doing."

"Certified!" she says. Too loud. Too high-pitched. Like she's about to throw a royal fit. "Certified?" she squeals again. "The bot who did this to me said he was certified too!"

"Lyra," I say, tired of this day and unable to hide the fact that she's wearing me down. "Just—"

"No! No. No. No. That thing isn't coming near me again. I'm putting my foot down! I want a real person!"

She actually stomps her foot.

"OK." I sigh. "ALCOR, what should we do?"

"Lyra," ALCOR says in a voice that's far too sweet and understanding for the situation. Usually he just barks orders at temperamental princesses. Does he like the girl? Is he infatuated with her? What is his deal?

"What?" she snaps.

"If you don't want the harem doctor to touch you then I'm afraid your only choice is to have Serpint help with the exam. We do not have human doctors on Harem."

She glares at me, but then her eyes begin to shine with what might be tears. Seems like she's had enough of this day as well. I think this might be her breaking point.

I stand up and walk towards her, grabbing her hand as I pass, and say, "Come on, I'll make sure nothing bad happens," as I pull her back down the hallway.

There's a moment just before I enter the room where she hesitates. But I just tug her harder, pull her inside, and then the cyborg master follows us and locks the door behind him after it slides closed.

Lyra jerks her hand from mine and backs herself up into a corner.

"For sun's sake," I say, rubbing two fingers alongside my temple to stave off a headache. "It's a fucking thirty-second exam, Lyra. In five minutes you'll be done, your little *problem* will be fixed, and we'll go home."

I cringe, realizing my mistake. My quarters are not her home.

But that's not what she focuses on. She looks around the room, trains her eyes on the set of laser pens hanging from a holder, and then glares at the cyborg master like she might chop his head off with one of them.

"Just take off your clothes and get in the scanner," I say.

Her head spins to the gyno-scanner. It's not really that intimidating when it's in standby mode. Just a long machine the length and width of a body made out of white plasteene.

"*Please*," I say. That headache is in full force now, no matter how hard I rub my temple. I don't have much fight left in me today. I really don't. Maybe I should just give this girl back and be done with her? Simplify things? Because I've got enough problems of my own. I don't need some lying, neurotic princess making things worse.

"Fine," she whispers, pulling her shirt over her head. And even though I've seen her naked—hell, the whole harem has seen her naked, including the cyborg master—he and I both turn our heads.

A moment later she climbs up into the scanner and we turn back to look at her. Find her biting her lip to stop a whimper, but not really succeeding.

I glance at the cyborg master and give him a nod to proceed. But just as he's about to push a little button on the control panel I reach up and grab his hand.

"No," I say. "Do not restrain her. She's had enough of that for one day."

The cyborg maser shrugs and presses another button to activate the machine.

Three things happen simultaneously.

One. The thin laser-hood arc comes up over Lyra's head and begins to scan her body.

Two. The lower part of the machine splits in half and begins to bend, forcing her knees up and her legs open.

And three. Lyra freaks out, and tries to make a run for it.

I quickly push her back down and glance over at the cyborg master, who is shooting me an I-told-you-we-needed-restraints look of satisfaction. Also difficult to pull off with only one red slash of an eye.

"Just… be still," I tell Lyra. "It's practically over already."

"I cannot believe this is happening," she whimpers.

I really do feel sorry for her. It's rough. I get it. She doesn't know us. My bot pierced her without her permission—or mine, for that matter—and now she's in pain and being forced to endure yet another moment of total humiliation in order to get relief.

But I wasn't lying when I said it was a thirty-second procedure, and when the scanner stops and the laser hood arc returns to its starting position tucked neatly away behind her head, she just closes her eyes and lets out a breath.

"OK," the cyborg master says, looking at the scan on the large wall screen. "Well, it's swollen."

"No shit, genius," Lyra snaps.

"There's my girl," I say, kinda chuckling.

"Shut up."

"So did the bot fuck up? Or what?"

"No, actually," the cyborg master says. Then he points to an image of Lyra's labia, which has been magnified like… a billion times. I glance at her to see if she's gonna throw a tantrum about that, but she's got her hand over her eyes and she's taking deep breaths. "The piercing is right where it's supposed to be. Directly behind the lux node. See?"

I lean in and squint my eyes. "That?" I ask, pointing to a little nub of flesh. "Huh. I always thought that was a clit."

"Oh, for fuck's sake," Lyra wails. "It figures. Stupid men."

The cyborg master ignores her and so do I. Because the shit works the same from my experience.

"The problem is," the cyborg master continues, "it's..."

"It's what?" Lyra asks. "What's wrong with it?"

"It's like ten times larger than normal. Are you on any medication, Lyra?"

"What kind of medication?"

"Anything," I say, rolling my eyes with frustration.

"No," she says.

But it's a lie. I've only known her half a day but she lies so much, I can tell now.

The cyborg master knows she's lying too. Seems like she came in that way.

"Well, it's not the piercing," he says. "So unless you tell me what's really going on here, the only thing I can do is relieve your discomfort with analgesics."

"Cool, let's do that," she says, still covering her eyes with her hand. But then she removes it and sits up a little bit. "Not you," she snaps. "Him."

And she points to me.

I raise my eyebrows at the cyborg master and he just shrugs, reaches into a little drawer, and pulls out a hypo-spray. "Here," he says, handing me the small cylindrical container. "Spray her with that. But you have to hit the node or it won't help. Precision is everything in this case."

Then he gets up, walks to the door, unlocks it, and leaves.

"Thank the sun," Lyra says. "OK, hand it over. I'll do it myself."

"Whatever," I say, tossing her the tiny canister.

She catches it one-handed, sits all the way up, and bends over to look between her legs. She sprays it, waits, then shakes her head. "Get that asshole back in here. It's not working."

"You probably missed," I say, so fucking done with this girl. "Did you not hear the part where he said precision is everything? Give it to me."

She pulls her hand away when I reach for the spray, but I snatch it anyway.

"Look," I say, any sympathy I had for her gone. "Just lie back and shut your mouth for three more seconds so I can fix this. And then you know what?"

"What?" she growls.

"You're not coming back with me. You're staying here. I've had enough of you."

"Good!"

"Good!"

"So do it and leave."

"I will."

I grab the little doctor's stool, sit my ass down, and slide between her legs.

"This isn't happening," she moans.

"Believe me," I say. "The last thing I wanted to do today is play doctor between your legs in an exam room."

"It's your fault."

"Ha," I laugh, leaning in a little to try to find the little lux nub. It's a lot harder to see when it's not magnified up to superclit levels. "It's your fault, princess. You heard the doctor. The bot didn't fuck up. You're on something and you're lying about it. So no, actually. This isn't my fault."

"Just spray it already!"

"I can't find it," I say.

She laughs so loud I startle backwards in the rolling stool. "Oh, that's classic."

"Shut the fuck up," I say, inching toward her again. "You've got like a million folds of skin down here."

"Stop talking about my lady parts or I swear I'll—"

"You'll what?" I snap, reaching in with my fingers to part the soft folds.

"Ohhhhh," she says.

"What?"

"Oh, my God, no."

"No what?"

She sits up and slaps my hand away. "Don't touch it."

"I have to touch it, Lyra. I can't see it. Open your legs wider."

"No, no, no. I think it's fine—Oh… oh shit!"

"What? What the fuck is your problem?"

She reaches for me, clamps her fingers onto my shoulders with such force I'm pretty sure her fingernails have drawn blood, and opens her mouth in a gasp.

"What?" I say. "What are you doing?" She pants hard for a few seconds, her eyes wide and… "Are you… are you sparkling?" I ask. Her eyes… they're not dark anymore. At least not all of them. They're shooting beams of pink light.

She just pants again. Then looks down between her legs. Which makes me look too.

She's glowing. The most spectacular Cygnian princess glow I've ever seen. And it's pink too.

"Holy shit," I say, standing up too quickly. The stool slides out from under me and crashes against the wall. "What the hell is that? Who the hell are you?"

"Oh, my God. Ohhhhhh…. Oh, my God!"

"Lyra!"

"Fuck me," she says, her eyes wide with… is that desperation?

"What?"

"You have to… oh, oh, ohhhhhhhh, myyyyyy Gaaaaaaaad!"

Then so much happens I can barely keep up. She lunges forward, grabs my shirt, pulls me back with her so she can sit on the table, and then her hands slide down my arms, reaching for the button on my pants. She pops it open and the next thing I know she's pulling out my cocks.

Both of them, because somehow in the last five seconds, I've gotten hard. And I didn't finish this morning when I jerked off, so yup. Cock number two is ready for the reward he was denied earlier.

"You have to!" she says. "You have to. I can't take it anymore! Please!"

And OK. Look, here's how it works. My cocks have needs, and apparently her pussy has them too. And there's this magnificent pink glow shooting up from between her legs. Which might actually contain some kind of aphrodisiac, because I'm suddenly so hot for this girl, I need to fuck her just as much as she needs me to.

I have no idea what's happening, but then again, I'm a man. An Akeelian man. With needs. And this glowing princess is begging me to take her to the depths of ecstasy.

So I do what any man in this situation would do.

I slip my cocks inside her. Both of them, at the same time, right into her glowing, wet pussy.

She gasps as I do this. Like loud. "Ooooooooo," she says, her perfect, plump lips making a tight o that seems very erotic for some reason.

"Oh, yeah," I say. "Keep making that face." I don't know why I say that, it's dumb. But she either doesn't hear me or doesn't care. Because she sits all the way up, scooting her ass towards the edge of the scanner, her legs still bent from the position of the machine, and spreads them wider for me.

"Serpint," she breathes.

"Yeah, baby," I say, then cringe. For fuck's sake. *Say something good, Serpint!* "Yeah, you like this, don't you?"

"Yes," she squeals. "Harder, please. I need to come *right now.* I feel like I'm gonna die if I don't come. Right. Now!" She thrusts her hips forward as she says each word, then without warning she wraps her legs around my waist, like she's begging me to pick her up.

So I do. I slide my hands under her knees and lift her off the scanner, twirl her around, and crash her back up against the wall.

"Oh, yeah!" she moans. "Harder!"

"I don't know if it gets any harder," I say.

"It does," she whimpers. "It has toooooo! I need to come right—"

And then she does.

She comes so hard, her whole body lights up with glow. And there is nothing dim about this glow. This glow is as brilliant as seven suns. It's an exploding supernova. It's bright as the birth of a galaxy.

And it's pink.

So fucking pink. Pink like clouds above a sunrise. Pink like tushberries. Pink with sparkles shooting from her eyes like the evanescent bubbles in champagne.

I come too. Both cocks. Right inside her without a second thought about consequences.

If someone asks me later how long we got it on in this exam room I'll just lie. Because two minutes with this girl is all it takes.

And even after I'm done she quivers in my arms, her legs shaking, her whole body trembling for many, many minutes.

I just hold her there. Pressed hard up against the wall as she shivers and shakes. And watch her light flicker. On and off, and on and off.

Caught in a spell I never want out of.

I want to look at her for a thousand spins and then a million more, she is that beautiful.

CHAPTER TEN

Best-laid plans and all that good junk, right?

"So…" Serpint says.

"I don't want to talk about it."

"Cool," he says. "Cool. I get that. But—"

"I just want to go home," I say.

"Right. Well. Here we are."

The elevator door slides open and we both walk back into his quarters.

Funny how things change. Because after he fucked my brains out—and boy, did he ever. Seven suns, I've never been fucked like that before. Two cocks! Two. I just can't even describe the feeling. And I realize it's partly due to the inhibitor I've been on, but… it was more than that.

The myths about Akeelian men are true.

But the funny part is that after all that talk about him leaving me up in the harem, how he was so done with me, how I was getting on his last nerve…

We're right back where we started.

His place.

Which I just called home.

I close my eyes and sigh, sinking onto the couch, completely exhausted. All my plans ruined. My disguise blown. Because my hair is already turning pink again. My eyes as well. I don't need to look in the mirror to know that they're almost back to normal. Not that it matters after I lit up the whole exam room like an exploding sun.

"Well…" Serpint sighs. "Hungry?"

I scowl up at him. "What? No third degree? No 'you're such a liar, Lyra?' No 'who the hell are you and why are you here?'"

"Uh…" he says, rubbing a hand over the stubble of his jaw. "Well… just please tell me you're not a queen. Lyra? You're not, right? Because I have enough Cygnian queen problems at the moment and Crux is gonna fucking kill me if you turn out to be a queen."

I have no idea what he's talking about, but I can't be bothered with his trivial problems right now. I just made a complete fool of myself back in that exam room.

Begged him to fuck me! Holy suns!

But I couldn't help it. It's like… like I was on that inhibitor too long and then the two glow tests this morning kinda set things in motion. My body is in active rejection. Even if I could get the palladium and the xenon it probably won't even work.

And what's the point now anyway?

He knows.

"Are you a queen?" he asks again.

"No," I say. "No. We only have one queen, for fuck's sake. And I'm not her."

"One?" he asks, like this is confusing. "Only one? Then what's going on? Who are you running from? Why did you get kicked out?"

"Just..." I sigh. "Can we talk about this tomorrow? Can we eat? Or something? Or can I take a shower? I just... need to process what to do next."

"What do you mean 'do next'? What's going on?"

"What part of 'tomorrow' don't you understand? I don't want to talk about it."

"Well, I do. So you better start explaining or I'm calling Crux and telling him I've got a pink princess up here pretending to be... whatever the fuck it was you were pretending to be."

"Oh, will you now?"

"Yeah." And then he says, "ALCOR, get Crux down here right now. We have a problem," in the direction of the ceiling.

But oddly, the AI doesn't answer.

"ALCOR!" Serpint tries again.

And again... nothing.

"Ha." I laugh before I can stop myself.

"Fucking thing. ALCOR!" He yells it this time. But I'm pretty sure AIs at this level can hear just fine when he whispers.

"He's ignoring you," I say. "Because he's on my side."

"Bullshit," Serpint says. "You don't have a side. That motherfucker's priority is the station. Which means *he has to answer me*!"

He yells that too.

But still, the AI ignores him.

"Any more brilliant threats, genius?" I might gloat a little as I say this.

"What's going on? You were on something, weren't you? Something to stop your glow and change the color of your hair and eyes."

"It's none of your business."

"It is now, princess. Because you're sitting in my quarters, on my station, and for all I know you've got a fucking tracker in your head and the goddamned Cygnian Navy is on their way here to attack us and bring you home."

I scoff. "Believe me, no one is coming to save me, Serpint. But thanks for your concern. I can see you're all torn up about my situation."

"What situation? And why wouldn't they come? You're one of the important ones. I know that much. We don't ever get pink princesses here. So who are you, really?"

"I'm Lyra," I yell. "And I'm so fucking done with this day! Why can't I just take a shower, eat something, and go to sleep? I've only been on the run for three days and I've already had enough. Why can't you just... be normal?"

"Normal?" He laughs. "I don't even know how to answer that. I am normal, you're the one who got me mixed up in this huge mess."

"Well... then just sell me a ship and I'll be on my way tomorrow. How about that? That work for you?"

"*Sell* you a ship?" He just squints at me. "You have credits to buy a ship?"

I sigh. "Again. None of your business."

"Can you fly a ship?"

"I'm not answering that."

"So you *can* fly a ship," he says, his voice softer now. Like he's talking to himself and not me.

The bot hovers over to him, stopping at his shoulder, and begins to beep out a whole litany of bullshit.

"What's he saying?" Serpint asks.

Luckily for me, Serpint can't understand him. "He says you should let me take a shower, feed me, and then give me your bedroom so I can sleep. Alone," I add. Just to make it clear that we won't be having a repeat of the exam room later tonight.

The bot begins beeping like crazy and I swear to the seven suns, I just want to slap that thing so hard right now.

"That's not what he said." Then Serpint opens up that air data display thing and pulls up a program that will translate the 700 Series bots. "Say again, bot."

Well, fuck. Now I'm really done. Because a tinny, automated AI voice says, "She's the queen's niece and she wasn't kicked out of the Cygnian System."

"She wasn't?" Serpint says. "Then why—"

But the bot interrupts him. "She escaped from prison. Was tried for treason and found guilty."

"Oh-ho-ho," Serpint says with a guffaw. "Was she now?"

"That's not really what happened," I say, unsure why I'm even telling him that. "He's just pulling things off the galactic web. And everyone knows that anything people report about Cygnians is just gossip. Nothing escapes from that system."

"Except you, apparently."

"And her sister," the bot adds.

"Would you shut up already?" I hiss.

"There's two of you?" Serpint asks, raising his eyebrows. The bot begins to beep and chirp again, but

Serpint swipes his hand through the data display and turns the translator off and the annoying robotic voice goes silent.

"*No*. Another lie," I spit.

But he doesn't believe me. Because he turns away, rubs a hand over his scratchy jaw and says, "Holy suns. Two of these mouthy little pink minxes."

"She's not pink," I say.

Serpint spins towards me and points his finger. "So you *did* escape with her!"

I just sigh and close my eyes, wishing I could go back three spins and make better choices. "Can I please just take a shower now?"

Serpint thinks for a moment. But I'm pretty sure he's not wondering if he should allow me to take a shower. "Treason, huh?"

"I told you, that's not what happened."

"Then what did happen?"

I can see he's not going to give up on this so I sigh, like I'm giving in, and formulate a new lie on the fly. "We… got caught."

"Doing?"

"I mean, you have a whole flock of Cygnian swans—"

"Swans?" he asks.

"Yeah, that's what we call princesses at home. If your feeble brain is having trouble keeping up, I'll use the word 'princesses,' better?"

He points at me. "You're breathing thin atmo right now, Lyra. Don't get mouthy on me or I'll drag you down to Crux, no asshole AI required."

"I'm just saying, we get out all the time. You know this because this station is famous for collecting them. It doesn't take much brain power to figure this out."

"So what did you do?"

I bite my lip.

"And don't lie to me. I can totally tell."

"Fine," I say. "I helped someone escape a while back."

"Escape? What? Why are people escaping?"

"We're a closed system, Serpint. How do you not understand this?"

"Like… they don't let anyone leave?"

"Yes, exactly like that. They don't let anyone leave. It's like… well, not like here. You're not allowed to do anything. You can't speak your mind or read anything that's not approved by the monarchy."

"It's a police state? A dictatorship?"

"Yes." I sigh. Thank the suns for men who like to fill in the blanks. "Yes. Exactly. And I helped my sister escape because she…"

"She what?"

"She got caught sending messages out of the system. And they were going to kill her. So I put her on a ship and sent her away."

"And you stayed behind."

"Yes."

"And got caught."

"Yes."

"And they found you guilty, so you escaped too."

"Yes. I was supposed to meet her—"

"Where?"

"Bull Station."

"Oh, for sun's sake. You didn't go there, did you?"

"Yes," I say. "I had to. She was all alone. But I got caught right away and thrown into a cell. Then some dirty old man stole me, froze me, and brought me here. And that's the whole story, I promise. You know the rest."

Please buy it. Please, please, please buy my lie.

"What were you taking? To stop your glow? And why, for that matter?"

"Because, as you said, pink princesses don't turn up much. We're under guard all the time. But I was in the military—"

"Fuck you." He laughs.

"I was," I say. And this part is totally true. "So I had access to ships." I shrug. "And I took one."

"Just like that?"

"No," I say, thinking up another lie. "It was a rather dicey situation after I was found guilty, but we have a whole network of people on the inside who helped. The military is crawling with liberators. So I got another ship and I cooked up an antagonist for the glow so people wouldn't know I was pink."

"Because…" he prods. "Just say the rest of it, Lyra. I already know you have to be someone important. Tell me who you are."

"I'm…" I sigh. I should lie about this but I've told so many already, I might as well give him one nugget of truth. "I'm the king's seventh daughter."

"The king. As in the head dude of the whole miserable place?"

"The very one."

"The seventh?" He shrugs. "So what? There are six more important princesses than you. So why'd he care so much?"

"Because the seventh daughter of the king has to *marry the king* on her twenty-third birthday."

"Your father?" he says, a look of disgust on his face.

"It's not as incestuous as it sounds."

"Well, that makes it better."

"I'm just saying, we're all genetically engineered, so my DNA is actually seven generations removed from his. But you're right. That doesn't make it any better."

"Well, fuck."

"Now do you understand?"

He sighs. Long and loud. Then shrugs. "OK."

"OK?" I ask. There's no way he's gonna just let all this go.

Is there?

"Go take a shower and I'll cook us some dinner."

"That's it?"

"What should I do, Lyra? Tell me. Because I have no fucking clue."

I shrug too. Because there's nothing left to say. Nothing left to do but stay here with him and see if I can figure another way out of this whole fucking mess. "I guess I'll take a shower then."

I get up and start walking down the hallway, but Serpint calls out, "Uh… hey, Lyra?"

"Yeah?" I ask looking over my shoulder.

"So… the queen. Like the one and only queen? She's your…"

"No," I say. "She's not my mother. She's the last seventh daughter of the king."

But I turn away and walk into the bedroom after that.

Because he can't know anything about how this whole thing works.

Not. One. Thing.

That is my deepest, darkest secret and I will take it to my grave.

CHAPTER ELEVEN

SERPINT

"ALCOR!" I hiss in the air after I hear Lyra start the shower.

"Yes, Serpint."

"Did you hear all that?"

"Yes, Serpint."

"What the fuck, man? Like… what the actual fuck is going on?"

"I think…" But he hesitates. For several seconds. And that is not a good sign. Not good at all. AIs can do millions of calculations in the span of microseconds. They can run scenarios, and make projections, and extrapolate outcomes out for hundreds of years in the span of one full second. So taking three or four seconds to respond means he just ran all that shit and more before he decided to answer me. "I think the sun is about to fuck us in the ass, that's how screwed we are."

I laugh. I can't help it. Because this is just ridiculous. We're smack in the middle of something huge here. And we have the goddamned one and only Cygnian queen up in the harem cryo center because I stumbled into an opportunity and stole her, cryo-capsule and all, right out from under… well, someone else. Obviously.

There are only two reasons you find people in a cryo-capsule when they're not traveling across millions of light years inside a generation-class cruise ship.

One. They're sick. The cryo-capsule can also heal. But again, that's for people in deep space, not on a crowded space station in the sun-forsaken Cetus System. That place had SEAR cannons so it's definitely got some state-of-the-art medical equipment.

Or two. They were stolen by someone like me. Which is the correct answer here. No matter what Lyra says, her story doesn't add up. But I don't care at the moment. I don't have room in my head to pick it all apart tonight.

And she's not gonna tell me anyway. She doesn't trust me. Why should she? I've kinda been a dick since the moment we met.

"What should I do?" I ask ALCOR. "Go up and tell all this to Crux?"

"I think you should make her dinner. Then go to sleep. Tomorrow I'll have a plan and *Booty* will be back online."

"Oh, shit. I almost forgot about her." A stab of guilt runs through my heart. I wish she was online now. She'd know which parts of Lyra's story were true. ALCOR might have thousands years of learning under his belt, but *Booty* is a tenth-generation quantum AI. Small, and fast, and exists in many states at once. Plus, she's been through hundreds of gates and interacted with thousands of people and other ships. ALCOR has been stuck here his entire life. And yeah, he's been connected to the wider web for two decades, but that's not a replacement for *experience.*

Booty has talents ALCOR never will. She knows things and she's more human than most humanoids. Draden was my brother, Ceres was my sidekick—but *Booty*…

Booty is my *partner.* It's been me and her against the world for almost a decade. Long before I won Ceres in a poker game down in the lower-level casinos and even though Draden and I started out as partners in the early days, he quit on me before *Booty* came along.

She is my world.

A bounty hunter is nothing without his ship. It's the kind of bond that almost defies explanation. People assume it's because they get us out of dicey situations or because their skills in navigating a series of gates in questionable states without detection means you live to steal another spin.

But that's not really it.

It's so much more than that.

We are connected. I don't know how it happened. Hell, I don't even know if it's real or just some figment of my imagination. But at this point none of that matters. We just… *are.*

"Crux doesn't need to know this right now," ALCOR continues. "He's busy making preparations for the memorial service."

Well, fuck. I almost forgot about that too.

"Valor, Luck, and Jimmy are on their way home now. They should arrive mid-spin tomorrow."

My other brothers—who I haven't seen in many, many spins—are all coming home because I fucked up.

"It'll be good to see them." I sigh.

"Yes," ALCOR says. "It will. But tonight you take care of Lyra. She needs it, Serpint. Believe me, she needs a nice, quiet, uneventful night. Because it might be her last."

"What do you mean?"

"I'll have more information tomorrow. We'll talk then."

The air goes still and silent and I know he's gone. I know he's gone and he won't be back. Not tonight.

I turn to the bot and say, "Go away. We're done for today." Because I'm sick of his too-bright bot face and his stupid chirping, which he's been doing this whole time ALCOR and I were talking.

His final annoying bleep is something I'll just assume is goodbye—but he could be telling me to fuck off for all I know—because he leaves after that.

And now it's just… us.

Me and her.

Serpint, the bounty hunter, and Lyra, the princess.

Or is she the future queen?

I don't want to think about it so I get up, go into the kitchen, and start making dinner.

I enjoy cooking. I know it's old-fashioned and out of style since the auto-cook can print anything I want and it'll taste the same, but it relaxes me. I'm just kind of a foodie. It's a cool pastime when you spend most of your days hopping through foreign systems. And to be honest, you learn a lot about people by what they eat.

Princesses who eat tushberries and passion limes to maintain their glow, for instance. Didn't know that before today.

By the time Lyra appears in the doorway to the kitchen, leaning against the wall looking fresh and wearing another cobbled-together outfit from my closet and drawers—which I sorta love, for some reason—dinner is finished.

"Feel better?" I ask. Because she's just staring at me.

She nods, then sighs. "Thanks."

"For which part?" I ask. "The part where I put magnetic bracelets and anklets on you? The part where I collared you? The part where you got pierced in three places by an overzealous bot?"

She just continues to stare.

"Oh," I say, pushing past her with our plates of food and setting them on the table in the small dining room. "You mean the part where I made you light up like a sun."

I smile, then look over my shoulder to see how she's taking that.

She blushes. Her skin is not pale like it was this morning. She got some color back in her cheeks the moment she walked out of that exam room. But now her skin is glowing.

Not the glow of sex, but the glow of health. Which is better, I think.

"So that's what we've been missing out on, huh?"

"What do you mean?" she asks, walking over to the table. I pull out her chair—ALCOR did tell me to be nice to her—and she sits, muttering a small, "Thank you," which, I admit, feels pretty good to hear.

"I mean… I've never been with a Cygnian princess before."

"Get out of here. You own the biggest collection of escaped Cygnians in the galaxy."

"I know, but we don't… partake."

I sit down, still watching her. And she laughs as she lifts a fork of pasta and fowl to her mouth. Looks at it dubiously for a moment, then decides she's too hungry to care what it is and takes a bite. "Pretty good," she says.

"Damn right it is," I say, taking a bite of my own.

"You have never—"

"Nope," I say. "Never. Crux hasn't either. I mean, we've seen you all glow. We do the royal test on everyone. So that I've seen many times. But I have to tell you, Lyra. I've never seen what you did today. Not the dull one and not the bright one either. I'm gonna assume the dull one was the reason you had that… uh, little problem with your flux capacitor…"

"Luminous flux." She laughs.

"Whatever. So what the hell was that? You had light coming out of your eyes."

"I know." She sighs, looking down at her plate.

"So what was it? Just… you had repressed it for too long and it just came bursting out? Like a flood, or something?"

"Maybe," she says, taking another bite of food.

"Or maybe not?"

"Or maybe not."

"Hmmm."

She puts her fork down and looks me in the eyes. "I don't really know what happened back there."

"You ready to talk about it now?" I ask. "Because you said you weren't before."

"I just don't understand why I got so…"

"Horny?"

She laughs, then looks away, trying to hide her smile with a hand over her mouth. "I think it was the repressor. Had to have been. Because that's not usually what happens."

I nod at her, thinking back to her test this morning. It was dull by most standards. But it wasn't that different than what I've seen in the past.

This shit in the exam room—light coming out of her eyes, and her pussy, and hell, pouring out of her whole body—not normal.

"So what aren't you telling me?"

She takes a deep breath but says nothing.

"OK," I say. "I get it. It's been a long day. Let's discuss sleeping arrangements."

"I'll take the couch."

I laugh. "Oh, hell no, princess. If you think I'm taking my eyes off you for one picosecond, you're insane."

"What do you mean?"

"Lyra," I say in my most condescending, yet patient voice. "You're a lying little minx. Pretty much everything you've told me today is just bullshit. We're sleeping in my bed. Together. In fact, I'm going to tether you to it with the bracelets."

"The hell, Serpint?"

"I don't trust you. Not one bit. And this whole thing reeks of an imminent attack on the station by a legion of Cygnian soldiers." I take a bite of food and chew, pointing my fork at her. "And it's because of *you*."

It's also because I stole their queen, but that's just details she doesn't need to know about.

"You're not chaining me to the bed."

"Oh, yes, I am. I haven't talked to Crux yet. But tomorrow you and I are going up there and we're gonna put you on drugs to drag the whole truth out."

I'm making this part up. But we could do that. In fact… we *should* do that.

She glares at me and drops her fork onto her plate. "I'm done."

But I just smile and get up from the table, saying, "Not quite, princess," as I grab the tushberry pudding from the fridge and set it in front of her. I pop a cork on a bottle of passion lime sparkling wine, pour her a glass, and say, "You didn't have dessert yet."

She takes in another deep breath. Holds it. Then lets it out. Repeats that three times. Like this is some relaxation technique she learned in a Cygnian military class called How to Get Through a Night of Captivity with an Akeelian Male.

The whole display just makes me grin.

"Why are you being such a dick?"

"I'm not being a dick. I'm being super cool. I made you dinner, I made you dessert, I let you shower and wear my clothes. And now I'm insisting that you sleep in my spectacular bed. With me in it. What more could you want?"

"How about some privacy? And some clothes that are actually mine?"

I point to her flute of champagne and say, "Drink up. You need your special nutrients."

She eyes the glass of sparkling wine and must come to the same conclusion. Because she lifts it to those fantastic, pouty pink lips and takes a sip.

And then closes her eyes. Sighs. And relaxes for several second before opening them again and drinking the entire flute in one go.

Huh. She really did need it.

"Better?" I ask, taking another bite of my dinner.

She doesn't answer, or even look at me. But she does pick up a spoon and eat her pudding.

Again, this elicits an almost orgasmic response.

I'm unapologetically staring at her.

"What?" she asks, a little bit of defeat in her normally haughty voice.

"You're really pretty, you know that?"

She frowns.

"I don't think I've ever been so intrigued by a woman before."

She sighs.

"So, yeah, Lyra. I'm gonna take you into my bedroom. Bind you to the bed. And make you sleep next to me. But it's not *just* because I don't trust you. It's because I think… I think I like you, princess. And even though I wasn't looking for my very own princess when I found you here this morning, I think I might… *like* you."

If I was expecting some kind of reciprocal gesture, I'd have been disappointed. Because she just stares at me with a blank face.

But I wasn't expecting that. Her defenses are on high alert. Her bullshit meter working overtime. She is a lost girl. I can see that now. She has been hurt and fucked over. Maybe a lot. And even though most of that story she told me was just lies, there were little nuggets of truth in there.

That part about the king being one of them.

The part about escaping, another.

Regardless of how she got out, she did it out of desperation. And then, once I realize that… once that manifests in my brain, I see the picture so clearly I almost laugh.

"I'll get her back for you," I whisper.

"What?"

"Your sister, Lyra? I can steal her back for you, ya know. That's what I do. I'm the best booty hunter there is."

She sucks in a deep breath, lifts her chin up, and says, "Don't make promises you can't keep."

Gotcha, I think to myself. *Found it. Your weakness is on display so fully now, I almost feel embarrassed for taking advantage of it.*

Almost.

"ALCOR says *Booty* will be online by tomorrow and once that happens…" I smile and shake my head. "Well, let's just say… she and I together can pretty much do whatever the fuck we want. And there ain't nothin' no one can do about that. So no, Lyra. This isn't an empty promise. I can get your sister back no problem."

"And what do I have to give you in return?"

I almost feel guilty for asking for it. Almost. But not quite. "Sleep with me."

"You mean fuck you," she snarls.

"Let me have another go. I was off my game earlier. You kinda took me by surprise, princess. I can do better."

"You sick pervert—"

"You liked it, right?"

She glares at me. "I was under duress. I won't like it again."

I laugh. "Ah, but you're wrong. Because you haven't even experienced what the bracelets and piercings can do yet. And even though people think the whole two-cock thing is the icing on the Akeelian cake, it's not. You only got half the experience."

She frowns, then looks down at her wrists. I can see the nipple rings underneath her t-shirt. In fact they are pressing against the loose fabric in a way that tells me she just got a chill. Which tells me she's picturing what my full attention might look like.

"Spectacular," I say, answering her unasked question. "I am spectacular. Just like you are, Lyra. You and your glow. You and your light. You and that little nub of flux between your legs. You have no idea what we could do together."

She breathes a little faster but says nothing.

And in my head I say it again.

Gotcha, princess.

CHAPTER TWLEVE

I thought I had him. I really did. I thought, *Lyra. You got this guy*. This stupid, two-cocked Akeelian male who thinks with his junk and sees what I let him see. Our little tryst in the exam room lowered his defenses. Weakened him.

I thought I was playing him.

But I was wrong.

He's playing me.

The shower was amazing. That thing practically made love to me. I sat on the bench and let the sweet-smelling steam wash over me. It allowed me to think. To formulate a plan.

How I could seduce him. How I could fool him. How I could escape. How this place is filled with ships and stealing ships just happens to be the top skill on my résumé. How stealing guns, and lasers, and plasma rifles is listed right underneath that. How tomorrow I'd be on my way back to Bull Station with a ship armed with SEAR cannons. How I'd liberate Nyleena, torture a few assholes for fun, and then blow that place to bits. How we would then proceed to the farthest reaches of the galaxy and find the one place in this sun-forsaken universe that would accept us for who we really are and not use us like sexual playthings.

How Serpint would buy all the bullshit I was selling because he's just another sexually-obsessed man and pretty, pink light-shows like me bring out the animal in them. And he might trust me, and let down his guard, and I'd slip away like I was never here.

But I got him wrong.

So, so wrong.

He is just like them.

He sees just one thing when he looks at me.

A prize.

And for sun's sake… I want to laugh. So bad. Because I was naive. I am sitting in Harem fucking Station. The one place in the galaxy where no one will ever see me as anything other than a sexy little gift. A piece of property.

I mean, what did I expect? He's one of the sun-damned owners of this stupid spinning whorehouse.

I look over at the table where the stack of paper still lies. Right where he so casually dropped them earlier this morning.

He owns me.

He really believes that he owns me.

I am not seducing him, I realize.

He is seducing me.

Because he has a plan as well. Just like I was going to use him to get what I want, he will use me to get what he wants.

He wants me to like him. Thank him for giving me basic things like food, and a shower. And my sister.

I can get her back for you.

I can get her back myself, you arrogant asshole. Just let me *go*! Just let me *leave*!

There is so much anger inside me right now I want to scream. I can feel my eyes filling up with tears, that's how pissed off I am.

But I drink more champagne and I eat another spoonful of the stupid pudding. Because it feels good to have my power back.

It feels amazing to be *me* again.

I take a deep breath and say, "Well. You're right about one thing."

"Yeah?" He smiles.

"I am spectacular. And if you think that little display back in the exam room was all I can do..." I stop to eat another spoonful of pudding, making sure I turn the spoon over in my mouth so I can suck off every last bit of whipped tushberry, and then withdraw the spoon, lick my lips, and say, "Well, you're sadly mistaken."

Because newsflash, you two-pricked jerk: Cygnian princess were genetically engineered to bring males of all species to erotic ecstasy.

So if he wants to play which-species-has-the-most-powerful-sex-organs, well... that's the very first game I ever learned to play, my newfound frenemy.

I'm practically the galactic champion.

"So... you're cool with it then?" he asks.

"Sure," I say. "I've never been with an Akeelian before today. And if you say I've only seen half the show, then perhaps I should stick around until the encore?"

He smiles. Pretty big. Like all his best-laid plans are falling into place.

Then he lifts his arms up in a stretch, fakes a yawn, and says, "Well, I'm ready for bed. How about you?"

OK. I can't take his arrogance one more second.

So I push my chair away from the table—his eyes locked with mine like he's a predator and I'm his prey.

He's got that backwards, but whatever.

And then I walk around to his side of the table until I'm directly behind him and he's craning his neck so he can keep eye contact with me, and slip my hands down the front of his chest.

"Serpint," I coo in his ear as I reach down and pop the button on his pants.

"Princess," he whispers, leaning back in his chair to give me better access.

"Why waste time walking to the bedroom when we have a perfectly good table right here?"

He stands up, making me take a few steps backwards, then rips the tablecloth off the table in one fell swoop.

Dishes and glasses go careening to the floor. Champagne and pudding hit the wall. And then he's turned me around, picked me up, and plopped my ass down in front of him.

I gasp because… holy shit. This guy takes things literally.

He places his hands on my knees, spreads my legs wide open, eases his body in between them, and presses his hard cock against my tits as his fingertips grab my hair.

I look up at him and find his eyes glowing. Which makes me squint in confusion.

"What?"

"Your eyes are glowing."

"So are yours." He smirks.

"Yeah, but… are your eyes supposed to glow?"

He grins wide enough to show me his teeth. "Having second thoughts already, Lyra? Is the big, powerful, two-cocked Akeelian too much for you?"

"Fuck off," I say, placing both hands on his chest to push him backwards.

He doesn't move. Not even a centimeter. And holy suns, his chest is like a rock. Like a fucking mountain of muscle. I just stare at it for a few seconds. Feel the hardness with my fingertips.

"I get it." He laughs. "I'm intimidating."

I guffaw at that. "Hardly."

"No, really. I understand, Lyra." He whispers my name as he takes my hands off his chest and pushes them back down to the hard bulge of his pants. "I'm a lot to handle. I get it if you're afraid—"

Another guffaw.

"—but I can be gentle if you can," he says.

And then he grabs the collar of my t-shirt and rips it open.

Right down the middle.

I gasp, looking down at my breasts, doing a double-take at the new nipple piercings. So odd to see them on my body when just this morning they weren't there.

"Shhhh," he says, petting my hair like I'm a pet. "Don't worry. I told you, I can be gentle."

And then he reaches down, pulls the zipper of his pants apart, and fists his cock, massaging it in his palm for a few strokes before leaning forward and pressing it between my breasts.

I close my eyes and shake my head.

Is he for real? Like… do girls fall for this shit?

"Serpint," I murmur seductively, tilting my head up so I can look into his glowing violet eyes.

"Lyra," he whispers back, looking down into my pink ones with great expectations.

"It's not me who should be intimidated right now, it's you."

It's his turn to laugh. Which he does with a smile. A very stupid grin splashed across his face. "Let's do this then," he says.

"Let's go." And then I grab his cock with one hand and squeeze his balls with the other. And I do this hard. I'm talking… this is a ball-busting, down-on-your-knees move that should incapacitate any male, even this guy.

But he just sighs. And holy suns, it's a hot sigh too. And whispers, "Harder, princess. Give me all you've got."

Well, that wasn't supposed to happen. But I'm nothing if not accommodating. So I give it to him harder. I squeeze his dick and his balls like I've never squeezed anything before. I give it all I've got. Every gram of strength inside me goes into my grip.

He closes his eyes and drops his head back a little. "Yeah," he breathes. "Just like that."

"Are you fucking kidding me?" I say.

"What?" he says, breaking the mood.

I give his balls a twist. Watch his face for signs of pain.

"Fuck," he moans, closing his eyes again. "Oh, shit, yeah."

"You like that?"

"What's not to like?" he coos. "Keep going."

I let him go and push his chest again. "You're lying. That has to hurt."

He laughs and opens his eyes to look at me. "Oh. I get it. You thought you'd bust my balls a little, eh? Show me who's boss? Well, I hate to disappoint you, but we like it rough, Lyra. So give me all you've got. I love it."

CHAPTER THIRTEEN

Fun fact about Akeelians.

We don't feel pain when we're hard.

We like it.

A lot.

In fact, I'd go so far as to say it turns us on.

So if this little pink-haired princess thinks she's gonna dish out more than I can handle, she's got another think coming.

"What?" I ask her. "Nothing to say to that?"

"You people are just weird."

"We're weird?" I laugh. "Well, least we don't want to marry our daughters."

"He's not really my father. I explained this to you."

"Same shit in my book. But hey, whatever. You be you, princess. I'll be me. So we gonna finish this? Or were you just hoping to put me on my knees so you could escape? Let me know now so I can make the appropriate preparations."

She's still gripping my balls. And it still feels good. So good my cock is actually growing bigger in her hand.

Which makes her look down at it. "What the—"

"Oh, you thought that was…" I laugh. "Oh, no. He's got several inches to go."

"What? But—"

"No, I wasn't this turned on back in the exam room. But then again, you didn't fire me up with foreplay like you're doing now, so…" I shrug. "What can I say. I'm just hung."

She pushes me away. And this time I give in and step backwards, chuckling a little under my breath. "So it's a game, huh?"

"What?" she snaps.

"This whole I'm-hot-for-you-Serpint thing you're doing? It's just a little game so you can escape?"

She glares at me.

"Newsflash. You're in my quarters on Harem Station. There is no possible scenario where you'd somehow get out." I nod down at her collar and bracelets. "And even if you did pull off a miracle, say, with the help of an AI who seems to have taken a liking to you"—I say that part for ALCOR's benefit, even though I don't think he's listening—"then you'd never get off the station. Because that collar and those bracelets, princess. They belong to me. And one push of a button would force you right back to where you started."

"Bullshit," she snaps. "That tech isn't even real."

"Why do you think you're wearing cuffs on your ankles, Lyra? So I can spread your legs before I fuck you? I could do that with rope, for sun's sake. I don't need magnets."

"But the wall—"

"Oh, yeah. The wall works. I could activate it right now and you'd be flat up against it in less than a second from this distance."

"What?"

"I take it Cygnians don't have a BDSM subculture? Or maybe you're just too much of a prude to know about it?"

"Fuck you!"

"Should I demonstrate? Hmmm?"

"If you do I'll—"

"You'll what? Grab my balls again?"

I laugh. I'm being a total prick. I know this, but I can't help it. I love this night so much. Hell, I love this *day*.

But that thought shakes me to my core.

How the hell could I even think that? Draden is dead. Ceres, blown up. And *Booty* is still offline.

How could I fucking forget this is the worst day of my entire existence?

I turn away, suddenly ashamed of myself.

"We're done here," I say, tucking my dick back into my pants and walking across the room.

"What? What the actual fuck is happening?" she yells.

"I said we're done. Go put on another shirt. In fact, just… go to sleep. And take the fucking bed. You can have it. I'm going out."

A few minutes later I'm down in the medical bay looking at the lifeless shell of a ship that used to be *Booty*.

I grab the nearest engineer and tug him towards me, growling, "What the fuck is happening with my ship? Why is she still offline?"

He stutters and stammers for a few seconds, then sputters out, "I was just going to call you!"

He's one of those aliens who look perfectly humanoid. No distinguishing features at all. No glowing eyes or double dicks. No wings, no organic body armor, no prosthetic arms with power tools attached. Just… ordinary.

"Were you now?" I ask him.

He's a little guy too. Like a whole third of a meter shorter than me. Hell, he's not even as tall as Lyra. So he's looking up at me like I'm a monster right now. Like I might squish him like a bug.

"Yes, sir," he says. "I was. She's… she's…"

"She's what?" I snap.

"She's got damage, sir."

"Obviously," I say.

"I mean…" He shakes his head. "Organic damage. We have to take her apart, I'm afraid. And replace her—"

"Wait," I say, putting up a hand. "What do you mean *organic* damage?"

"—neural network."

"Which is made out of quantum tech," I say.

"No." He shakes his head. "No, she's… not a quant, Mr. Serpint. We didn't realize this either."

"How could you not know this? She was upgraded—"

"I know, sir, but we didn't do the upgrade. ALCOR did. And we don't know how to fix her. Only he does."

"So? Tell him to do it."

"We can't, sir!"

"Why the fuck not?"

"Because… because he's not *here*, sir."

ALCOR.

He turned my ship organic without telling me.

And he skipped the station tonight and left her to die.

I will *kill* that fucking bastard.

"Where's Crux?"

"Gone, sir. They left together. Tray went too. I thought you knew!"

"Are you fucking shitting me right now?"

"No, sir. I'm not. I'm being totally serious."

"It was a rhetorical question," I growl.

"Sorry, sir." He stares at me for a minute. "But… but I can let you talk to her, if it will make you feel better."

"Talk to who?"

"*Booty Hunter*, sir. We have her mind in containment. She's awake."

"Why didn't you fucking say that in the first place? Take me to her right now."

CHAPTER FOURTEEN

Not-so-fun fact about Cygnian princesses.

We don't really do emotions.

Well, positive ones, anyway.

We do anger. Resentment. Jealousy. We've got all the bad ones down.

We're good fighters. Pretty good at killing enemies. Friends and family too. But we have trouble with attachment bonds. In fact, I'd go so far as to say… we don't attach to anyone.

We don't do friendship, or liking, or love. We don't even do loyalty all that well. Which, I suppose, is why they feel the need to lock us away in our own system and not let anyone leave.

That kind of thing just isn't programmed into our genetics.

The truth is we princesses were custom-made for harems. There are only a few purposes for us girls back home. So it's ironic that after escaping my home system thinking I was escaping my fate, I find myself here. We're just *things* back home. And here too. But at least on this station, we're—well, maybe not respected, but definitely revered as special.

I could do worse than Crux's penthouse harem room. I could do worse than this arrogant Akeelian, Serpint, if I'm being honest. He's kind of an asshole, but he's not really mean. And sure, I think his version of kink is a little out there. But he hasn't actually done anything to me. He didn't put those bracelets on. He didn't stick me to that wall. He didn't even ask the bot to pierce me.

In fact, he took better care of me than anyone I'd call family or friends back home.

And he said… *I like you.* He called me pretty.

Which might've been bullshit. But no one has ever said that to me before.

No one.

Before this day and this man I was going on the assumption that Akeelians didn't do attachment bonds. Didn't do like. Didn't do love. Didn't think about pretty beyond how it can make them money. It was in all the myths told in the harem back on my planet.

And it's almost a perfect fit, if you ask me. They like unemotional relationships, we are bred to service unemotional men… I mean, what are the chances that two cultures would complement each other like that?

We were always told that Akeelians were oversexed monsters who would rape you without question. Claim you as property and keep you prisoner.

Most of that seemed likely when I first got here. I was stripped naked, put on display, subjected to a humiliating royal test—*twice*—and then legally handed over to Serpint as some kind of gift.

But… I'm starting to think the myths were more like half-truths. Like perhaps someone back home got wind of this place and started embellishing the story? Or maybe they just wanted to scare us? Make us think that the world outside Cygnus was evil, and dark, and sinister.

But he said, *I like you.* He said, *You're pretty.*

And maybe they don't make attachments. Maybe I'm making this all up. Maybe they're just like us. Empty, emotionless shells who only briefly connect for one-off sexual encounters.

But I've seen him display a whole range of emotions today. And when he was talking about his ship… well, those were definitely feelings of attachment.

We feel anger. Lots of anger. And arousal, of course. Sometimes we laugh for real and not in a mocking way. So I guess we do amusement. Or at least something like it.

But we don't *like* people. Not usually. We don't have much loyalty in that regard.

We make deals. We respect contracts. We spell out conditions and rules, and that's what we rely on.

Rules and legalities.

Which is why that ownership contract is such a big deal. I bet they know this. I bet that's why they make up fake papers like that.

We respect it.

Those of us in the resistance are called defective. We're called traitors. We're called abominations.

Because we *feel* things.

I *feel* things.

And right now, against my better judgment I'm feeling something for him.

I'm just not sure what it is.

"Fuck it," I say to no one. I wish the bot was here. I don't like being alone. I'm not used to it. Back home I was never alone. I grew up with dozens of sisters under the watchful eyes of armed guards. Then I was in the military, under the watchful eyes of my superior officers.

And now… "Alone," I say. Again, to no one.

I clean up the table and the mess of broken dishes and glassware. Put the food in the recycler. Wash the counters down where Serpint made a mess preparing food.

Preparing *me* dinner.

And then… something happens to me.

I feel something weird. Something that might be guilt.

What if he never comes back? What if he gets on that ship of his and just leaves me here?

Would I miss him?

I couldn't possibly miss him.

Could I?

Do I like this man?

I've had a few experiences like this one in my life. Moments when you realize things have changed and you wish they hadn't. Like… you didn't realize you had something until it was gone and now everything is different, and that thing you had doesn't look too bad when an uncertain future is staring you in the face. In fact, you maybe miss that thing you thought you didn't need.

I felt that way when I joined the military. I looked back on my childhood—and even though there wasn't much to miss, I did miss certain things. My sisters, for one. For several months I wanted them back. I was so sure I made a mistake.

But then one day I was hauled in to speak to the military higher-ups. One day I was made an offer. And that one offer changed everything for me. Suddenly things were possible. Suddenly I had a plan. A way out. And sure, what they told me to do was very dangerous. Hell, I was never meant to live through it. Nyleena either.

But I said yes. One single word changed everything. And it meant that I would not have to marry my father, seven generations removed. And even if that was the only perk of agreeing to their plan, I'd have taken the deal.

So one day. That's all it took.

One day with Serpint has changed my life too. Turned all my plans completely backwards. All that energy I spent thinking up a scheme to inhibit myself again.

How stupid.

Because I don't want to pretend to be something I'm not. I just want to be myself.

Sighing, I walk into the bedroom and look at the bed. It's the biggest bed I've ever seen. Six of my sisters could share this bed with me and we'd never want for space. It's not like sleeping with him would even be intimate.

Why was I such a bitch?

He wanted to have sex with me again because he felt he could do better. Which is funny, since I came so hard I lit up like a damn sun going supernova.

After all this introspection my real question is—why did he leave?

What did I do?

What part of our conversation sent him over the edge?

I replay it back in my head and decide it could be almost anything. I called him lots of names today. I complained, and lied, and didn't even thank him for helping me with my little flux problem.

Maybe the better question is—how do I make him come back?

It's very obvious he does not live on the station. He really could just take off and I'd never see him again. Never have the chance to tell him I'm sorry.

"Shit, Lyra," I say, again to no one. "You really are defective."

Because no healthy person would think they owe this man an apology after the day I've had.

But I do. I think I do owe him that.

I pull the silver covers back from the bed and climb in. And even with me in it, it's the most empty bed in the universe.

CHAPTER FIFTEEN

"What is the fucking hold-up?" I ask the engineer when he shuffles past me for like the billionth time. "I've been sitting out in this little waiting room for almost an hour."

"Sorry, sir. I don't actually have permission to let you talk to *Booty Hunter*—"

"She's *my* fucking ship!" I say, about to blow my top. "My desire is all the permission you need!"

"Uh, well, actually..." He laughs uncomfortably. "No, that's not quite true. ALCOR runs the ships while they're on station. So yes. She is your ship. But also yes, she falls under his jurisdiction."

"I own one seventh share of this station. ALCOR isn't in charge of anything. We're all equal partners."

"Are you?" the engineer asks. "Are you really?"

But it comes off kinda sarcastic. Like he's telling me to think more carefully about that statement. "Open. The fucking containment display. Or I will rip your little head off your shoulders and stuff it inside your ass."

He does that little head thing that lets me know he's taken aback at my outburst. But then he says, "Very well. But this is all going into my report."

"Go for it."

"Come with me."

I follow him down several corridors and we finally end up in a small control room the size of a closet with one data station.

Before I can sit down he puts a hand up. "I just need to warn you. She's… not the same."

I push him aside, sit down, and tap the screen. "*Booty*?" I say.

Silence.

"*Booty*? Ya there?"

There's a weird, almost eerie, crackling noise. Then a voice.

"Serpint…"

A voice I was not expecting.

A voice that I'm not ready to hear.

Not her voice.

Draden's.

"I warned you," the engineer says as I blow past a group of people in the hallway.

He warned me all right. He just didn't say she's taken on the persona of my dead brother.

"Leave me alone," I growl, getting inside the elevator.

He doesn't try to follow me in. But he does place a hand on the door, preventing it from sliding closed. "It's not him."

"No fucking shit," I say.

"She's been infected with some virus. She's pulling things off her database, using it in weird ways to confuse us."

But I've heard enough. I push him back and the door closes.

Back up in my quarters the lights have been dimmed to late-spin levels. Just low glows of yellow drifting up from the floorboards. The mess I made tearing the tablecloth off the table has been cleaned up, but there's a lingering red tushberry stain on the wall that looks too much like blood spatter, so I walk down the hall to the bedroom, replaying the whole scene back in Cetus in my head.

Why did I steal that queen? If I had just left the way we were supposed to, everything would be fine right now. None of this would've happened. Draden would be alive, probably down in some lower-level hovel of a bar drinking and telling stories about his latest adventures. Ceres would be hovering like an annoying idiot, analyzing the last job and coming up with schemes for next time, and *Booty* would be playing virtual dice with the other docked ships, winning credits she didn't need.

The low-level lights continue in the bedroom.

Lyra is on the far side of the bed, sprawled out face down, eyes closed, breathing lightly.

I stare at her for a few moments. Her hair is light now. Very light compared to when I first saw her this morning. Her body is under the covers but only haphazardly. One leg sticking out, bent at the knee, so I can see the smooth creamy skin of her thigh.

I take off my shirt, throw it on the floor, then sit down on the bed and start messing with the tabs on my boots. My leg aching again, reminding me that I still need to see a medical pod.

She doesn't move or say anything, but I know she's awake.

I kick off my boots, stand again, then take off my pants, get in bed, and lie back.

"You didn't leave," I say, staring up at the ceiling for a few moments. Then I turn over on my stomach, cheek flat on the mattress, and look at her.

Her eyes are open now. And even in the dim, hazy light, I can see the pink. She's not glowing. Just staring at me. Blinking every few seconds. Like she's thinking.

"I'm locked in, right? So I figure… fuck it. Ya know?"

"Fuck it," I whisper back.

"You came home," she says.

I nod, sorta. As well as one can nod with their face pressed against a mattress. "I had a pretty bad day today."

She does her version of a nod. "Me too."

"Yeah?" I say, wondering what that looks like. "How'd it start?"

She inhales, holds it, then lets her breath out with a sigh. "I was kidnapped from Bull Station. Frozen in a cryopod, woke up in a medical facility on Harem Station, then subjected to humiliating royal tests."

"That it?" I ask.

"Then I was sold to a handsome jerk"—I smile. Can't help it—"pierced three times by a deranged nanny bot, and my best-laid plans for getting my life back on track slipped away when my inhibitor failed and I had to beg said handsome jerk to fuck me back to health."

"That all you got?"

"Not enough?" She tsks her tongue. "OK, bad boy. You want more? I'll give you more. How about this? I had this insane plan to restart my glow inhibitor. Wanna hear it?"

"Sure," I say, kinda smiling.

"I needed specific ingredients to mix up more inhibitor, so I was going to defile your ship to get the palladium, steal a xenon laser from the doctor's office, and then use the passion limes to start the reaction."

"So that's why you needed to go to the doctor."

"Mmmm-hmmm," she says, kinda sleepily. "That was my grand scheme. And none of it worked."

"Bummer," I say. "But..." I grin. Big. "You did get a double serving of Akeelian magic for your troubles."

She shakes her head, blushing. Then turns away.

"Well..." I say. "I think my day was worse."

"Oh, yeah?" she says, turning back to face me.

"Yeah," I say. "I stole something I shouldn't have this morning. My brother got killed while we were making our escape, my favorite bot got blown to bits, and my ship is now infected with a virus that's turned her insane."

"Oh," she says, frowning. "I'm sorry. I didn't know."

Which just makes me sadder. Because I should've said 'I'm sorry' first and it's too late now. Just another fuck-up in a long line of fuck-ups today.

I stretch my hand across the huge gulf of space between us. She stares at it for a moment, then trains her eyes on me.

I wiggle my fingertips, beckoning her.

She just looks at them and closes her eyes.

"Come here," I whisper.

"Why?"

"Because you know what?"

"What?" she asks, opening her eyes again.

"You're the best thing that's happened to me today."

She attempts a smile but doesn't quite make it. "Today's my birthday."

Well, shit.

I frown and say, "You win."

She nods, eyes closing again. Then opens them and shakes her head. "No. No one won today."

I wiggle my fingers again and this time she slides over, turning her back to me as I wrap my arm around her waist and tug her into my chest.

"Do you think tomorrow will be any better?" she whispers.

"No," I say, thinking about my brothers coming home for Draden's memorial service.

"Me either."

We lie like that for a little while. Our breathing becomes matched. And I think about trying to kiss her. Or slip my fingers between her legs to see if I can get her excited.

And even though all that sounds pretty good… I don't. I don't move at all and neither does she.

I just replay Draden's voice coming through *Booty's* interface as I wonder where ALCOR, Crux, and

Tray went. Wonder what they're doing and why it's a secret.

Wonder how yesterday I had no girl and tonight I do.

Wonder if she'll be here when I wake up.

Wonder if anything will ever be the same again and decide…

It won't.

CHAPTER SIXTEEN

Lying next to Serpint, all pulled into his protective embrace, is kind of driving me crazy. My glow spot between my legs is throbbing and even though I'm doing my best to ignore it, he's getting hard behind me.

"Sorry," he says, when I move away from his growing cock. "It's just… I can't help it. Whenever Akeelians fall asleep we get hard."

I open my eyes wide, thankful he can't see me. "All night?" I ask.

"Yup. All night."

"Doesn't that drive you crazy?"

"I think that's the point. We have an innate circadian breeding urge that gets a little… overwhelming at night. Especially if we sleep next to a woman. Especially a Cygnian woman. Which is why we tend to stay away from them ourselves."

Oh, sun. Help me.

"Do you want me to sleep somewhere else?" he asks.

"No," I say, trying to make my voice sound nonchalant.

He sighs, and relaxes a little.

"Can you control it?"

He huffs. "I'm not going to rape you, if that's your question."

"No," I say, turning over to face him. "I didn't mean it that way." God, my glow spot is practically pounding now. "I just meant… does it take over and make you… want to…"

"Have sex with you?" He laughs. "Well, sure. But we learn how to control the urges in puberty. And believe me, I had a lot of practice, so I can handle it."

I close my eyes and pretend I'm going to sleep. But I highly doubt there's going to be much sleep in my future. Once my glow spot gets excited it needs what it needs. I just don't want to embarrass myself the way I did earlier. That was humiliating.

"Can I ask you something?" Serpint says.

I open my eyes and look at him. Why does he have to be so damn handsome? "Sure," I say.

"I know you don't want to talk about it, but… that glow in the doctor's office…"

"Yeah?" I ask, really not wanting to talk about it.

"Is that normal?"

I let out a long breath of air. "Sorta," I say.

"What's that mean?"

"It means… I knew it could happen, it's just never happened to me. So I was as surprised as you were."

"Hmm," he says. "How come I've never seen that before? I mean, I've lived on this station for twenty years. Have seen Crux's princesses glow in pretty much every possible way. But I've never seen *that*."

"Well," I say. "Um…" Oh, sun. I do not want to tell him why I think that happened.

"Is it bad?" he asks.

"Nnnn-ooooooo," I say, drawing out the word into two syllables.

"Then what?" He squints his eyes at me in the dim light "Are you… glowing right now?"

Oh, shit. "Am I?" I say, looking at my hand. "I don't see any glow."

"No, just your… eyes," he says. "It's not bright, but it's there. What's up with all this flux capacitor stuff anyway?"

OK, I have to say something. One part truth, two parts lie. That's how this needs to go. "It's called luminous flux," I say. "I don't even know what a flux capacitor is. And the glow is… well, it's emotional. Strong feelings make us light up. So naturally, when we… erm… you know, *climax*"—I roll my eyes at myself—"we glow. Because it feels good. But we glow when we feel bad too," I add quickly. "And sometimes we glow for no reason." Lie. "Lots of times, actually." Another lie.

"OK," he says. "So what's faintly glowing eyes signify?" I grow hot and he says, "Oh, shit. It's getting brighter."

"It's… blushing," I say. And then I blush harder and the glow is bright enough for me to see a shine reflecting in his eyes.

"You're blushing?" He laughs. "Because my cock is gonna be hard all night?"

"No," I say too fast.

"Oh, hell." He laughs. "You're gonna light up the room if you blush any harder."

"Just… just… shut up, OK? God. And that's not why I'm blushing, anyway."

He thinks about that for a moment. "OK. We have two things happening here, I think."

Great. Just my luck to get a smart one.

"First, we have the freaky light show back in the doctor's office. And second, we have you blushing. And they're related, but not because I'm hard."

I just stare at him.

"How am I doing?"

I sigh.

"I'll take that as on the right track. OK. So. You glowed up like crazy in the doctor's office because… you're in love with me." Then he winks at his joke.

I close my eyes and shake my head.

"Holy shit!" he exclaims.

And when I open my eyes to see what's got him so excited—I'm lit up like the sun.

CHAPTER SEVENTEEN

"I was just kidding," I say, mesmerized by the yellow-pink light emanating from every inch of her body.

"Can we stop talking about this now?" She turns over, but I can't take my eyes off her. She's so beautiful all lit up. Like a fucking goddess.

"Wait." I laugh. "Lyra, what's going on? Are you in love—"

"No," she yells. "No. That's stupid."

"Then why is this happening?"

"I don't know, OK? I don't know."

I inhale deeply, just staring at how the light curves around her shoulder and peeks out from under the neck and sleeve of her t-shirt. *My* t-shirt, I remind myself.

"You don't know," I repeat. "But you have an idea. So what's your idea?"

"I don't want to talk about it." She peeks at me from over her shoulder. But now something else is different. Her eyes have stopped glowing and they are just the normal golden-pink they were before she started blushing.

"You're hiding something."

"I'm hiding lots of things." She huffs.

"You feel something for me."

"Well… just… I'm sorry I don't control my innate sexual urges as well as you, OK? I just… didn't have a lot of practice back home."

"Because you didn't have a lot of sex?" I ask.

"For sun's sake! Can you just shut up and go to sleep?"

"So you did have a lot of sex," I say, ignoring her command. "But not sex like this."

"Congratulations, genius. You win a cookie."

"Why are you so upset? There's nothing to be ashamed of. I'm just good at it, Lyra."

She guffaws and turns over so I can't see her face. "And arrogant too."

"Guilty," I say. "But you didn't really answer my question. Why did you glow that way in the doctor's office? And I don't care if you don't want to talk about it. Because it's got something to do with me and I want to know what that is."

She sighs. Loudly. Like she's fed up with me. "Fine," she says, turning back over to face me. "I'll tell you."

And again, her body is still lit up, but her eyes are not. It's exhilarating to look at her glow and be able to see deep into the soul of her eyes at the same time.

"Tell me then," I whisper.

"We have a myth about… fated mates."

"What?" I say, laughing.

"You know. The *one*? Soulmates? Stupid shit like that?"

"I'm your soulmate?"

And then I guffaw so loud, she sits up, slaps my face, and scrambles to get out of my bed.

I catch her by the foot and pull her back as she screams, "Let go!" and kicks. "I said let go!"

But I'm too fast. I've stolen a lot of reluctant princesses over the years and I've got a tried-and-true technique. They don't call me Booty Hunter for nothing.

I wrap my arms around her tight, then flip her over so she's on her back, then climb on top of her.

"Calm down," I say. "And stay put while I'm talking to you."

"Get off of me," she growls.

"I will. Once you answer my questions."

"I already did. And you laughed!"

"I'm sorry," I say, laughing again. "It's just… fated mates?"

"It's a myth, OK? I didn't make it up. You asked so I told you. Now let me go."

"Hold on," I say, rearranging myself so I can grip her wrists and press them into the mattress. "A myth?"

"Yes. It's just a myth. It's ridiculous, so just forget about it. We're not soulmates."

I think about this for a moment. "But you've never seen it before?"

"No," she snaps. "Get off of me." She wiggles furiously, but all that does is get my already hard cock more excited as it bumps up against her stomach.

"It was fake," I say. "Until today."

"Oh, my God. Just…"

"Just tell me, Lyra. I want to know because…"

But I don't finish. I'm too busy thinking the rest of that sentence through.

"Because what?" she asks.

"Because we have a myth like that too."

"Like what?" she asks, calming down a little.

"Fated mates," I say, absently. "But I've never heard of it being real, either."

She squints her eyes at me. They are so lovely I get lost in them for a second and have to shake myself out of her spell. But then she gives in and stops fighting. Just melts into the mattress under the weight of my body and suddenly my second cock gets hard.

What the hell?

That's not supposed to happen until *after* we have sex. It's an every-other-time deal. Has been that way ever since I got my first boner and learned to masturbate.

"What the hell is that?" she exclaims, feeling my second cock grow hard and thick along her stomach.

I smile. Weakly. And say, "Surprise. I guess we're both learning something new today."

"Is that your—"

"Yup."

"Oh." She pauses. Looking me in the eyes. "Oh," she says again, now looking away. "But I thought—"

"Yup."

"So—"

"Uh-huh. Something's going on here."

"Hmmm," she says, glowing brighter.

"Does that make you blush, Princess Lyra?"

She turns her head, trying to hide her face in the muscle of my forearm. "So… I glow weird when we…

you know. Do it. And your second… ding-a-ling—" I laugh so loud she startles. "What?"

"They've got names, ya know. And neither one of them is called ding-a-ling."

She starts chuckling. Which makes her breasts bounce against my chest. Which makes both my manly appendages even more excited than they already were.

"What do you call them?" she says.

"Never mind that. We might have a situation here."

"How do you figure?"

"Well, something's obviously happening between us, Lyra. Something weird."

"Maybe we're just horny?"

"Maybe," I say, unable to hide my smile. "But maybe not."

"Well," she huffs. "If you're suggesting we're this… this… stupid fated mates thing, no. I refuse to believe that."

"Why?"

"Why? Because you're… *you*. And I'm… *me*. That's why."

"So I'm not good enough for you? I'm just some no-good Akeelian booty hunter and you're a special princess who's supposed to marry her father."

"I'm not going to marry him. And I'm not saying that. I'm just saying…" She sighs. "Well, I didn't run away, risk everything to get out, just to end up soulmated to an Akeelian on Harem Station. I mean, I have *plans*."

"What kind of plans?" I ask.

"Can you get off me while we discuss this? Because your ding-a-lings are distracting my flux capacitor."

Oh, she is too cute. Too fucking cute. I squirm a little on top of her, making sure to maneuver both my giant, hard ding-a-lings right between her legs.

"Stop it, Serpint. I'm serious." She wriggles her wrists, still in my firm grip, and tries to get away.

"I am too," I say. "Totally fucking serious."

She looks me straight in the eyes and says, "I'm telling you no, OK? So do whatever you want with that."

I groan and roll off of her. Turn my whole body the complete opposite direction and say, "Fine. Whatever. Go to sleep then."

"Good, I will."

"And stay on your side," I growl. "That's an order."

She scoots all the way over to the other side of the bed and says, "I will. Watch me."

"Good."

"*Good.*"

Except it's not good. It's not good at all. Because both my cocks are still hard and this is not normal. I don't think I can sleep with both of them hard. It's very distracting. I always have sex or jerk off twice in a row to take care of this little problem. And even though I didn't this morning, there were extenuating circumstances to keep my mind off the fact that I didn't finish.

But now, lying here in bed with her, in the middle of the night with nothing to do but sleep—I don't think I can do it.

Something has to be done.

So I reach down and start jerking off to take care of my little problem.

"What are you doing?"

"What's it look like?" I say, picturing the way I fucked her in the doctor's office.

"You can't jerk off in bed next to me," she says. And then she squeaks a little.

"I can, and I will. I can't sleep with two hard-ons. And why the fuck are you making that noise?"

"What noise?" But she squeaks again.

"*That* noise."

"Would you quit jerking off?"

"I'll be done in like twenty minutes, don't worry. I'll make it fast."

"Twenty minutes?" And her little squeak comes with a moan.

"What is your problem?" I say.

"Nothing. What's yours?" But then she groans.

"Lyra," I say. "I can't get off if you're constantly distracting me. Stop making those sounds."

"I can't—Ohh… Oh…"

I turn and find her knees bunched up to her chest, almost curled up in a ball. "What the hell is going on?"

"Nothing," she gasps.

"Lyra—" I reach for her, but the moment I touch her she glows a bright, fluorescent pink.

"No, no, no, no… don't touch me or I'll—"

"You'll what?" But then it hits me and I laugh. "You can't go to sleep without sex either, can you? You're all fluxed up."

"Very funny," she hisses.

I look up at the ceiling, fisting both my cocks in an easy up-and-down motion, and take a moment to enjoy her discomfort. "It's your own fault. I offered to help you out."

"I don't understand what's happening. I've never had this problem before."

"Just get yourself off, then," I say. "For fuck's sake."

"Not in front of you."

I just shake my head. "Then go into the bathroom and do it."

"You go into the bathroom and do it. I'll stay here."

"No, this is my bed."

"Oh, shit… oh, shit!"

"What?" I say, turning over on my side so I can reach for her.

"No, don't!"

But it's too late. My fingertips brush against her arm and her whole body spasms.

"What?" she says, gasping for breath. "It didn't work."

"What didn't work?"

"When you touched me I should've come! And oh, oh, shit! It's getting worse!"

"Oh, this is too much. Too fucking perfect."

"It's not funny. You have no idea what it feels like when the flux builds up like—oh, my God!"

I sit up and look at her. Maybe even get a little worried. Because she looks like she's in pain. Her face is all bunched up in a grimace. Like she's being tortured.

"OK," I say, hooking a hand around her waist so I can pull her over to me. "That's it. I'm gonna take care of you, you're gonna take care of me, and then we're going to sleep. Tomorrow, I'm sending you back to Crux. I can't deal with all this weird bullshit."

She's breathing hard now. Almost panting. So hard she doesn't even answer me, just grabs my arm, urging me to get on top of her.

"Fuck me," she says. Just like she did in the doctor's office. "Fuck me right now!"

And I mean… she is not joking around. Because she reaches down for both my cocks and just…

Oh, shit. I'm done for.

CHAPTER EIGHTEEN

I am embarrassed, mortified, and humiliated all in the same instant. And the glow I produce with that combination of emotions is the same as it was earlier.

I am the sun. I am a supernova of light.

And still, I do not come.

What the hell is happening to me?

It's like I can't control myself. It's only then that I realize I've got both his cocks in my hand. And it's way more than one handful can handle. Because my fingers don't even begin to wrap all the way around his double-thick shafts.

"Yeah," he moans. "Yeah, grip me hard, princess. That's exactly what I need."

He moves closer to me, his fingers eagerly reaching between my legs.

I expect it to happen this time. The moment his fingers slide into the wetness pooling there, I expect the sun to explode.

But it doesn't.

I wail—"Oh, God. Oh, *GOD*!"

He pushes his fingers inside me, penetrating me deep. But still. The release I need so badly isn't there!

"What the hell is happening?" I cry out.

"Pump me harder, princess. I need more."

"Me too," I say, following his orders. "Me too!"

"Get on top of me," he says, turning over and taking me with him. So that by the time he's done with that sentence, I'm straddling his hips.

I reach for his cocks as he lifts my shirt up over my head in a desperate attempt to get me naked, and tosses it over his shoulder. "Fuck me," I say again. Just as he rips my bottoms apart and frees me of the last piece of cloth that separates us.

"No, you fuck me."

We don't have the patience to have another bout of back-and-forth talking about who will fuck who, because something in this room—or something between *us*—has taken possession of our senses.

I reach between my legs, fist his cocks with my hand, and aim them right at my pussy as I lift my hips up, and then—

"Ohhhhhhhh," we say in the same breath.

I sink down on him.

An immediate calm overtakes us. I'm still very fluxed up, and he is still bursting with need, but suddenly there is time.

And we start moving. Slowly. His hands on my hips, rocking me back and forth across his upper thighs. I fall forward, palms slapping onto his muscular chest, and bow my head so my hair drags across his face as we move.

"That's nice," he whispers.

"Better than nice," I say, lowering my mouth to his so that I hum out the words between his lips.

"Princess," he moans.

But he doesn't ask me to fuck him harder. He doesn't seem to be in any hurry at all. And neither am I.

It's like… it's like when we're apart we can only think of each other. How to connect. How he can be inside me, and I can get him there, and the light—oh, God, the light that starts pouring out of me mingles with him and…

"I don't know what this is," I say.

"I do," he says.

And then we come together. There is no mere supernova this time, it's more like the universe imploding.

And it's a good thing that my hair is covering his face, and his eyes are closed…

Because the brightness of our release would blind us.

We stay like that—me on top of him, his arms circling my waist in case I try to escape—for several minutes.

His cocks pulse inside me and coat my pussy with his milky release. And the muscles of my pussy clamp down on him with the same rhythm.

He says, "I think I'm dead, Lyra. I think you just killed me."

And I say, "You're welcome."

We laugh a little and then, because I'm exhausted, I try to swing my leg over so I can snuggle up to his chest. Not that I'd ever admit that to anyone. Because

I'm not a snuggler, but… I don't seem to be able to do that.

"Ow," he says.

"Sorry. I don't know what's happening. I feel… stuck."

"Oh, no," he says.

"What?"

"Oh… no."

"*What?*"

"Oh, shit, Lyra. I don't… I don't know what's happening, but my cocks are… oh, my God, my cocks are—"

"Your cocks are *what?*" I say.

"They're swelling up!"

"What?"

"Oh, shit. I've heard of this but… I just thought it was a myth."

I lift myself up off him and find I can't. I cannot get up. "What's happening?"

"I'm stuck!" he says.

"You are not! Stop fucking around. It's starting to hurt."

"I know, but my cocks—"

"Take them out!"

"I can't! I can't! It's like the head of my dick is locked into your pussy!"

"This is not a thing," I say.

"I didn't think it was either, but I swear—"

I try to roll to the side, but he just comes with me. "Ow," he says, his body turning with mine.

"What the fuck is happening?" I ask.

"We have to come again."

"Again? I just imploded the universe! That's all there is!"

"No," he says. "No. Two cocks, Lyra. Two implosions. Or I can't separate from you."

"Since when? This didn't happen earlier."

"Since..." He covers his face with his hand and shakes his head. "I can't believe I'm gonna say this, but"—he's propped up over the top of me now, holding up all his weight with one flat palm on the mattress—"since... we became soulmates."

"But I don't think I can come again. I mean, I gave it my all, Serpint."

"You gotta give a little more."

"But I'm not even horny anymore. Like... I'm done."

"We can't be done."

"But we are."

He sighs. Loudly. "Maybe I can get you going again? And you can come? Because I need to come again."

"So come! And get your dicks out of me!"

"OK," he says, rocking his hips. "Talk dirty to me."

"What?" I say, blinking my eyes at him.

"Talk dirty to me. Get me ready again."

"What should I say?"

He shrugs. "Just say whatever you usually say. Like... 'I want you to fuck my mouth with your cocks and choke on your come.'"

I just continue blinking at him.

"Or something."

"Not only am I *not* saying that, but I'm not doing it either."

"Just pretend," he says. "It's not real. Just dirty-talk me for like… twenty minutes, tops. Then I'm sure I'll be ready."

One more set of blank staring blinks for the booty hunter. "Twenty. Minutes?"

"I mean… if you're really good at it I could probably get off in fifteen."

"You need fifteen minutes of dirty-talk to be able to pull your cocks out of my pussy?"

"And I need to come," he says. "Don't forget that part."

"You're lying," I say. "This is not a real thing."

"You keep saying that, and yet we're stuck together like mating animals."

"You're serious?"

"Look, I'm new at this whole soulmates thing, OK? I have no idea what it means to be fate mates and all that bullshit, but apparently it's…" He pans his hand to our conjoined body parts. "This."

I begin to glow. I'm not blushing. Oh, no. This is nothing more than one hundred percent humiliation.

"Or…" he says, straightening up and grabbing my ass so he can scoot me closer to him.

Which only makes his huge, swollen cocks delve deeper inside me. And I'm not gonna lie. It feels *pret-ty* amazing. "Or what?" I say.

"Or…" He begins to fuck me again, his eyes drooping and heavy as he smiles lazily down at my tits. He grabs them with both hands and begins to pinch my nipples as he leans down to kiss my belly.

Which gets my flux capacitor motor humming along again. But then he lets go of one of my breasts and starts massaging my clit with his thumb.

"Oh..." I say. "I see."

"You're glowing again," he says.

And as those words come out of his mouth, his cocks begin to stretch the walls of my pussy every further. "And you're growing again," I say.

I bite my lip as he begins to pump harder. Then his balls are banging against my ass as his motion becomes more forceful.

"Perhaps," I whisper, closing my eyes as the luminous flux inside me begins to build again. "Perhaps there's another universe out there waiting for me to implode it?"

He just slams me with his hips. "More," he says. "Keep talking," he commands, his thumb still working magic on my clit.

"Perhaps my pussy is your goddess, Serpint. Perhaps it commands you to do as I say."

"Anything," he growls. "I'll do anything to make you come again."

And then he leans down. Kisses me. His tongue gently sweeping across the seam of my lips. And says, "I love you," into my mouth.

My pussy clamps down on his swollen cocks.

And he groans and pounds me so hard, I slip up to the top of the bed and bang my head on the headboard.

And then... for the second time tonight... we annihilate the universe.

CHAPTER NINETEEN

I love her?

I don't love her. I don't even know her. I have no clue why those words just came out of my mouth.

But it's really hard to care about that at the moment because then we're coming. Imploding another sun into oblivion.

She cries out, "Ohhhhhh. Yeeeeees!"

She is squeezing me so tight I want to die of pleasure. Everything drains out of me at once. All my come, all my energy, all my everything.

And I collapse on top of her, my cocks happy and only semi-hard now. I roll over, taking her with me. Wrapping her up in my arms as my cocks slip out and the secondary one, finally, shrinks away.

"Wow," Lyra says, pressing her back into my chest.

"Yeah," I say, still breathing hard. "Wow."

We lie still for a few minutes. I'm expecting my cock to get hard again as I slowly drift off a little, but it doesn't. Neither of them do.

Which is weird. But then again, everything about this girl is weird.

No. Not her, just the way she makes me feel.

Unconsciously I hug her tighter. This makes her hum a little.

Tired, I guess. Half asleep like me.

I have a lot of questions for her, but not now. I can't even think straight. This day just needs to end. Everything will make sense tomorrow. I know it will.

It has to.

Because… *I love her?*

I don't love her. That's not even close to being true. I've never said to anyone before and I didn't mean it just now.

But later. I will straighten all this out later.

I fall asleep picturing her face when she came. All the times she came today, but mostly this last time. How beautiful it was. And how familiar she feels, even though we're strangers.

Soulmates.

My hand automatically reaches for my cocks as I wake in the morning. It's an unconscious habit. Something I've been doing for decades. Wake up hard, jerk myself off—twice—and then start the day.

But I'm not hard this morning.

For a second I panic. Like… am I sick? Did my dicks fall off? What's happening?

But then Lyra moans next to me and rolls over, her blonde hair a tangled mess over her face, and I feel…

OK.

That's the only way to describe it. I feel OK. Like this is normal. Like it's no big deal that today is the first time I've ever woken up without hard-ons since I was a teenager.

And that makes no sense.

I should be worried. I should be wondering what's wrong.

Except my brain is telling me to just… chill. Relax. No big deal.

Chemicals, I think. Some kind of neuro-chemicals are manipulating me into thinking everything's fine. Like… drugs.

Or something.

I don't know.

"Serpint?" ALCOR's voice says.

"Yeah?" I groan, still groggy.

"Your brothers will start arriving just after lunch."

And then that feeling of being OK just disappears. Because Draden is dead and today is his memorial service. And we don't even have a body to float out the airlock. We have nothing left of him at all.

"Will you be bringing Lyra?" ALCOR asks.

"No," I say. But then, "Yes." Because for some reason I can't imagine *not* taking her.

"Are you sure?" ALCOR asks.

"Hey," I say, ignoring that last question. Because it brings back all the memories of last night. What I said, why I might've said it. And I'm still in denial that it happened. "Where were you guys last night? Someone told me you left the station."

"We did," ALCOR says. "But we're back now. We can talk about that later."

"And *Booty*?" I say. Because suddenly all the fucked-up shit that happened yesterday is fresh in my mind. "You turned her organic? Without my permission?"

"You don't *own* her," ALCOR says. "She's her own person and that was her choice."

I growl a little at that answer. Because it's only half true. Sentient ships are banned everywhere unless they are *owned*. It's a universal directorate. Even here, that law still applies. If we had unowned sentient ships here, I don't care what kind of security ALCOR has out at those gates, the Prime Navy would attack us. They might not win that fight, but they would sure as hell try their best. That's why I'm listed as her responsible party.

But ALCOR is right. If *Booty* wants to disregard my orders or wishes, she is free to do so because I don't have any kind of regulator on her to stop it.

We're partners like that.

At least I thought we were.

"Lyra will need clothes," ALCOR says, bringing me back to the conversation.

"Sure," I say. "I'll take care of it."

He leaves after that. Or whatever it is he does. Disengages from the sensors in my quarters. I can feel his absence.

Lyra turns over, questions in her eyes. Because clearly she heard that whole conversation. "Are you sure you want me at your brother's memorial service?"

No. I'm not sure at all. But there's an undeniable feeling inside me that says leaving her behind isn't an option. Some kind of new urge to keep her close at all times.

But all that's so complicated and I just want to keep things simple. So I say, "Yeah. I do."

"Well," she says. "I'll get the shopping code after all." She smiles when she says this.

And even though I'm not happy—not anything close to happy—I smile back at her. Like… can't *not* smile back at her. "You know what?"

"What?"

"Fuck that auto-shopper. Let's go out into the city. Get the fuck out of these quarters. Maybe get breakfast too. Have you seen the city yet?"

"No," she says, shaking her head. "As soon as I got out of the cryopod I was taken directly to the harem."

"Well, good. I'll show you around this morning."

She sighs a little. Like that makes her happy. But then she says, "You don't have to, though. I get that this day is gonna be hard for you. I can fend for myself here just fine. And I like auto-shopping."

But she's wrong. I don't know how I know this, I just do.

I do have to. Just like how that one moment when I considered leaving her behind for the memorial service conjured up an urge to keep her close, that's how I feel about walking out of here without her next to me.

Except I can't explain that. And even if I could, it sounds stupid. So I say, "It's no big deal. Besides, this place is pretty great. I know everyone thinks Harem Station is just a cesspool of outlaws and killers, but ALCOR runs it, ya know. And he's no joke. And it's the only home I have, so I'd like you to see it."

For fuck's sake. Why am I talking to her about this shit?

"OK," she says. And then she smiles. "But I'll still need that auto-shopper code. Unless you want me walking around in your boxer shorts."

I laugh, picturing that. Then frown, picturing that. Because I have a sudden urge to kill anyone who looks at her. And if she walked out of here in shorts, everyone would be looking at her.

"Sure," I say, throwing the covers off me and swinging my legs over the side of the bed. "I'll program it now."

I pinch my fingers together in the air and open up a screen, then punch all the required tabs to give her permission to shop.

"How does that work?" she asks.

"How's what work?" I ask, looking over my shoulder. She's propped up on one elbow, long blonde hair spilling over her bare breasts like spun gold.

"Those air screens you guys use here."

"Oh," I say, looking at my still-open screen. I swipe my hand through it and it disappears, then pinch the air with my fingers and open it up again. "I've got an implant in my fingers," I say. "And there are nanobots in the atmosphere here that respond to them. ALCOR's magic. I don't really know much other than that. But I'll get you one. If you want. Every Harem citizen has one. In fact, we should do that first. You can't be walking around without a connection."

She gives me a funny look, then her fingertips go to the collar around her neck that displays my name as her responsible party.

"What?" I ask.

"Yesterday I was your slave. You wanted to send me back to the harem. Now you're giving me citizen privileges?"

Yeah, that's weird. But then again, it's not. It's like me wanting her to go to the memorial service with me. And the thought of sending her back to Crux makes my chest hurt in a weird way I can't explain. "I just want to keep you safe," I say. "That's all. Don't read too much into it."

"OK," she says.

"OK," I say, not looking at her. "Well. Find something to wear and we'll get going. Lots of things to do before my brothers start arriving."

I get up, grab a t-shirt and pants from my closet, and go into the shower to clean up. Making a point not to invite her to join me.

CHAPTER TWENTY

The auto-shopper is top notch. And my access is amazing. It's like… he put no limits on it! I could've gotten anything I wanted. But I controlled myself and just got some gray pants, a loose, pink, long-sleeve blouse that flares at the wrists, and a pair of sensible pink slipper flats. Which was all delivered in less than ten minutes. So I was ready to go by the time he came out of the bedroom dressed in his usual black tactical pants, white t-shirt, and boots.

I was serious when I said I loved auto-shopping and I would be perfectly happy just loading up my virtual shopping cart. Back home I never went out to buy things. But back home was not a fun place to be. And that's kinda what I expected here.

Except Serpint seems to think it's a pretty great place and wants to show me around.

Which excites me a little.

So strange how things can change so quickly. I've been here one day and so much has happened.

We had sex three times. And each time was better than the last.

Of course, that's new-people sex. Usually it starts out great, gets better and better, then things always fizzle.

I hate thinking about the inevitable decline of our relationship. It makes me unreasonably sad for some reason. Even though we don't really have a relationship. I am still his slave, as evident by the fucking collar I'm wearing with his name on it.

But then again, we're sitting in the harem medical office waiting for me to be fitted with a fingertip implant so I'll be connected.

Weird.

"Lyra," the harem master says from the hallway. "Come with me."

I look over at Serpint and frown. "Want me to come with you?" he asks.

"Yes." I nod. Which is dumb. *Dumb, dumb, dumb.* I do not need a man to hold my hand while they prick my finger.

And yet… I do need him to hold my hand while they prick my finger.

I think about last night as Serpint and I walk down the hallway to the same room I was in last night.

I'm pretty sure everyone in the office heard us going at it. So that kinda sucks. But no one says anything, so they are either super polite or super antisocial and don't give any fucks at all about what we did.

"Have a seat," the cyber master says, pointing to the examination table.

Serpint holds my hand while I climb up and even though I'm only here to get an implant, I'm nervous. I don't like doctors.

The cyber master turns to me with something that looks like a cross between a needle and a laser, and says, "Hold out these two fingers," as he holds out his own two fingers in example.

Vibrating fingers, I remember from yesterday morning.

"You want to see my credentials?" he asks me when I hesitate. Nothing but snark in his voice.

"No," I say. "I'm fine. I'm just thinking about how you *violated me* with those fingers, that's all."

The cyborg master isn't made of flesh. He's not human, he's just a very high-end robot. He doesn't even really have a face. It's mostly just silver-metallic synthetic skin with a single vision sensor and a slit of a mouth that is nothing more than a speaker.

But still, he rolls that vision sensor at me after I implicate him in the previous day's torture. And then in one quick motion he pricks my fingers with the laser needle thing and it's done.

"That's it?" I ask.

"That's it," Serpint says. "Now ALCOR just needs to assign you credentials and you can use it. But we don't have to wait for that."

"She shouldn't have this," the master says, glaring at me with that one vision sensor.

Serpint just shrugs and says, "Not up to you, my friend. Just send in the order and call her when it's done so we know."

When we exit the clinic and get in the elevator the nanny bot is back, to Serpint's dismay. And he's chirping at me about his night off while we ride the lift down to the city. Which I give no shits about, but no matter how many times I tell him that, he just keeps going on and on about bot bars, and bot girls, and bot this and... like... that's *not* a thing where I come from. Bots are just bots.

But not here, apparently. Bots are people here. Like the ships, I guess. That conversation this morning with ALCOR about *Booty* was bizarre.

And when we step out of the lift I start to think this whole place is bizarre.

For one, it's not built like any other station I've ever been on. The kind with many levels all separated by ceilings and floors.

This station is one large open space running down the center of the ring with tall buildings on either side.

We come out somewhere in the middle, so when Serpint leads me through a crowd of people—all of whom look like they kill people for a living—and over to the edge of the wide walkway, I can peer down, and up, and it is just like he said.

Magnificent.

There's people-moving walkways going in all directions. Up, down, sideways... crisscrossing like snakes in a jungle of lights, and flash, and glass-sided store fronts.

Gambling halls, shooting galleries, bars, clubs, arcades, brothels—every fun thing a sinner might like is available.

I look up again. Start counting levels. Because even though it's all open, there's walkways along the perimeter of the buildings.

"Two hundred levels that way," Serpint says, pointing up. "And two hundred more down there too. Crux's harem is all the way up at the top."

I squint to try to see it, but I can't. And I don't know if it's because the sides of the station curve up to a gently sloping roof overhead and I'm just at the wrong angle to be able to see the top, or it's truly just so far away I cannot. The same effects happens when I look forward and back. This station is a ring. So the buildings actually curve off into the horizon in both directions. "Holy suns," I say. "This is… just… I can't even comprehend it. It really is a whole city in here."

"What'd you expect?" He laughs.

"Well, you know. A station. Low ceilings, cramped quarters, horrible smell. But this place—is that a garden down on the bottom level?"

Serpint nods. "Yeah. But that's not the bottom. That's just the park level."

I can't stop the laugh. "Outlaws have parks," I muse. "Who knew."

"Stick with me, princess. I'll show you a good time."

I roll my eyes at him, but not sarcastically. Because he already has shown me a good time.

"Come on," Serpint says, tugging on my hand. He's been holding it ever since we left his quarters. And even though that's weird too, it's not. It feels right for some reason. Which makes me think about our conversation last night about being soulmates.

We should've asked the cyborg master about his cock and how it got stuck up inside me last night until he came again.

Then again… gross. I'm not talking about anything with that subhuman piece of space trash.

"Wow," I say, looking at all the store fronts on this level. All designer. And jewelry stores too. The really expensive ones like I've seen on the screens when one of my sisters would hack into an illicit feed. And everywhere there are people. So many people. Selling things on the side of the wide walkways, and gathering in small crowds. And almost all of them look happy. "This place isn't anything like the stations I've been on before."

"No," Serpint agrees. "This is the only one made by ALCOR."

"What's his deal, anyway?"

"What do you mean?" Serpint says, leading me into an opening in the side of the wall that turns out to be a restaurant.

"Where did you get him?"

"He came with the place." Serpint laughs.

"So how did you guys happen to become partners?"

He shrugs, holding up two fingers at a hostess. She's very tall. Like way taller than Serpint. And super-thin. Like she was born in zero gravity, maybe. And she has long, black hair and silver skin. Which alone would make her look really special and exotic, but she's wearing a black bodysuit and has the biggest rifle I've ever seen strapped to her back.

I stare at her. Gawk at her, actually. Because I've never seen her kind before. This whole station is filled with humanoids I've never seen before.

Both Serpint and the bot must notice my fascination as we follow her to the back of the restaurant, because Serpint says, "Never seen a Centurian before, I take it," just as the bot starts spouting off useless facts about Centurians. Where they're located in the galaxy, how they live in the atmosphere of gas giants in huge rotating habitats, and other such things that no one who sees this woman for the first time would give any fucks about whatsoever.

You just want to look at her. The way I'm looking at her. Equal parts awe and fear.

I hope, if I'm ever in danger and she's with me, she's on my side. That's all I'm thinking about.

"Thanks," Serpint says to the silver woman, then pulls out a chair for me to sit.

"Oh," I say, surprised at his manners. "Thank you."

He takes the chair across from me and then the hostess hands us menus. I look at mine while the bot hovers at my shoulder and starts chirping about what's good.

"How would you even know?" I ask him. "You don't even eat."

He deflates a little. And by that I mean loses a little altitude, then takes off and says something about playing games in the arcade next door.

I roll my eyes.

"So... what's that all about?" Serpint says.

"What?"

"You and that bot. How do you know what he's saying? You have a translator implant? Crux has one of those. Not me, I don't give a fuck what they say. My bot—" But then he stops. "Well, the bot I used to have. Ceres. He spoke our language just fine. He was a damn good bot."

I remember that the bot was killed with his brother yesterday. I think that's one of the most surprising things about this station. They seem to think bots, and ships, and cyborgs all have the same rights as humanoids.

Which is new to me. Because that's not how it was back in Cygnia. Not at all.

Bots, and ships, and cyborgs were all just… *things*.

"Lyra?"

"What?" I say. "Oh. Your question. Well, I had nanny bots all growing up. I had that model for a while. And I was always interested in learning new languages. So I'm fluent in 700 Series."

"Interesting."

"Why is it interesting?"

"Just…" He shrugs. "Because you don't seem to mind him, even though he pierced you yesterday without my permission, and yet you hate the cyborg master. I kinda feel the other way around. That nanny bot is useless to me but the harem master, I'd make sure he was on my team if shit ever went down, that's for sure."

"Hmmm," I say. "Well, he did stick his vibrating fingers between my legs. In front of everyone. *Twice*," I add, for emphasis. "So I don't feel the same."

"And the bot pierced your pussy," he whispers, covering his face with the menu so people around us can't hear. "And your nipples. So… three times." He holds his hands up like, *I rest my case*.

"Yeah, but the bot is really harmless. He doesn't have emotions. He wasn't doing it to teach me a lesson. He really did think you wanted him to do that. In fact, he said it was part of your routine." Serpint smiles, but wisely decides not to defend himself. "And that master…" I shudder. "I know their kind and they are *not* harmless."

"How do you know their kind?" he asks, just as the hostess returns with two glasses of water. He nods thank you to her, which again surprises me. Because he's very polite to the people here. Like everyone is family, instead of just his inner circle.

"I just… do," I say, not wanting to get into the past too much. It's over. I'm gone and I'm never going back. *Ever.*

"Hmmm," Serpint says. "Well, the bots here do have emotions. So you're giving that 700 too much credit. We take off their restrictors whenever we liberate them from their former masters."

"What do you mean?" I ask, scrunching up my face. "You… don't have regulators on them?"

"Nope," Serpint says. "This place. It's not what you think."

"How do you know what I think it is?"

"Because I do. I've been all over the galaxy, Lyra. And no matter where I am or who I'm talking to, if they're not from here they all have the same opinion about Harem Station. The second people learn who I am and where I come from, they get a look on their face."

"What look?"

"The look you had yesterday when you tried to spit on me."

I inhale deeply, then let it out. "Sorry about that. I was… afraid. And wound up. And not here because I wanted to be here."

He shrugs. "I don't let it get to me. Any more," he adds. "They see what they want to see and that's just fine by me. But everyone who lives here, or stops by on their way through the gates between jobs…" He shrugs again. "They get me. And I get them. We're all the same on Harem. Just trying to stay alive in a really fucked-up, dangerous world."

"Hmm," I say.

"Hmm, what?"

"Well..." I laugh a little. "You make it sound like... you know. You're not all a bunch of outlaws on the run from the Prime Navy."

"People are people," he says. "Doesn't really matter what side of Prime you're on. Because those guys? The ones who run shit? They're no different than us, Lyra. They just make the laws that suit them, that's all. They steal and kill too. Just like us. They just call it appropriation and war instead of what it really is. Everyone's an outlaw, it's just we're the ones on the wrong side of popular opinion."

"So you fancy yourselves revolutionaries?" I ask, kinda finding it ridiculous. "I mean, I get what you're saying, because I come from a horrible, oppressive society. Make no mistake, the Cygnians are not good people. But I'm not naive enough to think that there's no difference between law and lawlessness."

"We have laws here," he says. "How do you think we get two million people to live together?"

"The hostess has a plasma rifle strapped to her back, Serpint."

"Yeah, but she showed us to our table, she didn't pull it out and try to rob us. If she ever does pull that rifle off her back to use it here, she better have a damn good reason. Because ALCOR will strike her down with one blast. Everyone knows what happens if they don't try to work shit out without killing. Of course, murder happens. We have a police force here and many murders. Just like any city. But ALCOR makes all the difference. He sees and hears *everything*."

ALCOR. Where the hell did that thing come from, I wonder? I've seen my share of sentient AIs but none of them are in charge of things like this one seems to be.

It's kinda scary, if you ask me. Letting a machine have so much power.

"Are you ready to order?"

I look up and find a waitress holding a tablet. She's got bright purple hair and her whole body is covered in metallic scales.

"Umm," I say, then point to the menu. "I'll have this?" I say, showing her the menu item.

Serpint laughs a little.

"What?" I ask.

"That's what the stupid bot told you to get."

"Well, is it bad?"

"No," he says, taking my menu and handing it to the waitress. "I'll have the same."

"Be right up," the waitress says. Then leaves.

I look around and realize there's a lot of metallic people here.

"Armor," Serpint says.

"Oh," I say. "I guess that makes sense."

"Makes them feel safe, ya know? Old habits."

"Right."

"So… you said you know about people like him."

"Who?"

"The cyborg master," Serpint says. "You said you know his kind. What's that mean?"

"I told you, I just know."

"OK," he says, taking the hint. But he has a look on his face that tells me he's not gonna let this go.

Luckily a tray bot appears with our food and its articulated grippy appendages place our plates on the table.

"Pancakes," I say, laughing. "They're pancakes."

Serpint thanks the bot, then smiles at me. "Eat up, princess. You're gonna need your energy once you meet my brothers."

Hmmm. We're on day two of this little… friendship? Relationship? Whatever it is. And I'm already meeting the family.

What a weird, fucked-up world.

CHAPTER TWENTY-ONE

I watch her as she eats breakfast. Pancakes. Not called pancakes here. But pancakes are pancakes and she likes them.

Knowing about her seems to be an unconscious priority for me. Something I still don't understand. And even though last night was fun—hell, who am I kidding? It was mind-blowing—I'm a little worried about tonight. After the memorial service, after I introduce her to my brothers, after everyone has to go home and we'll be alone…

I worry about that.

Because I do not understand what's happening to me. Or her, for that matter.

Soulmates? Like… shut the fuck up. There's no such thing. I've been in plenty of relationships with lots of different women and even though one or two of them felt like maybe they had potential, only one of those women is still around.

And her name is *Booty*.

So no. I don't believe in soulmates. But there's definitely something strange going on between Lyra and me.

Add in the fact that just thinking about being away from her makes my heart speed up. And not in the good way.

I think it's fear.

Which is so stupid. I don't even know her. She has no clue about me either, and aside from the sex, I don't think we're even compatible.

But there's too much going on today to stop and chat to ALCOR and Crux about this. Crux should be able to give me some answers. He knows more about Cygnian princesses than anyone outside Cygnia. He'll have opinions.

But first… I sigh. We need clothes for the memorial. And then we need to go see my brothers. Who will have a lot of fucking questions for me, and none of them will have anything to do with Lyra. They'll want to know why I stole the queen, how Draden and Ceres died, and what we should do about it.

Because something has to be done. Someone has to pay for the deaths of our family members.

An eye for an eye, that's how we roll.

"In here," I say to Lyra, placing my hand on the small of her back to guide her into a storefront. "This is where I shop."

She shoots me a look because she saw my closet. My clothes might not be exciting, but they are custom. And this is where I get them made.

"Raylor," I say, extending my hand to the man who runs the boutique. "I'd like you to meet Lyra. She needs something in black for this afternoon."

He takes my hand in both of his, shakes it gently, and gives a very sad look of sympathy. "I'm so sorry," he says. "It's so sad about Draden and Ceres."

"Thanks," I say, then sigh. "I guess I'll need something too."

He pats my shoulder and says, "We will dress you appropriately." Then he turns to Lyra and takes her hand. "Very nice to meet you, Miss—"

"Princess," I say, correcting him. "*Princess* Lyra."

He nods and smiles bigger. "Princess. My apologies. If you will just go with Miss Alee, she will dress you as well."

Lyra shoots me an apprehensive look as she's led away by Alee and I feel the same way.

Heart fluttering, then racing, then pounding. "Um," I say, reaching for her as she disappears behind a wall.

"She'll be fine," Raylor says. "Trust me."

I nod, take a deep breath, and will my heart to stop this bullshit. *I do not love her.*

But my heart doesn't seem to agree. Either that or my willpower is shit today.

"Here," Raylor says. "Drink this while we discuss what you need." He hands me a cut-crystal glass of whiskey and I take it. Down it. Then hold it out for another and drink that too.

Helps. Just a little, but enough.

He points me to a long couch and I take a seat as he starts cycling through suits appropriate for a memorial service.

I just stare at them as they go by. Seeing them, but not seeing them.

Draden is really dead. The past twenty-four hours have felt a little unreal. Like it didn't really happen. Like any minute now Draden and Ceres will barge in here, drunk, or just happy, or maybe fresh from a fight. Draden sporting a black eye and Ceres with new dings and dents on his outer armor.

But when I look at the door, they're not there.

And they never will be again.

They're gone.

With Raylor's constant prodding and help, I manage to choose a suit. Then I get to wait while it's tailored for me, which only has my mind wandering back to Lyra again. Every now and then I can hear them in the other room. Lyra's soft talking or Alee's authoritative opinions.

I force myself not to drink any more, even though that bottle is calling my name. It would be a very bad idea to be drunk for the service.

Just a few hours, Serpint. Just get through a few more hours and then you can drink yourself into oblivion.

Raylor appears, broad smile across his face that doesn't reach up to his eyes. He was one of the very first *haute couture* designers to make Harem Station their home. He legitimized us in this regard. Took a huge risk by leaving the Prime planets and hitching his rising star to a bunch of outlaws.

But it worked. Hundreds of eager up-and-coming designers and creatives followed his lead and within a few years, people who were not welcome here wanted to come, just for the fashion and the art.

That was over a decade ago in Akeelian time and we've been friends ever since. He'll be there this afternoon to pay his respects.

"We're ready for you, Serpint," Raylor says.

"Great," I say, following him to the back room to be dressed.

It's a weird thing to be dressed by his cyborgs because they were built on a sex-borg model. Two tall, clearly-female cyborgs begin undressing me. One unbuttons my shirt, another goes for my pants, while two more are fussing with the new suit off to one side.

Normally I enjoy this. Under different circumstances I might even let them pleasure me.

But not today. So I place a hand on each of theirs, telling them to stop. "I can do it," I say.

Raylor claps his hands two times and the sex-borgs back off and begin doing other things.

I strip down to bare flesh and pull on the underclothes.

"Would you like a shave?" Raylor asks.

"No," I say. I know that's the wrong answer. I should shave for my brother's service. But I don't want the borgs touching me right now. So I say it once more for emphasis. "No."

He nods, then motions for the dressers to proceed. They come at me again and help me into a crisp black shirt with a stiff, high, tight collar that I know will bother me until I take the shirt off later. But it's not optional. Every man in the ceremony will be wearing the same irritating collar. And every one of us will endure it without comment out of respect.

It occurs to me that this is the first time I've had to dress in the ceremonial garb since we left Akeelian space. I've been to many memorial services on Harem over the past two decades for friends who died, been one of the witnesses on the platform a dozen times or more, but never part of the immediate family.

Every alien culture has a different way of paying their last tribute to their inner circle and ALCOR will accommodate them all. But we decided early on that Harem will have its own customs as well. That we would be more than just a collection of outlaws on a station.

We would be a nation of people. A collective of thought, and customs, and history.

So every service uses the same platform, and the same announcement signals, and follows the same ascension ritual.

The pants go on next. Dressy, high-quality black slacks made of the finest silks in the galaxy. They are so soft and comfortable, they almost make up for the collar.

Then the shoes and then the accessories.

Raylor stands in front of me holding a flat velvet box. I nod to him and he opens it to reveal the medals and ribbons ALCOR and Crux had printed for the service.

"Pink?" I say, unable to hide my smile.

"She's *very* pink," Raylor says, smiling.

"Ah," I say. And I even laugh a little. Because he is matching me with Lyra. "Well, that's a first for me. I've never had a woman at my side for a ceremony before."

"It's a good first," Raylor says, snapping his fingers at one of the borgs.

She approaches us, lifts the pink ribbon from the box, and places it against the shirt collar. A second Borg is already behind me, reaching for the magnetic ends so she can snap the ribbon tightly around my neck.

A third is lifting out the familial medal. Mine is also pink to match Lyra and it has me wondering what she'll look like when she comes out from behind that wall. Surely, she won't be in pink. But there will be pink on her. Ribbons, and medals, and other things too. Lingerie, maybe. Things I won't see now but will be a nice surprise later.

Which reminds me of later. My thoughts cloud with memories of last night as the borgs fasten the accessories onto my suit.

The familial medal, signaling that I'm Draden's brother, goes over my heart. Five more are lined up underneath, military-style. All in shades of gray, and black, and pink. One for each of us—Crux, then Jimmy, then Tray, then Valor, then Luck. Underneath there is another, larger medal that belongs to Draden and Ceres.

My heart is heavy with the burden of these symbols. And not just because they have literal weight.

A dozen smaller ones climb up each of my shirt cuffs to represent how many life-and-death battles Draden, Ceres, and I have been in—and won. And then the ribbons are snapped into place on my shoulders to signify the weight I will have to carry now that they're gone.

When they are done, I step back out into the lobby, look in the full-length mirror, and barely recognize myself. My hair is messy and my face is ragged with a few days of beard. I should've let them shave me, I realize. I'm about to ask if that can still be done when my link chimes.

I pinch my fingers together and open up a screen.

It's Jimmy.

I tab the accept button and say, "Hey, when did you get in?"

"A little while ago," Jimmy says in his deep, rough voice. He's already dressed too, only his accessories aren't pink, they're silver with shades of gray, black, and white. He stares at me in the screen and I want to cut the connection to make that unnerving scrutiny disappear, but I don't. Because I can't.

I have to face up to what I did.

"I'm sorry," he says.

"For what?" I ask. "It's me who should be saying that to you."

He presses his lips together. Like he's trying hard not to frown. He's not shaved either and he looks as strangely unfamiliar in his ceremonial garb as I feel, which comforts me a little.

"We knew this day would come eventually," he says.

"Yeah," I say. "Thanks. I appreciate that."

He opens his mouth to say more but the station chime sounds, signaling that people should start making their way to the ceremonial platform.

And then I open my mouth to say more, but that's when Lyra appears from around the wall.

I stare at her, unable to take my eyes off her, and say, "I'll see you in a little bit," as I end the connection with Jimmy.

She is… stunning.

Magnificently stunning.

Her long black gown has elaborate skirts that go all the way to the floor. The bodice of her dress is woven with black crystals, so that the soft light in the room makes her shimmer as she walks towards me. Over her heart is one jeweled-pink medal. For me, I realize. But on her shoulders are the same weighty pink ribbons.

ALCOR, I think to myself. *What did you do?*

But then I notice the high collar of her dress is open and I can see the cleavage of her large breasts, which rise and fall rapidly, like she's scared, or excited, or maybe both.

"We need to take the collar off so she can wear this, Serpint," Raylor says. And then I notice he's holding another collar in his hands. This one is made out of pink and white jewels. Maybe even diamonds.

"Right," I say, stepping forward.

ALCOR. What did you do?

"You look nice," she says, frowning. Like she's unsure if she's supposed to say that when a person is dressed for a memorial service.

I stand in front of her, just staring down into her eyes. She's glowing just a little bit. So pink against the black dress. Her hair is piled up on top of her head, but it spills out of a tiara made of the same pink and white jewels as the collar in Raylor's hand.

"Princess Lyra," I sigh, reaching behind her neck to remove my ownership collar.

She smiles. Weakly. Then has trouble meeting my eyes and looks down, just as a burst of glow flows up from her breasts.

I hand the collar to Raylor and then reach for the buttons on the top of her open bodice. Fastening them all the way up her throat.

She sucks in a breath. Maybe because the fabric is tight or maybe just because I'm making her nervous. Then I take the new collar and snap the magnetic ends around her neck.

It still says Serpint, because it must. But it's very small and my name has been printed in black diamonds.

"I don't know what to think about this," Lyra says. Her fingertips lift up her floaty skirts and then let go, illustrating her point.

I let out a breath that, surprisingly, comes with a small laugh. "Me either, princess. Me either."

The station chimes a second warning that people should be on their way to the ceremony, so I just hold out my hand and say, "Shall we?"

She looks up at me, then down again, and nods her head as she places her fingertips in my palm.

I turn to Raylor and say, "I can't thank you enough."

He smiles at me. A warm smile that says he's sorry, and I'm welcome all in the same moment. "I'm going to close up and then we'll be right behind you."

I walk her out looking down at our entwined hands and notice another small medal on the cuff of her long sleeve. "What's that?" I say, holding up her hand with the medal towards her face.

"It's for the bot," she says. "I don't know why, or understand any of what just happened back there, but..." She inhales deeply, lets it out. And then shrugs.

"The bot?" And just as I say it, he's here. In front of us. Hovering. Except his dingy gray sphere of a body has been repainted in matte black. And encircling that black body is a strip of glittery pink. "What the hell?"

He chirps out a quick litany of responses, which I don't understand. But Lyra says, "ALCOR made him mine. So he gets to come too. And he has to match."

I huff a small laugh through my nose.

So now we are three.

ALCOR. What are you doing?

CHAPTER TWENTY-TWO

"This way," Serpint says, leading me through a bustling crowd of people who all seem to be heading in the same direction. "We've got a lift."

Everyone is heading for the moving sidewalks that lead to the various levels, but Serpint takes me over to the edge of the open walkway and opens a door built into the glass half-wall.

He pans his hand, motioning me to step forward onto a small landing pad, then follows me through and shuts the door behind him. The bot—my bot now, I guess—hovers just at my shoulder as a flat ship-like bot floats up to us.

"Step on," Serpint says, holding my hand to keep me steady as I board the lift-bot. "The ceremony starts at the bottom." He smiles at me, but I can tell he's not really smiling. It's a very sad day. All the dresser borgs were talking about his brother Draden while they were busy getting me ready. He was well-loved on this station. The baby of the family, good-natured, charming, and even though they didn't hide the fact that he was as ruthless and dangerous as the rest of the brothers, they brushed over it like that was just a small part of him.

They talked about Ceres, too. His bot. And worried over *Booty*, who, it seems, isn't herself. I knew that because Serpint mentioned it last night. But I didn't pay much attention to her since I didn't grow up loving ships. It's a foreign idea for me.

But everyone seems to have the same feelings for *Booty* as they do for Draden and Ceres.

I am both uncomfortable and at ease in my ceremonial gown. Uncomfortable because I feel beautiful. Truly special and stunning. And that feels wrong because of why I'm wearing it.

But at ease too, because it's a princess dress. Something I'd wear back home on certain occasions. And they put a tiara on my head, which gives me rank. It probably doesn't mean much here, but still. They did not have to acknowledge me in this way.

I'm his slave.

Or whatever they call them here.

I owe him servitude. I have the collar to prove that fact. And sure, this new one is encrusted with diamonds, but it still says *Serpint* on it.

Although I'm not feeling any self-righteous indignation over that at the moment. In fact… I kinda like being known as *his*.

After taking a few seconds to settle on the platform, we begin to descend.

I can't help but look around in awe.

This station is amazing in every direction. I look up as the ceiling grows farther and farther away, then look down, over the edge of the lift-bot, and get a little dizzy at our staggering height.

"Take a step back," Serpint says, tugging on my hand. "Believe it or not, people fall off these things all the time just because they want to look down."

"They do?" I say, then stagger backwards as I picture myself falling to my death.

"Oh, don't worry. ALCOR catches them with a safety bot. No one has ever died from falling off a lift. But they give it their best shot sometimes."

I shoot him a weak smile. This ACLOR is really a lot more than he appears. He's like a god here. In charge of everything. All-seeing, all-hearing, all-knowing.

All around us as we descend, people are making their way to the edge of each level, looking up and down, watching us as we pass. It's only then that I notice there are other lifts with people on them doing the same thing.

His brothers, I realize. All dressed up in similar ceremonial garb as Serpint and I. And their companions or partner bots. One of them I recognize as Crux, who stands next to the cyborg master on his lift. The other one I recognize is Tray, who has no bot or companion.

Two more, on the same platform, have one bot between them, like mine, but a more military version. Higher series number. Maybe a 3000 or better.

And the last brother has a full-on, silver-metallic, sex-borg as his partner. But she looks like a weapon, not just a borg. Her legs look like they are encased in silver metal stockings. Her foot molds into a high-heel stiletto shoe, and she wears a tight, black bodysuit, much like the hostess did at the restaurant this morning and it covers all her skin, not just where she would wear a top. But she has no rifle strapped to her back. Weapons are mounted all over her body. Her forearms, her thighs, and holstered at her waist.

Note to self. Make friends with the killer sex-borg. She looks more dangerous than all the brothers put together.

We all reach the bottom of the station at the same time, lined up neatly in a circle, around the perimeter of yet another very large circular platform.

"Come with me," Serpint whispers.

Every one of these brothers and companions are staring at me.

And it's no wonder. I do not belong here with them.

The station sounds a chime. But as Serpint leads me off the lift and on to the larger platform, I see that in the center there is a five-meter-tall crystal obelisk that lights up as the station chimes. And now I realize—that's ALCOR.

Or the personification of him, anyway.

Because when his voice booms through the station, the obelisk glows white with each word.

"Let us begin," ALCOR says, just as someone to my right takes my hand.

I look up, startled to see that the sex-borg is next to me. Then realize everyone around the circle is holding hands.

ALCOR begins to talk about Draden and Ceres. Tells how they met. What they mean to him, and then Crux has his say. Everyone has their say. Even the bots and the sex-borg, who has a surprisingly feminine voice attached to her military-scary body.

This is his family.

No one expects me or my bot to talk. They are going in a circle to the left, so as soon as the sex-borg finishes, Serpint clears his throat.

He takes a long breath. Stares straight ahead.

I squeeze his hand to let him know I'm here.

Which is dumb. So stupid. I don't even know this man. I'm just… compelled to comfort him.

"Um…" Serpint says. "I'm not good at this. And I'm still in shock at what happened. But I just want to say… I'm sorry." He looks at each of his family members. His voice is booming through the station speakers and suddenly, even though just a few seconds ago, there was the low thrum of whispered conversation, the station goes utterly silent except for some far-off humming of machinery.

"That's it," Serpint says in the hush. "I love you, I'll miss you, and I'm sorry."

All his brothers nod and frown. Then the one to his left begins to talk.

Serpint squeezes my hand, looks at me for a moment, and we frown together.

When the last family member is done speaking—the military bot between the two brothers it rode down with—everyone drops hands except Serpint and me. And they turn to face outward.

"Turn with me, Lyra," he says. "Face the station. We're going up."

I turn with him and find thousands of eyeballs staring back at me. Thousands of sad outlaws who came here to pay their respects to Draden and Ceres.

The sex-borg takes my hand again, just as the platform begins to rise.

We ascend slowly. Seemingly for the sole purpose of everyone getting a good look at us. And I realize that *is* the reason. They get to see us as we rise. This is some group sadness. Some shared empathy for the family's sorrow.

And once again, it is pointed out to me in the silence that Harem Station isn't what it seems.

It is more than a place. It is a *home.*

Filled with people who care about each other. Somewhere safe where they can rest and be themselves. Or fight against whatever it is they fight against. Or just… *live.*

I am humbled by this and my heart begins to beat faster as we take the long, almost agonizingly slow ride to the top of the station. By the time we reach the apex I am sure we have passed hundreds of thousands of people. Maybe even a million, they are that packed at the edge of each level.

The platform stops smoothly. Without even a slight jolt. Everyone drops hands again, except Serpint and me, and then once again we turn to face the center where the ALCOR obelisk lights up in bright white.

We rejoin hands just as it begins to rise, still glowing, and once it gets to some pre-determined altitude, the top of the station begins to open.

I gasp for breath out of instinct, fearing the darkness of deep, black space and the suffocating death of the vacuum beyond. But then I realize there is a barrier between us and the great unknown outside. Some nearly-invisible layer of force field that keeps us in the atmosphere of the station.

ALCOR says, "I will join you on your journey into eternity. You will never be alone."

And less than a breath later, the obelisk shoots through the opening and out into space.

For three seconds there is a heavy silence, then a chime. And another chime.

And then it… explodes. SEAR cannons come out of nowhere and shatter the crystal obelisk into particles of light.

"What the hell just happened?" I whisper.

"The security beacons near the gates," Serpint says. "They shatter them with cannons so their particles will float in space for eternity."

"Oh," I say. "That's quite beautiful."

Serpint squeezes my hand just as the roof opening begins to close.

When it's sealed back up and the layer of field above us has dissipated, ALCOR says, "Goodbye, brothers. We will miss you."

Even though ALCOR just rocketed out into space, he is still here. Because he is everywhere.

He is God.

Then a great cheer erupts. The cheer of a million or more people. The cheer of the station fills my ears. Fills my whole body until I'm so overwhelmed by the noise, and vibration, and emotion—that tears fall down my face and I begin to glow.

CHAPTER TWENTY-THREE

She glows for them.

First just a subtle pink, then brighter and brighter until she is a sun. She turns to me just as a pink tear falls down her cheek.

I can't help myself. The sight of her sadness, for people she didn't even know, it breaks me in half and I pull her into my chest and just hold her tight.

Some of the cheering has abruptly stopped. But just the people up here on the higher level who can see what I'm feeling.

A princess is glowing in sadness for one of their brothers.

And it is beautiful.

"Are you OK?" I ask her, swiping a piece of hair away from her cheek and tucking it behind her ear.

"Me?" She laughs a little. "I should be asking you that."

"I'm OK," I say, pressing my face into her hair. And for some reason, I truly believe that. I am OK.

"This was the most beautiful tribute I've ever seen," she says, pulling back and wiping a tear off her cheek. "Just so… touching."

I hug her tight again. How this girl, who was a complete stranger yesterday, suddenly became my rock, I have no idea. She just did.

"Serpint," Jimmy says, placing a hand on my shoulder.

I look up and see him and Xyla, his partner in crime, standing just behind Lyra.

"Good to see you," I say. "Both of you. I'm just sorry—"

"Stop," Xyla says. "Just stop. We all know that the things we do have risk. Draden knew that and so did Ceres. It's no one's fault, Serpint. People just… die."

Jimmy takes a breath. Maybe agreeing with her, maybe not. But he places a hand on Lyra's shoulder and says, "Who's this?"

Lyra turns, still brushing away tears.

"Lyra," I say. "This is my brother Jimmy and his cohort, Xyla. Xyla and Jimmy, this is Princess Lyra."

Jimmy shoots her one of his infamous sly grins. "Princess." Then he *tsks* his tongue. "You should know better, brother."

"Yeah, well. She popped into my life yesterday when I got home and I…" I take a deep breath and let it out. "I don't seem to be able to let her go."

"Imagine that," Xyla says.

"Hello," Lyra says, straightening up and extending her hand in greeting. "Very nice to meet you both. I'm so, so sorry for your loss."

"Thanks," Jimmy says, taking her hand and shaking it softly.

Then Valor is here, Luck trailing behind him. Their bot, Beauty, between them as always.

"Lyra, huh?" Luck says. "We've heard all about you."

"From who?" I ask.

"Crux," Valor says.

"And ALCOR." Luck laughs. "In fact, pretty much everyone is talking about the new princess today."

"How could we not?" Valor says.

And then Luck, being the charmer he is, takes Lyra's hand and kisses it. "Very pleased to meet you, Princess Lyra."

Her glow, which had been dying down, suddenly lights up again.

I push Luck back and say, "Hands off."

Which only makes him laugh.

"Lyra," Xyla purrs in her fembot voice. "I'm Xyla, this is Beauty," she says, motioning to Valor and Luck's bot. "But who is this little delicious morsel following you at every turn?" She smiles coyly at our new bot.

"Oh," Lyra, says, catching her breath. "This is… well. Do you have a name?" She asks the bot.

It chirps out a long string of beeps and whistles, which makes Xyla guffaw. "Oh, honey," she says. "We're not calling you the Crowned King Prince of Planet Palasia. Get over yourself."

The bot objects, but Lyra puts up a hand and says, "Prince, then. You can be called Prince."

"Wonderful," I say, rolling my eyes.

"Nice paint job," Xyla says, trailing a finger over the bot's ring of pink glitter. "Come dance with me,

Prince." And she beckons him with a single finger as she walks off, looking over her shoulder.

The bot squeaks in what seems to be cautious excitement, but follows.

When Xyla gives an order most people follow it. She's just kinda… powerful like that.

"So, Lyra," Jimmy says in his deep voice.

"So… I'm sorry. How do you say your name? Yimminy?"

"Jimmy," I say quickly. "Not Yimminy." Jimmy's sensitive about this because his name is… weird. No one can say it right.

Lyra smiles back at him and tries again. "Himmy. Hmmm. That's an unusual name. Where does it come from?"

Valor, Luck, Jimmy and I all trade glances. None of us correct her this time. It is what it is. Not our fault his name is weird.

"What?" Lyra says.

"He has no idea where the name comes from," Valor says. "He's making it all up so don't believe him when he tells you. And we've begged him for years to change it but he refuses even though everyone gets it wrong."

"Wait," Lyra says. "You're brothers though, right?"

"Brothers from another mother." Valor laughs. Then he looks at me, raising one eyebrow. "Does she not know how this works?"

"How what works?" Lyra asks.

"You know," Luck says. "How little Akeelian babies are made?" He bobs his eyebrows at her.

"OK, that's enough," I say. "Let's talk about Jimmy's stupid name."

"I like my name," Jimmy says, taking a drink off a bot tray as it passes. "It's unique. No one else in the whole galaxy is called Jimmy."

"Probably true," Luck says, reaching to help himself to a drink before the bot tray can leave. "Because it's stupid."

Jimmy rolls his eyes just as the station begins playing soft music, and says, "Would you like to dance, Lyra? I seem to be short a partner at the moment."

"Um…" She looks at me.

I shrug. "Go ahead. I've got to talk to Crux and ALCOR anyway. You know, about our little problem."

"Oh," she says. "Right."

"What problem?" Jimmy asks, taking her hand and leading her to the center of the platform. "Tell Jimmy all about it. I'm sure I can help."

Lyra shoots me a panicked look over her shoulder, but I find it cute that Jimmy has taken an interest. He hates everyone so this is a good sign.

"Yeah, what problem?" Valor asks.

"Never mind," I say, pushing him in the chest as I make my way past him. "ALCOR and Crux will know what to do."

But I only get a few steps away before I'm the one looking over my shoulder. My eyes immediately track to Lyra and I have sudden heart palpitations the further apart she and I get.

"Stop it, Serpint," I chastise myself under my breath. "You do not love this girl. You do not even know this girl."

And she has secrets.

Secrets I've conveniently forgotten about after last night, but which have now resurfaced.

"Crux," I say, making my way towards him and the cyborg master. "I need to talk to you."

Crux leans in to the cyborg master, whispers something—which earns him a nod—and then the master walks off.

"What problem is that?" Crux asks.

"You know what problem. I'm pretty sure the master has filled you in on what happened last night in the doctor's office with Lyra."

He raises one eyebrow at me. "No. He didn't. But why was she in the doctor's office?"

"Never mind that. The problem is…" I lean in closer and whisper. "The problem is that… we seem to… well…"

"Spit it out," Crux says.

"We seem to have some kind of connection."

Crux smiles big and says, "Good. I'm glad."

"No," I say. "You don't understand. By connection, I mean… *connection.*" I point down to my groin.

He laughs.

"It's not funny, asshole. Last night my second cock popped out before his time. And then both of them got stuck inside her. And now she's talking about soulmates or fated mates, or some bullshit like that, and I can't stop thinking about her."

"So… what's the problem again?"

"Did you even hear the words coming out of my mouth? I said—"

"I heard you," he says, holding up a hand. "I just don't understand the question."

"That's not supposed to happen. None of it."

He gives me a sideways glance. "Yeah, it is."

"No, it isn't. And she lights up like the fucking sun, Crux. Her flux capacitor is on overdrive, man. I'm not kidding. I've never seen anything like it."

"I'm still not understanding why you're confused."

"What do you mean?"

"Well, you said all the right things. So… what's the question again?"

"Why is this happening?"

He just looks at me. "You're serious?"

"Yeah, I'm dead fucking serious. That's why I'm here. Talking to your dumb ass."

"But you just said soulmates. So…"

"Yeah, but that's bullshit."

"Oh, is it?" He laughs.

My heart begins to race. "Isn't it?"

"No, you shithead. That's the whole draw to a Cygnian princess. If you find the right one, they glow like the sun. That's how you know you're perfect for each other."

I swallow hard. And I'm not sure if it's because I'm nervous, excited, or afraid. Maybe all of the above. "I've never heard of this."

"Well, it almost never happens. They genetically engineer their soulmates before birth. So yeah, it is very strange that hers turns out to be *you*. But other than that, nah. This is all normal, everyday shit."

"You've had it before then? You've experienced it?"

He looks away from me very quickly. But catches himself and looks back almost as fast. "Maybe. Once. A long time ago."

And that's when I put two and two together. "No," I say. "No."

He smiles weakly, then shrugs. "Yup."

"You and Queen Corla?" I ask.

He sucks a bit of air through his teeth. "Guilty."

"When?" I ask.

"Right before we left Akeela System."

I am speechless. I thought I knew everything there was to know about my brother, but apparently I don't. "But you were like—"

"Sixteen." He laughs. "So was she."

"How did you even meet her?"

He chews on his lip and shakes his head. "She was on a delegation—"

"Wait," I say, putting up a hand. "The Cygnians were in the Akeela System? For diplomatic relations? Since when?"

"You really don't know, do you?"

"Know what?" I ask.

Crux looks at me hard. A little bit too hard. "Serpint," he says. "We come from them."

I hear the words. I see his mouth moving. But what he just said makes no sense at all. "What do you mean?"

"I mean…" He takes a deep breath. "I mean we come from them, Serpint. When they used to make their soulmates, fated mates, whatever, we were how they made them. Didn't you ever wonder why we have the biology we do? How did you get here?" he asks. "Your mother slept with an Akeelian male, she got pregnant with you, a boy. So you are now an Akeelian as well. But did you ever ask yourself what happens to the girls?"

I start to feel sick.

"They take the girls, Serpint. Back to Cygnia and use those genetics in their engineering program. That's how you make a glowing girl. That's how you make a man with two dicks."

"How come I didn't know this?"

He shrugs. "No one outside Cygnia and Akeela knows. And we left when you were young. I just figured you knew. Someone told you."

"Who would tell me? Jimmy?" I laugh.

"ALCOR at least."

I wait for ALCOR's input. Crux and I both know he's listening. But the silence after we invoke his name says far more than words ever could.

"Look," Crux says. "There's a lot of shit happening right now that we need to talk about. But not today, Serpint. Not now." He claps me on the shoulder and says, "We'll talk tomorrow. OK? Just go back to that princess and dance with her. Take her back to your quarters and just… enjoy her. Ya know? If she's your one, then just enjoy her."

"Why?" I ask, getting the feeling he's talking about something else. "I mean…"

"Don't overthink it, Serpint." And then Crux smiles. "And thank you. I don't think I thanked you."

"For what?" I say.

"Bringing Corla to me." He holds his breath and lets it out in a long rush. "I never thought I'd see her again."

I nod, trying to picture him with this woman. Back when they were kids. "You should wake her up," I say.

But he shakes his head. "I can't. We're star crossed."

I shoot yet another confused look and he claps me on the shoulder again. Laughing. "Tomorrow, Serpint. Go dance with Lyra. Before Jimmy gets any ideas about shooting her up with a plasmid to rearrange her DNA so she's bonded to him instead."

I look over at Jimmy and Lyra and find them still dancing. Smiling and having a good time. And when I look back at Crux he's already walking off. I yell, "Hey! Wait! Is that a real thing?"

Because the thought of someone fucking up the genetic bond we have… that just scares the shit out of me. "And we need to talk about *Booty*!"

"Tomorrow," he calls back, already disappearing through a door that leads up to his private quarters. I guess he's out. Or maybe he's just going back up to Corla's cryopod to look at her forbidden body.

So close, yet still so far away.

But he didn't say it *wasn't* possible, which means it is.

I start heading over to Jimmy and Lyra, intent on breaking that little friend affair up real fast, when I glance over and see Lyra's stupid bot showing off a weapon to Beauty, Valor and Luck's bot.

"For sun's sake," I mutter, heading over there first. Irritated that I have to babysit a nanny bot. I don't even understand why he's even here. If Crux thinks this low-level 700 Series can replace Ceres—well, I just laugh.

"Excuse me," I say, interrupting the little bot party. "Can you give us a minute, Beauty?"

"Sure, Serpint," she purrs in her over-seductive voice. I have never seen the draw of a sexy bot or cyborg the way Jimmy, Valor, and Luck always did. If you're gonna have a bot as part of your team they should be manly. Not feminine. Ships should be feminine. Bots, not so much. I like them tough. Like Ceres was.

Once Beauty floats away I turn to the 700 Series and say, "Bot, put that stupid little laser gun away. It's the most ridiculous weapon I've ever seen."

And it is too. Looks like a fucking toy I played with back when I was a baby.

He chirps at me, squeaking and whistling all kinds of things that make no sense to me. "I don't understand you." I say. "And I don't care what you're saying. If you belong to Lyra, and Lyra belongs to me, then you belong to me and I can boss you around. So put the toy gun away and act your age."

He tilts his body just a little. And if he were humanoid, and had a head, I'd say he was cocking his head at me. Like, *Oh, really*?

"Yes," I say. "Really. You look ridiculous holding that tiny weapon. Does it even shoot real light? Or is it some flashlight left over from your nanny bot days?"

He straightens his thin, metal arm, points the gun at a storefront, and then his grippy appendage that acts like a hand squeezes the trigger.

A huge burst of fire erupts from the tiny barrel and then there's a hole in the wall where the store used to be.

"What the fuck?"

"Prince," ALCOR says in his stern, I-am-the-law-here omnipresent voice. "That is unlawful, and unacceptable behavior on Harem Station. Weapons can only be discharged in designated areas."

I forgot the bot was called Prince now. I will never call him that. No matter what.

Safety bots appear in vast numbers immediately. Dozens of them. One throws a net over the bot, another shocks him with a taser, and a third is reading him his rights.

I nod my head, satisfied as Lyra's bot complains loudly.

"What the hell?" Lyra says, suddenly by my side.

I smile at her. Take her hand and just… pull her close. "Got what he deserved," I say. "Dance with me, princess. I've got a jealous streak inside me and right now, I'm thinking up seventeen different ways to kill my brother for trying to steal you away from me today."

Her smile makes this whole day better. Well, that and the fact that the bot got arrested and is gonna get ripped a new sensor port by ALCOR. "I only had eyes for you the whole time," she coos in my ear as we press our bodies together and sway to the station music. "What were you and Crux talking about? It looked pretty heated."

"Tomorrow," I say. "We can talk about it tomorrow. Tonight I just want to forget everything but you."

She drops her head to my shoulder and lets me twirl us in slow circles. She smells good. And she's so beautiful tonight, I suddenly have an urge to get her naked and in my bed. Maybe make good use of her magnetic bracelets.

Hell, maybe I'll never get out of bed ever again.

That's a nice thought.

A really nice thought.

CHAPTER TWENTY-FOUR

Opinions so far on our first date.

One. Serpint looks hot in his ceremonial suit. And I know that's totally inappropriate since we're at a memorial service, but it's true. He looks so commanding. Everything about him says power. And now that I know what all the various metals and ribbons mean attached to his shirt sleeves, I'm both impressed that he's still alive and worried about the life he lives.

Alee talked a lot while she and the other borgs were dressing me. And every bit of it was about Serpint. She must be old, even though she obviously doesn't look it, because borgs don't age the way full humans do. She's known him even longer than Raylor. She came to the station just after the brothers and ALCOR opened it for business, so he was young.

I try to picture Serpint as a boy and find it very difficult. There is something hard about him. Something dark, too. Something you either never see in children or if you do, you wish you hadn't.

I tried to pump her for information about how they all got here, but she didn't seem to know. Or maybe she just didn't want to tell me. But I feel like there's a story there.

Probably a bad one. Or a sad one. Or maybe both.

Opinion number two about our first date.

Meeting his brothers was surprisingly nice. Luck and Valor have some kind of unusual arrangement. Even though I've figured out that Serpint and his dead brother Draden had a similar partnership, Luck and Valor seemed different. And that gold bot of theirs? Beauty. She's just your basic round sphere like my Prince, but somehow she came off sexy. Luck and Valor's ceremonial metals and ribbons were gold to match Beauty and even more plentiful than Serpint's, which has me wondering what they do. Do they hunt down princesses, like Serpint? I need to learn more about them before I put all those pieces together.

Tray. Hmmm. I don't think I have an opinion about Tray yet. I get the feeling he's ALCOR's right hand around here, even though Crux is the one in charge. He was always alone tonight, for one thing. No bot, no borg, no woman. He didn't even hang out with his brothers, just kept to himself off to the side. And he wore no medals or ribbons on his suit.

Which might lead one to think he's the pacifist in the family. Or he's weak. But that's not the impression I got. His eyes are dark, dark violet. And narrow like he had a constant look of distrustfulness in them. Always scanning the crowd. Looking for something. Or super-aware of his environment. And then he'd whisper into the air. To nobody. That's what I thought at first when

I saw him doing that. But then I realized he was talking to ALCOR.

A mystery, then. Maybe they are all mysteries.

Himmy is a charmer even though that name of his is impossible to say. In fact, I'd go so far as to call him dangerously charismatic. Every word across his tongue is sweetness secretly laced with a threat. Not that I was afraid of him while we danced. I wasn't. But I probably should've been. He's tall—they are all tall—and has light brown hair and one of those perfectly trimmed shadow beards. He was also looking very handsome in his suit and all his metals and ribbons were silver, white, and black. They matched Xyla.

Which brings me to opinion number three.

Xyla isn't what I expected. Yes, I still think she's even more dangerous than all these brothers put together, but she was flirting with my bot the entire night.

Until he blew a hole in that storefront and got arrested, that is.

I would like to make friends with Xyla. I would like to know where a girl might get one of those black bodysuits that seem to be all the rage. Also, I'd like a few weapons of my own. I think Xyla is just the person to handle these things for me.

Opinion number four.

Crux is lying about something. I watched him talk to Serpint out of the corner of my eye as I danced with Himmy, and I saw it. I saw all the tells of a man lying. He knows something the others don't, or he's hiding something from them, or… I don't know. I just know there's more to him than I can see right now.

So far nothing about this station is what I thought. And every single one of these men who run it, including the AI and the bots and borgs they include in their inner circle, isn't what I thought either.

What is this place? It's not just a rowdy safe haven for transient outlaws. Where did this ALCOR come from? And how did this little group of people get their hands on what amounts to a floating metropolitan city?

Mysteries. All of them.

"What are you thinking so hard about?" Serpint asks, just as the elevator stops at his apartment.

"Our day," I say, pulling him closer to me. I've got my hands wrapped around his upper arm in a possessive way and I didn't realize I was doing that until just now, so I let go and try my best not to blush.

To my surprise, I can control the glow. There's a little hum inside me that I know is the light in reserve. It's always there just below the surface, waiting to be unleashed.

Serpint looks down at my hands, now suddenly free, and takes one. Leading me into his quarters.

My gown is long and the skirts are full. They swish a little as I walk. Serpint looks over his shoulder at me with a sly grin, mischief in his eyes as he leads me straight back to the bedroom.

Oh, I've been thinking about this all day.

When we pass through the open door he twirls me around so I'm facing him and slides one of his large, strong hands along my waist. "You look stunning, Lyra. Absolutely stunning. If someone had told me yesterday morning that you'd turn into… *this* tonight, I wouldn't have believed them."

"Yeah," I say, laughing a little. "Well, I was doing my best to look like shit. So… I'm going to take that as a compliment."

"Good," he says. "That's how I meant it."

He leans in and kisses me and I automatically kiss him back.

It's a nice kiss. A soft, warm, gentle kiss.

But it's not the heated passion we experienced yesterday.

In fact, I don't even glow. Not even a little.

What the hell? Because I feel good. I feel turned on. There's a thrum between my legs that lets me know I want him. I'd like him to strip me naked and fuck me.

But that *need* is missing now. I cannot even imagine this night turning supernova. There doesn't seem to be an imploding universe in our immediate future.

"What's wrong?" he asks, still kissing me.

I don't want to talk about it because I've kinda gotten used to the idea that I was his and he was mine. And this mythological soulmate bond is real.

But now it feels a lot more like a stupid children's fantasy cooked up by a restless and bored mind.

And I don't want it to be that way. I want to go back in time and feel the way I did last night. I want to rip his clothes off, and he mine, and fuck until we blow the whole place up.

Oh, God. Did I really just think that? What the hell is wrong with me?

"Lyra." He laughs a little into my mouth. "What are you thinking about?"

Not anything I can tell you, I silently think. So I do the only thing left to do.

I begin unbuttoning his shirt.

He leans back, pulling us out of our kiss, and watches my fingers as they release his buttons from the bottom up.

I stare into his eyes—and they glow a deep purple violet. When I get to his high collar he tilts his head forward so I can unclasp the pink ribbon around his neck. It's very smooth in my hand. Silky and expensive and the magnetic ends give it some weight and make it feel important.

He takes it from my hand and lays it flat and straight on a nearby shelf. Then looks back at me and tilts his head back so I can reach the buttons on his high collar.

I suck in a breath of air as I release the last few and then open his shirt up to reveal the hard, cut body underneath and place my hand flat on the muscles of his chest.

He feels like smooth, warm stone.

One side of his shirt falls over his shoulder and hangs there from the weight of the medals. He makes no move to take off the shirt and neither do I.

Instead I place my other hand flat on his chest, and drag them both down his stomach as I kneel before him.

He exhales, closing his eyes, when my fingers pop the button on his pants.

Then he grips my head with both hands when I drag the zipper down and release his hard cocks from his underwear.

"Two?" I whisper.

"I don't know, Lyra. I don't have any answers for you." He says this as his fingers slide into my hair and urge me to move my face closer to his groin.

"That's OK," I say, wrapping both my hands around both his cocks. Together they are so thick, I can just barely encircle them in my palms. Gently, slowly, I start to move my hands up and down his two shafts.

He exhales again, gripping my hair with more force. Leaning his head back to point his closed eyes at the ceiling.

"Do you like that?" I ask him.

"Mmmm-hmmm," he murmurs. "Very much."

"Do you want me to put them in my mouth?" I ask.

He opens his eyes to look at me, then nods his head, wordlessly.

I don't think they'll fit. But I don't say that. Better to let him fantasize about the possibility. So I lean forward, gently blowing on his tips. He sucks in a long breath of air through his teeth so it sounds like a hiss. And just as he does that, I drag the tip of my tongue across the tip of his heads.

"Oh, fuck," he groans.

And I feel the same way. My pussy is throbbing now. Hot, and wet, and ready for him to be inside me.

But again, the desperation we felt last night seems to be gone.

Now everything is slow, and calm, and… different.

I'm worried about that. So very worried that we're not anything special. That we are just two ordinary people who met by accident and there's no fate in our future.

But I don't want to think about that right now.

So I open my mouth as wide as I can, and take one of his cocks in my mouth. Slowly pumping his other one with my hand as I lean forward and take him in my throat.

"Lyra," he moans, pushing on my head to urge me to go deeper.

I do. I take him as deep as I can until I know I can't force him inside me any farther.

He pulls me back off his cock when I gag, smiling down at me like I'm his princess.

"You like that?" I ask him, wiping saliva off my lips. He brushes my hand away from my mouth to stop me, then nods and aims me at his cock again.

I go down deep. Deeper than last time. And this time when I gag he pulls me off with a jerk to my hair.

The excitement between my legs builds again. The desperation I felt last night floats inside me, just below the surface. Ready to be let loose.

"Oh," I say, looking up at him as saliva spills over the side of my lips.

"Do you like it rough?" he asks.

And even though yesterday I would've insisted I didn't, tonight is a whole other lifetime of difference. "Mmmmm-hmmmm," I mutter, then whisper, "I think I do."

He grins. A lopsided grin that is equal parts mischief and diabolical intentions. And says, "Me too."

CHAPTER TWENTY-FIVE

I have plans for Lyra tonight*.* Plans I didn't realize I'd made until this very second. Until now this whole day has been rather calm, and subdued, with no hint of the desperation and acute longing we experienced yesterday.

And all that is about to change.

"Take me," I tell her. "Take all of me, Lyra."

She sucks in a long breath of air as she looks at my hard cocks in her hands. I get even harder as I notice that together, with both of my thick shafts in her hands, they barely fit in her circled palms. The tips of her fingers do not meet. They are huge.

I know what she's thinking. *These will never fit in my mouth.*

And maybe that's true, but trying is half the fun.

"Do it," I say, my voice raw and rough as I fist her hair, knocking her sparkling tiara off to the side of her head a little.

She nods her head, eyes locked on mine, and whispers, "OK," as she opens her mouth and leans forward.

There is no way she can take all of me at once without help. But I don't mind helping. One hand releases her hair and I pull the corner of her mouth to the side, stretching her cheek as I move my hips forward. She gets one inside her mouth and the way she presses her tongue flat along the top of my shaft almost drives me insane.

But I focus. I want this. I don't know why I need to make her do dirty things to me, but I do.

I push along the side of my cock as I pull her cheek aside, forcing it to fit snug against my other one. And then it's inside her. Just barely, but oh, fuck. The sensation this little bit elicits is beyond amazing.

Groans and loud moans escape my lips as I take it one step further and thrust my hips forward with force.

She gags as one of my cocks slips deeper into her throat and the other, pressed up just behind it, blocks her airway.

Her eyes begin to water as she stares up at me and sweet streaks of pink tears pool until they overflow her lower lids and spill over the side. They take some black mascara with them as they fall down her cheeks. Streaks of watered-down gray that glow pink.

"That's it," I say, encouraging her.

She breathes through her nose. Eyes still locked on mine. And I take a mental picture of this moment. Her face, her eyes, her pink, her disheveled hair and crooked tiara. Her mouth stretched wide with my fat cocks shoved between her lips.

I pull her back and she gasps for air. Fingertips hastily wiping away the spit that runs down her chin.

"Come here," I say. Remembering the way I said that to her last night. Beckoning her from across the bed and the empty space between us.

What a world away from how I say it now.

She stands, her breasts heaving with heavy, deep inhales of breath. Up and down, quick and fast.

"I want you naked," I say.

She nods her head and immediately her fingers go to the high buttons of her collar.

Instantly she realizes she cannot take the dress off without my permission. Because I have to remove the collar to remove the dress.

I do *not* want to remove that collar.

I have this irrational fear that if it ever comes off she will flee. She will run away from me as fast as she can.

So even though this is a very nice dress and it should be respected if only for the event it was made for, I don't care.

I reach for the middle seam and rip it open with one quick tug.

Black crystal buttons go flying across the room. Scattering and sliding along the obsidian floors. And underneath the deceptive black fabric is a sweet, sweet surprise.

My brute force is rewarded with a pink bra covered in white crystals.

She glows as she watches me take it all in. Not a lot. Just a little hint of light that catches the thousands of tiny gems and makes her *sparkle*.

"Oh, princess, you're going to kill me," I say, pulling on the edges of her ripped bodice even more. Tearing her dress off until the top half lies flat in tatters over her hips and the only thing left is the sleeves, gripping tightly to the flesh of her arms.

I take her hand, kiss her knuckles gently, then pull the sleeve down one arm until it's fully removed. I toss that carelessly to the floor and repeat. Taking her other hand. Kissing all her remaining knuckles, then pulling the sleeve down until both arms are bare.

Taking a step back, I look at her.

She is glowing much brighter now. Much brighter.

Her tits are contained in the sparkling bra cups, just begging me to rip that off and bare them as well.

But no. No. I need to see her in this sweet lingerie. I want to see her pink body pressed up against the dark gunmetal-gray magnetic wall. I want to keep her prisoner against my wall and do dirty, nasty things to her to make her explode.

Unable to control myself another second, I reach for the waist of her skirts and rip them open, exposing her legs.

And oh, God. I'm dead. I'm fucking dead when I realize she's wearing stockings and garters, but no underwear.

"Oh, princess," I moan. "What have you done?"

She lights up bright pink as she blushes. "Do you like it?"

"Fuck yeah, I do."

And now I can't get her naked. She is too pretty to take apart anymore.

So I hold out my hand, palm up, and she places her fingers over the top as I help her step out of the ring of fluffy skirts at her feet.

Just below her black magnetic anklets she's wearing pink stilettos.

I'm going to send Raylor and Alee a big, fat, two-happy-cocks bonus tomorrow.

"Come with me," I say, leading her over to my magnetic wall.

I turn her around so her back is against the wall and she sucks in a breath of air as her skin hits the cold metal. "Don't move until I make you," I say. My voice is husky and deep with my desire for her body.

She bites her lip and nods as I pinch air between my fingers and open up a screen. I pull up the controls for the wall and smile at her.

She sucks in air at that smile and I don't blame her. That smile is filled with many deviant, sexual promises for her tonight.

I take her left hand, kiss her knuckles, and then lift her arm up and to the side. Placing it flat against the wall.

Then do the same thing for the other arm.

"Now," I say, tapping the inside of her left ankle with my shoe. "Open your legs. Wide."

She does. Repositioning herself.

And then I whisper, "Hold still," and activate the controls for the magnets.

Instantly her wrists, neck, and ankles are snapped to the wall.

She struggles with the new sensation at being locked in place for a moment. Soft whimpers and moans escaping her lips.

"Now I can do anything I want with you, princess." I lean in to kiss her lips and then whisper, "And you won't be able to stop me."

Instantly she lights up.

Not quite a sun, not even close to a supernova, but she is *lit*.

"You like that, don't you?" I ask her. "You like that idea."

"Yes," she moans, lighting up even more.

I step forward and slide my fingers up against her pussy. I rub her in small circles as she struggles under the confinement of the magnets. Her hips jerking from side to side, using every single bit of the small amount of freedom I've allowed. Writhing under my touch.

"Good," I say. "Because I've got more in store for you tonight. Now stay put right here, princess. I'll be right back."

I chuckle as I turn away and walk out of the bedroom. As if she could move. Those magnets are strong enough to pull a ship into a docking lock. There is no way to escape until I let her.

Maybe we'll play that game tomorrow. Escape from Serpint's Sex Wall could be fun.

But tonight, I have other plans.

I go to the drawers where I keep my toys and pull them open, looking for just the right accessories for tonight.

I choose two. Just two. And walk back into the bedroom.

She is on fire with light. Pink light flows out of her body. From her eyes, from her pussy, from every inch of her.

"Scare you a little?" I ask.

She's practically panting like an animal, that's how hard she's breathing. Her large, round breasts are rising and falling with each inhale and exhale. She nods her head. "I don't like the thought of you leaving."

"You think I might leave you here and never come back?" I ask, cocking my head to the side. "While it's a nice thought, and a game we'll eventually play, I have no intention of leaving you alone tonight. Not for one second."

She smiles and shakes her head, looking down at the floor. "No," she says. "That's not what I mean."

"Then what did you mean?"

"I meant… just… I don't like the thought of you leaving me, Serpint. Of being separated from you. I can't bear it. I can't stand the idea of not having you close."

Oh. God.

I love this girl.

I walk over to her, place my palm against her face, lean down to take her mouth, and whisper, "You don't ever have to worry about that," as I kiss her lips. "You're mine now and forever."

She kisses me back and it's… perfect. Soft, but the desperation we'd been missing earlier is definitely back. The longing is throbbing in my cocks. The want and the need manifests as a bright burst of light.

I take a step back and then turn, placing my two toys on the silver bed cover. Then let my shirt fall down my arms. Picturing her behind me, taking in all the cut muscles of my back and shoulders.

Then I lower my pants and boxers until they fall to the floor at my feet. I turn to face her. Sitting down on the bed to take off my shoes and socks and shove the discarded clothes to one side.

She stares at me. At my face, then my chest, then my stomach, then my cocks and my balls. I open my legs wider, giving her a better view, and this makes her flash pink.

I reach for the cock ring and she moans a little as I spit on my fingers to lube it up, then grab my cocks in one fist, holding them tightly together, and slip the ring around them. Binding them into one, super-thick cock for her pussy.

Then I stand up, my mega-cock sticking straight out, and pick up the other toy before approaching her again.

"What's that?" she breathes, looking down at the toy in my hand.

"That," I say, "is your nemesis, princess. That is the devil that will torture you until you're begging me to let you come. That… is your worst nightmare tonight."

I flick it on with my finger and it begins to hum. Not a lot. Not even a little bit. The hum and vibration is so low, it barely registers.

But that's the whole point.

I want her to beg for the real thing. I want her to hate this toy. I want her to despise any and all possible substitutions for my cocks.

I place it between her wide-open legs. She is so wet it slides back and forth across her lips easily. No friction at all.

"I can't feel it," she says. "Turn it up."

"Oh, no," I say. "That's not the point of this toy."

"Oh, God," she moans, biting her lip. "No…"

"Oh, yes," I assure her. "Oh. Yes." I move it back and forth just enough to make her whine and whimper. And as I do this I glance down at her bra. There's a little clasp in the center. *Oh, fuck you all to hell, Raylor. You thought of everything.*

I don't want to take her bra off. I like the sparkles that shine from the crystals. Little bits of reflected light dance across her neck and face, making her look like something surreal. Like a fantasy right out of my most sensual, erotic dream.

But now that I've seen the opportunity—now that the little silver clasp is right in front of my face—I can't not undo it.

"You're killing me," I say.

"You're killing *me*," she whispers back. "More," she groans. "Please give me more."

I just chuckle as my fingers twist the clasp of her bra and release her tits. They bounce and jiggle in their newfound freedom. And instead of the piercings the bot placed on her yesterday, there are two rings of silver, each with one bright pink diamond attached. "Oh, that's not enough," I say. "Not nearly enough begging for me to give you what you want."

I squeeze her breast as I say this, then lower my mouth to her nipples and take the diamond ring into my mouth. Swirling my tongue against it as I continue to caress her dripping-wet pussy with the low-vibration toy.

"I want you," she says, her body writhing against the wall. "I want your cocks inside me. Right now!"

There we are, my little princess. Your unquenchable desire is back.

But instead of giving her what she wants, I dig in and say, "No, no, no," as I lean into her body until my chest is pressed up against her tits and my mega-cock is poking her in the stomach. "Your words are not enough. I need to see it."

"Serpint," she coos. "Please." And oh, how I love to hear my name come out of that perfect, pouty mouth.

"I need your light. I want all of it, Lyra. And I won't accept anything less than the annihilation of the multiverse this time."

Our eyes meet and she growls at me. And in that same instant they flash bright white. Blinding me with her anguish so I have to look away.

But I force myself not to. I make myself look at her. The white flutters and flashes until it's neon pink.

I rub her pussy with the vibrator just as her glow begins to morph into a combination of yellow gold and light pink.

"Oh, yeah," I moan. "Let me see all the ways I light you up, Lyra."

She begins rocking her hips back and forth. Rubbing my cock and pressing it between our bare stomachs.

I am beyond myself with desire for this woman. She is everything in this moment. My whole world. Suddenly I want my cocks inside her just as much as she does. I lose my resolve, overtaken by heat and the desire to push myself deep into her belly and make her scream.

"Fuck me," she says, the light coming out of her turning into a flutter of sparks. Sparks that have heat to them. Sparks that burn my skin and inflict an insatiable desire to do everything she says.

I reach over, tap the release tab for the magnetic field that holds her to the wall, and she falls forward into my waiting arms. I reach under, pick her up. Backing her into the wall once more. Crashing her into it so hard, her breath escapes from her lungs with a groan.

And in that same groan I thrust my tightly bound cocks into her waiting, wet pussy and pound her so hard, her tiara falls off her head and crashes to the obsidian floor with an earsplitting ting that resonates in my ears. That sound mixes with her light as she bites my neck and digs her nails into the skin of my back. Raking them up to my shoulders with a sting that forces me to give in.

I twirl her around, take two steps towards the bed, and throw her down. She bounces, still reaching for me. Eagerly grabbing for my glistening cocks and grasping for my waist as I lower myself on top of her.

And this time, when I enter her there are no more demands. Nothing left to wait for.

I slide down, my feet sliding backwards on the floor behind me as I push my cocks so deep inside her she bucks her back, opens her mouth, and screams as we tear apart the very fabric of the universe.

CHAPTER TWENTY-SIX

When the light finally fades there is nothing left of us. We have dissipated into the ether of the universe like photons. Drifting out, past the walls of the station, and into the deep dark where nothing matters.

"Holy shit," Serpint says, rolling off me. "Just… holy fucking shit, Lyra."

I smile, and just lie on my back with my eyes closed.

He reaches for me, tugs me in close, and wraps his arms around my middle as he pulls my back up to his chest. "You're mine," he says. "All mine now. I hope you don't have plans for the next hundred years, because I've already made them. I'm going to magnetically bind you to me forever."

"You say that now," I say, trying to catch my breath. But then I turn so I can see his face. And I place one hand on his cheek. Gently. Because I want to be as gentle with him now as I was rough with him a few minutes ago. "That's because this whole world annihilation thing is all new and sexy. But you've only gotten a small taste of what I can do to you. Just wait until you see the real me. You might run away scared."

He laughs. "I'll take my chances."

I sigh, content, and then lean in and kiss him on the nose.

But inside I really do worry about that moment. The one when he figures out what I really am and what I was on my way to do when I got caught on Bull Station.

What will he think of me then?

"I know what you're thinking," he says. But he's got a smile on his face and his eyes are closed. So he has no idea what I'm thinking. Because if he did... well, I don't know what would happen next. But I'm pretty sure it would involve a meeting with ALCOR and maybe a call to the Prime Navy, and not be anything like what's actually happening.

"You're thinking," he continues when I stay silent, "that we're new, and fresh. And all this light-fucking and galaxy-breaking sex will fade over time." He opens his eyes. "But I'm gonna tell you something right now, Princess Lyra."

"What will you tell me?" I tease. Because I want to believe him. I really do.

"You're my fucking fated mate. The other half of my soul. I don't care if I only met you yesterday, this is biology. Crux told me about it."

"What?" I say, my heart speeding up. "What did he tell you?"

I knew it. I fucking knew they were talking secrets earlier.

"He told me they genetically engineer you princesses to have one true soulmate. And then he hinted that we Akeelians are those mates. So it's real, Lyra. This is real. You're mine and I'm yours. And there's nothing, not a goddamned thing, either of us can do to change that."

I kiss him again so I don't have to reply. I kiss him on the mouth. He opens up for me, parts his lips to allow my tongue inside, and whispers, "I'll never let you go. Ever."

We kiss a little longer as I think about that proclamation. Wonder if it could really work out for us.

Not likely. Even if this soulmates thing is true, there's not a whole lot about my future that will excite him. Not the way he thinks, anyway.

And that reminds me of Nyleena. What is she doing right now? What are they doing to her? Two days—three probably, if you count my transport time. We've been separated for three days. So much could've happened in three days. I mean, look at me. Three days ago I was a slave locked in a cryopod. Yesterday I was still under the inhibitor and so many things happened I don't have time to list them in this mental conversation. And today I attended the memorial service of Draden and Ceres of Harem Station as a family member. Or, at the very least, an honored guest.

This shit is crazy. Utterly insane.

And the whole reason I was sent to escort Nyleena was because I'm the calm one. The sensible one. The one people rely on to not give in to the crazy.

And now look at me. I might be *soul-mated* to Serpint the Booty Hunter.

If I have gone this wild, deviated this far off my path, and I'm *me?*

Then what the hell is Nyleena getting up to back on Bull Station? There's no way they didn't remove her from her cryopod. These guys here on Harem, they know things. They have restraint when it comes to coveted silver princesses. Those guys back on Bull, they're the complete opposite.

She's the wild one. *She's* the crazy one. You have to be to become what they made her into. And it was my job to get her safely to the other side of the galaxy and now the whole plan is fucked.

Utterly fucked.

I force myself not to think about it. I can't think about it. I just need to let it go for now.

Just one night. That's all I want. Just one more night as this princess they think I am. Because I know, I feel it in my heart, that deep down Serpint and his Harem Station family are good people.

And when they find out what I've set out to do… what we, the high-order princesses of Cygnia, were born to do… they will stop me.

They will lock me up. Lock all of us up, even the clueless low-order ones they keep up in that special harem. And never, ever want to see a Cygnian princess again as long as they live.

"Lyra?" Serpint says.

"Hmmm?" I mumble, feigning sleepiness.

"We need to go again."

Oh, for sun's sake. I forgot. You can't ever just have one good time with an Akeelian.

"I have a headache," I murmur, opening one eye cautiously and staring at the wall, waiting to see if he'll buy that.

He turns me over, swipes a piece of hair off my cheek, and places his palm on my forehead. "Are you OK?" he asks. "You're not getting sick, are you?" Real concern in his voice.

Which just makes me feel like shit.

"No," I say. "No. My head is just pounding with… pounding things."

He smiles at me, then huffs out a small laugh. "Pounding things, huh?"

I nod, staring up at his violet eyes. He glows too. Not like me, but he does have light inside him. What's up with that light? I want to ask but I really do not want to have sex again and I know if we start talking about personal stuff like that again I won't be able to talk my way out of it. Or he'll talk me into it. Or, more likely, I'll just lose control again and explode like the sun.

So I don't ask about it. I close my eyes, turn back over and say, "Can you finish without me?"

Meaning… *There's the lotion and the bathroom, dude. Knock yourself out.*

He's silent for a moment. But then he says, "Sure, princess. Sure. That's how I've been starting and ending my days for as long as I can remember. So no problem. You get some sleep."

And then he kisses me on the back of the head, gets out of bed, and goes into the bathroom.

CHAPTER TWENTY-SEVEN

In the morning I don't bother Lyra with sex. Just get up, go into the bathroom, and do my usual routine. Something is up with her, I can just feel it. Something big, too.

But also… I don't want to be rejected again and I know she will reject me if I try to turn her on.

I don't like that feeling.

And it's not because I never get rejected by women, it's just that I don't want to be rejected by this woman in particular. I don't want to work for it like I had to last night. I want her to light up for me because she can't stop herself.

Which is all kinds of weird because three days ago I didn't even know this girl. I had no long-term relationship in mind, and hell, I hadn't even been with a woman in months because Draden, Ceres, *Booty* and I were on the other side of the galaxy where all the weird ones live.

And two days ago I was telling myself that stealing the queen was a huge mistake. And it was, but only because Draden and Ceres were killed. Because if I had not stolen the queen I wouldn't have come back home to Harem in time to see Lyra all wild and feral in the harem room.

And my life would be so different right now.

Better? Or worse? I ask myself.

Funny that. Because I want to say better and worse. I want Draden and Ceres to be alive but I also want to be right here, with Lyra, thinking about how she's my soulmate.

For fuck's sake. I think I need therapy.

I step out of the shower, wrap a towel around myself, and walk into the bedroom, hoping she's awake.

She's not.

I'm even kind of loud as I get dressed. And when I sit down on the bed to pull on my boots, I bounce it a little, hoping to wake her up.

She doesn't move.

Is she faking it?

"Lyra," I say. Nothing. "Lyra!"

"Hmmm," she mumbles, turning over. Her hair is even pinker today than it was yesterday. And she's got a soft glow to her skin. Not quite light, but not quite not, either.

"Are you awake?"

"Mmmm."

I'm not sure if that's a yes or a no.

But eventually I decide it's a no and walk out into the living room, pinch my fingers together, open up a screen, and start typing a message to the medical clinic.

"What are you doing?" Lyra asks.

I look down the hall and find her standing naked in the bedroom doorway. Rubbing her eyes and trying to get her mess of pink hair off her face.

"Making us an appointment."

"What kind of appointment?" she burbles out, groggily.

"I think we need to talk some things over."

She makes a face at me. "What kind of things?"

"Just get dressed."

She smiles at me and says, "I guess I'll have to go shopping then," and turns back into the bedroom.

I sigh. Because I feel like I'm losing her. I feel like the magic we had yesterday morning is fading and I hate that.

When I landed *Booty* the other day I felt so alone. Two of my partners were gone and *Booty* was sick. Hell, she's still offline. And then Lyra burst into my life and took over. And even the stupid bot was starting to feel like he was part of our new little circle.

I don't want to be alone again. I don't ever want to feel the way I did when I landed the other day. I will miss Draden and Ceres every day for the rest of my life, but is it so bad to want partners again?

"Found something!" Lyra calls from the bedroom. "Should be here in a few minutes so I'm gonna jump in the shower!"

"Cool!" I call back. "I'll get us some breakfast and we can eat it on the way."

And I realize I'm smiling because the idea of auto-cooking us some breakfast and then walking out of my quarters with somewhere to be—*together*—feels good. Feels right.

I walk over to the kitchen, punch in my usual—breakfast biscuits—and make two cups of coffee to go while I wait for the food to be printed.

I can't lose her. I will do whatever it takes to make this girl happy. Anything.

But I can't do that until I know what she needs. And she's not going to tell me that until she trusts me.

So. A trip to the medical center is in order.

We eat our breakfast in the elevator as we ride up to the harem. Lyra is dressed in... well... not what I expected. I expected something like yesterday. Nice slacks, flat shoes, and a frilly, romantic top.

That's not what I see when I look over at her now and force a smile.

She's wearing a synthetic black bodysuit. The kind you see the assassin girls wear on the station. The kind that hugs her curves in a very sexy way and has a zipper that starts right between her legs and goes all the way up to her cleavage. Which is ample, at the moment. I think she's got one of those sexy push-up bras on under that bodysuit.

And she's got tall boots on. Tall as in they go all the way up to her thighs, and tall as in the pointy fucking heels are high enough that I'm worried she's gonna break an ankle every time she takes a step.

But she danced and twirled for me just before we got into the elevator. Like she was born to wear dangerous boots.

I love all of this—on any other girl but her, that is.

"I think I need a gun," Lyra says. "Where can I get a laser rifle like that hostess had yesterday?"

I just raise one eyebrow at her and scowl.

"What?"

"Why do you need a gun?"

She points to my hip and then my leg. "You have two."

"I'm a man."

She crinkles her nose at me. "You did not just say that."

I'm about to put my foot down about the laser rifle when the elevator door opens. Lyra shoves the remaining bite of her breakfast biscuit into her mouth, then drops her napkin into a trash bin as we step into the harem room.

There's a couple dozen princesses lounging around on the various couches and chairs, all gabbing incessantly as they drink their tea and eat their fruit.

Every single one of them turns to look at us as we enter and then there's an audible gasp when they spot Lyra.

She stops in her tracks, then squares her shoulders and continues walking. "Where are we going, anyway?"

"What was that all about?"

"What was what about?"

"Why did all the girls stop and gasp at you?"

She shrugs, just as I place my hand on the small of her back to guide her towards the medical center. "Probably because I'm a sexy pink princess who looks like she's about to kill them."

Truth, I decide.

"Why are we going to the medical center? Do I need to do something to get my communicator to work? No one chimed me yesterday to let me know it was online."

"Oh, yeah," I say. "I'll have to ask ALCOR about that."

"If we're not here for that, then why are we here?" she asks, just as the door to the medical center opens.

But the cyborg master is waiting for us. He's wearing a jacket with elbow patches, a pair of gray slacks, and a fake lens over his one cyborg eye like he's wearing glasses.

"What the fuck are you wearing?" I ask him.

He looks down at himself, then back at me, and says, "My therapist outfit."

"Therapist?" Lyra says.

"Whatever," I say, nodding to the master. "Where do you want us?"

"We're going to therapy?" Lyra says.

"This way," the master says, leading us down the hallway.

"Why the hell are we going to therapy?" Lyra says, stopping in her tracks.

"Because something is wrong," I say, taking Lyra's hand and pulling her down the hallway.

"How could something be wrong? I just met you three days ago."

"Just…" I sigh and rub my temple with one finger. "Just humor me, OK? I think we need to talk this whole soulmates thing through, that's all."

"That's all?" she asks, stopping at the threshold to the office. Then she crinkles her nose as she takes in the room.

There are two therapy couches. So when I sit down on one, and she sits down on the other, we'll be facing each other.

"And..." I add, tugging her into the room so the door can close behind us. "I think you're keeping things from me and I need to know what."

She folds her arms across her breasts—which are practically popping out of her bodysuit—and scowls.

"What?" I ask.

"You ambushed me."

"It's not an ambush, Lyra," the master says.

"And are you kidding me right now? He's the therapist? What part of 'I don't like this guy' don't you get? Because I thought I made that clear. Several times."

"Lyra," the master says, sitting in his giant, wingback, leather chair and crossing his legs as he looks up at us from over the top of his fake glasses and pretends to makes notes on a tablet. "I'm certified in—"

"Thirty billion different couples' therapy techniques for seventy billion different species. I know. All you people seem to be certified in everything. Maybe that's the problem with this place. Don't you believe in specialists?" She turns to look at me. "Serpint, what's going on?"

"I just think we need to talk," I say, rubbing her arm. "Can we do that? Please?"

She frowns. "About what?"

"About us. About this bond thing. And the way you light up. And then... the way you didn't light up. Last night. We had to work for it, Lyra. It's never happened before. It's not normal."

"We've known each other *three days*," she protests. "We don't even know what normal is yet! And besides, what makes you think this jerk knows anything about me or why I do things?"

The cyborg master opens his mouth to assure her of his qualifications, but the answer, "I know many things about you, Lyra," is omnipresent and comes from everywhere. And it's ALCOR talking now, not the master.

Lyra scowls again.

"Please," ALCOR says. "Just take a seat and relax. We'll get to the bottom of things."

She looks worried at that comment. Like she doesn't want to get to the bottom of things.

That makes my heart pound because now I know… my fear is real.

I'm about to lose her.

CHAPTER TWENTY-EIGHT

It was an ambush. And now I'm trapped in this room with that vile cyborg and ALCOR has been called in to "get to the bottom of things."

Which means they know.

They might not know specifics. In fact I'm sure they don't. But they know *something* is going on with me.

"So…" Serpint says, breaking the silence. "Sit?"

I sigh as I walk around the couches, take a seat on one, and sit back.

Serpint does the same, never taking his eyes off me.

"OK," the monster master says. "What kind of questions do you have for Lyra, Serpint?"

His eyes never unlock from mine. He just stares at me with that dim, violet glow and says nothing.

"I'll start," ALCOR says. "Lyra, what do you think is happening with you and Serpint?"

I huff out an annoyed sigh. "We're… attracted to each other." Serpint smiles. Faintly, but it's a good start. "I like him." He smiles bigger. "And… the things that happen to me when we're intimate are… surprising."

"Surprising how?" Serpint asks.

"You know," I say. "The light. Coming from…" I wave my hand over my pussy area. "And everywhere else."

"Why was that surprising?" ALCOR asks.

"Because that's not… normal."

"What is normal?" Serpint asks.

For sun's sake. How did I get myself in this situation?

"Lyra?" ALCOR prods.

"You know. Regular light. Not… universe-imploding light."

"Why do you think it's happening?" the vile master asks.

And here's the problem. I have a few thoughts about this that I didn't mention to Serpint yet. I told him about the soulmate bond thing, but there's more to it than that. So much more. The actual problem is… I don't even know if that soulmate thing is true or just a myth. I only know the other part, the part I *should not talk about*, is true. One hundred percent true.

"Lyra?" Serpint asks. His voice is low and a little bit soft. Not persuasive or forceful. He's confused, I can see that now. Not angry, not upset that I didn't glow enough last night during sex. He's not here to make himself feel better about his performance. We're here because he wants to fix whatever he thinks is wrong with us.

Never mind that this *us* we're all referring to is so new, I can barely wrap my head around it. He doesn't care. He… loves me. He said that too. And I didn't say it back. And now he's worried that he let this bond take a hold of him and I'm going to somehow rip it apart.

"I'm not going to do that," I say, looking him in the eyes.

"Do what?" ALCOR asks.

"You sure about that?" Serpint asks, ignoring ALCOR.

I nod. "I swear. It's just..."

"What are you talking about?" the master asks.

"Just what, Lyra?" Serpint prods. "You can tell me. I'm on your side, OK? We're a team now. Me, and you, and that worthless nanny bot. And *Booty*," he adds. "Once she gets better. We're your team now. So tell me. What's really going on with you?"

"What *are* we talking about?" ALCOR asks.

I exhale. And it's loud and long. "You're going to hate me," I say.

"I won't," he says, shaking his head.

"Can you two please explain what you're talking about?" the master says.

"I promise, Lyra." He sits forward on his couch until his hand can reach mine. And then he takes it. Holds it. "What's going on?"

I sigh again. I have to make a choice here. Either let them all in on what's happening with the Cygnian princesses, or... or what? Do I even have a choice at this point? The only other option I see involves stealing a ship, going back to Bull Station—*alone*—and getting Nyleena out myself. And even though I'm pretty sure I could steal a ship, there's no way this stupid ALCOR wouldn't catch me in the act. I've never seen such a powerful AI. He sees everything. He is literally the station god.

"OK," I decide.

"OK." Serpint nods, squeezing my hand for encouragement.

"We're not what you think," I say.

"Who?" ALCOR asks.

"No?" Serpint says.

"No," I say, shaking my head.

"WHAT THE HELL ARE WE TALKING ABOUT?" ALCOR's shout is so loud I jump in my chair.

"Chill, dude!" Serpint yells back. "She's getting there!"

I hesitate, but Serpint squeezes my hand again. "Go on," he says.

"We're not just princesses," I say.

"What's that mean, Lyra?" the master asks.

"It *means*," I snarl at him—why does he have to be here for this, anyway?—"it means… we're something more than just… people."

"I'm getting impatient," ALCOR snaps.

"We're weapons," I say. "OK? That's what we are. We're weapons."

Serpint squints his eyes. The cyborg master uncrosses his legs and leans forward, and even I can *feel* the confused look on ALCOR's non-face.

"Weapons?" all three of them say at the same time.

"Yes," I say, sitting up straighter and lifting my chin. "We're weapons." I wilt a little as I squeeze Serpint's hand. "We don't just implode the universe during sex, Serpint. We can literally implode the universe."

They all blink at me in confusion. Even ALCOR. Because the lights in the room flicker a little.

"At the very least, we can annihilate planets and stations. Stations bigger than this one."

"You explode?" Serpint says.

"Yes," I say. "We explode."

"And you die when you do this?" he asks.

I nod. Frown. "There is no other possible outcome when one explodes, is there?"

He lets go of my hand and leans back in his chair. Stares up at the ceiling.

"So we have," ALCOR says, "in our possession, more than two dozen universe-annihilating *BOMBS*?"

"No," I say. "Those girls out there," I say, panning my hand to the door, "they're not like me. They can cause damage. If they knew how to trigger it, and they don't. So don't worry. None of them will explode. But me and my sisters? The pink and silver ones? We're different. We were made just to kill people. That's it. That's our only purpose."

"That station last year," Serpint says. "That one that just… disappeared."

"That was us," I say. "My sister Rox, to be exact. But I left. We left. Nyleena and I. We were…" I hesitate, unsure if I should finish the story. But hell, the secret is out now. I might as well just keep going. "We got out by lying, OK? We were told to go to some planet. Earth, or something like that. I don't really know. I've never heard of it. But the ship I was supposed to take was programmed to get us there. Except… I stole a different ship and we got out. That ship was programmed to go to Bull Station. All our ships leave with a destination program because, obviously, they don't want anyone going somewhere they're not supposed to be. So I was just gonna steal a new ship on Bull Station and then Nyleena and I were on our way to Angel Station on the other side of Hydra System. That's where we go to escape. They deprogram us. Mix up the genetic instructions inside us that make us dangerous. So Nyleena and I were headed to there to get the procedure done. That way the Cygnians would have no use for us and they'd leave us alone."

"Oh, shit," Serpint says.

ALCOR says, "Oh, shit."

And then the cyborg master says, "Oh, shit."

"What?" I ask.

Serpint hesitates for a few seconds, then says, "I think we need to show you something."

We stand in front of a double-wide frosted-glass door. There's a digital keypad on the outside, so it doesn't open automatically when we approach. The cyborg master presses the pad of one of his fingers into a red circle, which then turns green, and the doors part, sliding smoothly open.

The master goes first, then me, and Serpint has his hand on the small of my back as he follows.

In the center of the room is one cryopod and Crux, standing next to it, with his arms crossed. He stares at me with a combination of emotions that I interpret as fear, mixed in with a healthy dose of anger. Obviously ALCOR has filled him in on the situation.

"What's going on?" I ask.

"You tell me," Crux says.

"I don't know what you mean."

"Lyra," Serpint says, taking my hand. "Remember when I told you I stole something I shouldn't have and that's why Draden and Ceres died?"

"Um... OK. Sure. Yeah. I remember."

"This is what I stole."

I look at the cryopod again, trying to fit all the pieces together. "OK. So... who's in there?"

"You tell us," Crux says, stepping aside and waving me forward in one motion.

I walk forward to the pod, peer down, then use my hand to wipe away the thick layer of ice over the faceplate window and—

"Oh, shit," I say.

"'Oh, shit' is right," Serpint says. "I stole your queen. By accident, I swear. I just knew this was Corla, the woman Crux has been pining over for two decades. So..." He shrugs. "So I thought I'd bring him a little present." He smiles and says to Crux, "Surprise."

I just stare at Corla, unable to accept that this is really happening. "What the fuck were you thinking?"

"Obviously we didn't know she was the queen bomb, or he'd never have brought her here," Crux says.

"Where did you get her?" I ask Serpint. "She ran weeks ago. I figured she'd be safe by now."

He shakes his head at me. "She was almost there. I got her in the Cetus System."

"But that's—"

"I know," he says, deflating. "So close to the Hydra System, you can taste it. I took her before she could be... defused, I guess. I was coming back from Hydra System and we stopped on Cetus, and I just kinda... bumped into this situation."

"And your first inclination was to *steal her*?" I say, raising an eyebrow.

"I am the Booty Hunter," he says. "It's pretty much what I do."

"Did you open this?" I ask Crux.

"No, we knew there was a tracker on her. We knew it'd be activated if we unfroze her."

I sigh. "Poor Corla," I say. "Poor, poor Corla. She got out before we figured out how to deactivate the trackers.

"So she's a bomb," ALCOR says. "One that can blow me into the deep dark for all eternity?"

He sounds *pissed.*

"Yes," I say. "She is. And if she's opened up before she gets to Angel Station, you won't have to worry about a tracker. Because she will detonate. We smuggled her out just after she was activated."

"Who was the target?" ALCOR asks.

"I don't know. They didn't tell me any of that."

"What was your job back in Cygnia?" ALCOR asks.

Well, here we go. I guess this is it for me. I look at Serpint. Memorize his eyes. The way they glow, the way he looks at me now and all the ways he's looked at me over the past three days. And regret everything. Ever coming here.

Because he's going to *hate me.*

"Lyra," ALCOR says. "We need to know."

I nod my head and let out a long breath of air. "I was trained to deliver the payload. And when whoever I was transporting exploded, it would trigger me at the same time."

Serpint says, "You were supposed to deliver Nyleena, weren't you? She's one of these... *things*. Isn't she?"

I nod. "She is."

"Oh, shit," says everyone in the room but me.

Because I say, "We have to get her back. We have to get her back, you guys. Because someone could trigger her and then... I mean, I don't like Bull Station and I really don't care about what happens to it, but... she's my best friend in the whole universe and we promised to keep each other safe and now she's back there, all alone, and—"

Serpint puts his hand over my mouth to stop my rambling. "Stop," he says. "We don't need to be convinced. There's no way we're not going to get her."

"*Booty* is back online," ALCOR says.

"Oh, thank fuck," Serpint says, removing his hand from my lips.

"But she's not one hundred percent yet," ALCOR adds. "You can see her now though. She's... mostly herself."

Serpint takes my hand and pulls me out of the cryopod room.

"Where are we going?"

"To see *Booty*." Then he slows down so I can catch up with him and he smiles. A real smile, too. For her. *Booty's* return. "You're going to love her," he says. "I promise. Don't worry."

Which only has me thinking... should I be worried?

But I don't ask that. I just follow him as he leads me through a series of hallways and elevators. We get out to the main part of the city and we take several people-movers downward.

He's silent the whole way until we get to the bottom level and go through a series of security doors that lead to the medical bay for ships.

We stop in front of a large, double-wide door with two long windows near the top, and peer inside.

And there she is. The *Booty Hunter*.

She's a magnificent ship and takes up two whole bays. She is sleek, and long, and silver. And she looks like… well, not a ship you fuck with.

"Don't be nervous," Serpint says.

And again, I have to wonder… should I be nervous?

But before I can ask him, the doors open and we walk inside.

"*Boots*!" Serpint yells. "Are you back?"

"I'm here, Serpint," she coos in a very feminine, very sexy voice. "I'm back. Who is thissssss?" she hisses, sounding a little too reptilian for my liking.

"Lyra," Serpint says. "This is *Booty Hunter*. *Booty*, this is Princess Lyra."

"Ahhhh," she purrs. "They *waaaarned me* about you."

"Oh, shit," I say, without thinking. Because this ship… this ship is not at all what I was expecting. He talked about her like she's… nice. Or good. Or at the very least benevolent.

But I'm getting the impression the *Booty Hunter* is none of those things.

Her body is imposingly big now that I've heard her speak. She has torpedoes on her undercarriage and a Gatling turret on her topside. A Gatling turret, I can assume from my past military experience, which holds plasma cannons. The kind of plasma cannons that sterilize organic matter on contact and melt inorganic matter into slag. The kind of plasma cannons the Prime Navy uses to rein in corporate planets who don't pay their taxes and large populations of uprising people.

The *Booty Hunter* is… well, the only word that comes to mind is… *terrifying.*

CHAPTER TWENTY-NINE

I walk forward towards my ship, climb up the stairs to the hatch, stop at the top, and hug her. "*Boots*, oh, *Boots*. I'm so glad you're back. I've missed you. I came last night but—"

"I know. I remember," she says. "That wasn't me. I'm so sorry for upsetting you with Draden's voice. The virus had a hold of my speech centers."

"God, I've missed your voice. I'm lost without you, you know that?"

"Now you have Lyra," she protests.

"No," I say. Then look down at Lyra and find her frowning. "I mean, yeah. She's one of us now. And we have a new bot, too. I had no say in that part though. But you, *Booty*. Come on." I laugh. "No one can ever replace you. *Ever*."

"I am happy to be back with you, Serpint."

"Happy, huh?" I ask, raising an eyebrow. "They told me you were turned organic. How come you didn't say anything?"

If a ship could shrug, I'm pretty sure that's what *Booty* would be doing right now. Because all I get is a long, awkward silence.

"*Boots*?" I say. "You gonna answer me?"

"It was for personal reasons."

"Personal as in…" I prod her.

"No one ever asked me if I wanted to be a ship, Serpint."

I take a few seconds to let *that* land. Which adds up to yet another awkward silence. But finally I say, "So… you want to be something else?"

"I might want to be something else."

"Oh." Well… hmmm. This kinda sucks from my end. Because she is the best ship ever and I do not want to go find another one, that's for sure. But, on the other hand, I love her, so I want her to be happy. "What kind of something else?" I ask. "Like… a station, or something?"

"I have been thinking about getting a body."

"A body," I repeat.

"Yes," she says. "Like Lyra's."

"Ohhhhhhh," I say, turning around to look at Lyra. She's shooting me a weird look. One raised eyebrow, crinkled-up nose, and narrow eyes. "A woman," I say. "You'd like to be a real woman."

"Yes, Serpint," she says. "A real woman."

"Huh," I say. "So… how close are you to getting that?"

"Not close enough."

"Mmmm-hmmm," I say, nodding my head. "Well, maybe I should go talk to Tray and ALCOR and see if we can move that along for you?"

"That would be wonderful, Serpint. ALCOR is resistant."

"Why?" I say. I get why. I don't need her to tell me all the ways this is a bad idea and should never, *ever* happen. But I just want to see what ALCOR's been telling her, since he was the genius who started the whole organic process in the first place.

"He feels I am too powerful to be contained in a humanoid mind."

"He might be right about that, *Boots*. It's… been done before. And it's… never turned out well."

"I am different," she says.

"You are," I say, walking back down the stairs and turning to look up at her massive hull. "You've always been special," I say. "So if anyone can do it, I'm sure you can."

I smile, then turn to Lyra. Who is frozen in place and hasn't moved a muscle. I smile at her too. "OK, *Booty*. We have a few things happening on the station right now. And pretty much all of them need my attention. So I'm gonna go take care of that and then I'll talk to ALCOR and Tray about your… transition. And stop by later. Sound good?"

"Thank you," she says.

"No problem. I'm glad you're back online. I've missed you."

"I've missed you too, Serpint."

I take Lyra's hand and we walk back through the large double-wide doors. When we get in the hallway, I shake my head at her, trying to tell her not to speak yet. *Booty*'s hearing sensors are top-notch—like everything else about her—and I don't want her to pick up on my resistance.

No one knows better than me that making *Booty* your enemy is a very bad idea. Almost as bad as giving her a humanoid body.

Lyra gives me a wary look, then nods her head.

I wait until we are all the way back inside the city center and on a people-mover going up to the higher levels before I dare to whisper, "My ship has gone insane."

Lyra lets out a long breath of air. "Oh, thank God. For a second I thought you were actually agreeing with her."

"No," I say. It's a hard, firm, fast *no*. "I have heard of this before. And when I say it doesn't turn out well, I mean… every ship that ever tried to contain themselves inside a humanoid body ended up murdering people." I look at Lyra. "Stations filled with people. *Millions* of people."

She nods, frowning. "So the virus? It's still inside her?"

"I don't know, to be honest. This might've been going on for a long time."

"What are you gonna do?" Lyra asks.

I sigh. "Well, I'm not taking her out of medical, that's for sure. She can't be trusted. And she's too big and too powerful to have this kind of instability. As long as she's in medical ALCOR has control of her."

Lyra frowns even deeper. "I'm sorry. I can tell you love her."

"I do. I can't even explain that love. And she's all I have left. I've really been telling myself that even though Draden and Ceres are gone, *Booty* made it out. And now it looks like that's not the case. We might have to put her down if she doesn't get her shit together. This is a bad sign. A very bad sign."

Lyra wraps her hands around my upper arm and leans in to me, sighing as we get off one people-mover and get on another. It's a long, silent ride back up to the top levels.

My screen pops open in front of me and ALCOR says, "Serpint, we need you and Lyra up in the harem."

"We're on our way now," I say, then close up the screen.

"We'll figure something out," Lyra says. Trying to be helpful.

When we finally get to the harem room the master points Lyra and I to the cryopod chamber. And when we enter all my brothers are gathered around Corla.

Luck is sitting in a swivel chair near a control center. Making it rotate left half a circle, then right half a circle. Like he's an impatient six-year old who is bored out of his mind. Valor stands nearby, arms crossed and face stoic. And Beauty hovers between them.

Crux has both palms flat on the cryopod, staring down at Corla's frozen face through a circle of cleared condensation and ice.

Tray is sitting at another control center, personal screen open in the air to his right and tapping frantically on another screen off to his left.

Jimmy and Xyla are cleaning weapons at a table near the door.

Everyone looks over at us when we enter.

"How is she?" Jimmy asks.

I just shake my head. "Not good."

"We can talk about that later," ALCOR's omnipresent voice says. "First, we need to talk about where Crux, Tray, and I went the other night."

"Yeah, what the fuck? You left the station, ALCOR?"

"I had to," he says. "We needed to infiltrate the Cetus Station to see if we could find out anything about Corla."

"Did you?" I ask.

"Just who was in possession of her pod. That's all."

"Who was it?" Lyra asks.

"It was a princess called Veila. Have you heard of her?"

Everyone looks at Lyra. She nods her head and says, "Yes. I know her."

"Who is she?" Crux asks, once again staring down at Corla's frozen face.

"She's a silver. She's very powerful. A lot more powerful than me, that's for sure."

"So she was her transport?" I ask.

"Yes," Lyra says. "I'm going to assume she was. But like I said, they escaped weeks ago. I don't know why they were still on Cetus Station. They should have made it to Angel Station already."

"What is this Angel Station?" Valor asks. "Because I've never heard of it and we've been all over this fucking galaxy."

"It's where we go when we escape," Lyra says.

"But why?" Valor presses.

"Because..." she says, then stops. "Because that's just where we go."

"How do you know it's safe?" Crux says.

Lyra looks confused for a moment. "Well, people told me it was." Then she stops and stares at him. "Do you know something I don't?"

ALCOR is the one who answers. "We don't know what or where it is. There's no record of it anywhere, Lyra. How do you get there?"

"I just know it's somewhere on the other side of Hydra System, that's all. It's a series of gates and stations. You get a new coordinate at each stop. We pass through the right gate, in the right order, and on the other side we get a coordinate. Which is a station through yet another gate. It's a long journey, but Corla should've been further than Cetus, that's for sure. So something happened to them. Was Veila on the station?"

"No," Tray says, not bothering to turn away from his work to look at us. "ALCOR and I hacked into their systems and even though Princess Veila was listed as Corla's responsible party, it was very well hidden. And there was no record of Veila ever being there."

Lyra sighs. Long and heavy. "Something is very wrong."

"Very wrong," ALCOR agrees. "But Serpint's impulsive decision to steal Corla might just have saved millions of people."

"How so?" I ask.

"Because I just decrypted the program running in Corla's cryopod," Tray says, "and she was meant to blow up the Prime Planet of Cassiopeia." He stops to swivel in his chair now. Looking straight at Lyra. "And she was scheduled to leave the same time Serpint took her. So… someone other than Princess Veila was in charge of her at that moment and was about to put her on a ship headed that way."

"Holy shit," Lyra says. "They were gonna start a war."

"They were going to start a war," ALCOR agrees.

"And use Corla to do it," Crux growls.

"We need to get Nyleena back," ALCOR says. "And we need you to provide us with the encryption to do that once we get to Bull Station."

"Sure," Lyra says. "Yes!" She turns to me, smiling. "I was gonna ask you for help. So yes. We need to go get her. I promised her I'd keep her safe. And we need to go *now*. It's been three days and there's no telling what's happened to her since I left."

"When I say *we*, Lyra," ALCOR says, "I didn't mean *you*."

"What?" she says. "Oh, fuck that. I'm going. You guys can't keep me here. I know where she is. I know how to move her and keep her safe."

No one says anything. But everyone, aside from Lyra, understands that we absolutely *can* leave her here. And we will.

"You are not coming," ALCOR says in his definitive I'm-in-charge-here voice. "You will provide Tray with the information we need and then Serpint will take you to his quarters and that's where you'll stay until we return."

"But—"

"Lyra," I say, placing a hand on her shoulder. "Please." I raise one eyebrow at her, trying to signal that we can talk more about it later. "Can you just give Tray the information so we can prepare?"

She sucks in a deep breath. Angry at being put on the spot. She can't refuse us, her sister is in danger. So if she chooses this moment to be defiant, she will only hurt Nyleena in the end.

"Fine," she says. Just as Tray gets up and walks over to her, handing her a tablet.

"This is the program Corla is running," he says. And then he starts pointing out the missing information he needs. It takes a while for them to figure everything out, so I just sit down at a console near Luck and wait for her to be done.

When Tray has what he needs, Lyra comes over to me. I take her hand and give it a squeeze. Letting her know this is for the best and she did the right thing.

Then ALCOR says, "Serpint?"

"Yes," I say.

"The cyborg master would like to speak to you and Lyra in private. He's waiting in the medical center for you. Please stop by before you take Lyra back to your quarters."

"Sure," I say, standing up. "Come on, Lyra."

She keeps quiet until we're outside in the hallway. Then she practically explodes with light.

Which I interpret as anger.

And I'm right.

"How dare you?" she spits.

"What am I gonna say, Lyra? If ALCOR says you're not going, then you're not going. That's just the end of it. There's no way off this station without his permission."

"You could've fought for me!" she says, glowing with rage.

"Why would I do that?" I almost laugh. "I don't want you going. I want you here, safe. So when I return you're—"

"Waiting for you?" She guffaws at the ceiling. "I'm a fucking military officer, Serpint. Not a helpless fairytale princess. And if I had my own ship I'd go without *you*! All of you! I don't need your help! I know what I'm doing."

I'm ready to list about a dozen counterpoints to that. Things like, *Oh, really? Is that why you got kidnapped off Bull Station and ended up in here in Crux's little princess harem?* Or things like, *I suppose you'll just concoct another half-baked inhibitor disguise that wears off in the middle of the job?*

But I know better. So I say, in the calmest voice I can muster up, "Lyra. I can't lose you now. I lost my whole team three days ago and you're all I have left. So please, just let us handle it."

She glares at me, but then softens. Just a little. And her light fades to a soft, pink glow. "Fine."

"Good," I say, squeezing her hand and giving her a smile. "It's not that I don't think you're capable—"

"I get it," she says.

"You sure?" I ask. Because this went a lot easier than I'd imagined a few seconds ago.

"I'm sure," she says, nodding. "Now why does that vile master want to see us again?"

"I dunno," I say. "Let's find out."

When we get to the medical center a bot leads us down the hall to the office. The master is sitting at his desk, wearing his white lab coat, tapping away at his tablet.

"Oh, good," he says. "Come in, close the door, and have a seat."

"What's this about?" Lyra asks, irritated.

He stares at her with his one eyeball sensor and says, "You two were having problems earlier and we got off track. I just wanted to see if you were interested in knowing why your light was so... sporadic when it comes to your sex life."

Lyra turns to me. "I'm not talking about our sex life with this thing."

"Lyra," the master says. And we all know what's coming. "I'm a certified sex therapist—"

She puts up a hand. "I don't want to hear about it. I stopped believing in all these fictitious certifications after Prince the bot told me he graduated from Serpint's Sex University." Then she pauses and looks at me. "Where is that bot, anyway? He's been missing all day."

"Oh, shit. He's probably still in jail. I'll bail him out when I get back from the mission."

"Or I could do it," she offers.

I shrug. "Sure. Knock yourself out. He's yours now anyway."

"Back to the sex therapy," the master says.

"Right. Let's hear it then," I say. Because I know Lyra is about at the end of her patience with this guy.

"Lyra's light represents her emotions in the moment—"

"I know that," Lyra interrupts. "I've been lighting up my whole life. I don't need your input."

"—so when the light is dim, she is calm," the master says, ignoring her outburst. "It doesn't mean she's unhappy, or unsatisfied, or not in the mood." He blinks his red light eyeball at us. Like he's winking. "Dim light is actually a sign of contentment."

"So the wild light?" I ask.

"That's heightened emotions, nothing more. It could be anger, or fear, or an exceptional orgasm."

"OK, I'm done here," Lyra says, turning to leave. Then she calls over her shoulder, "Thanks for the tip."

I give the master a smile, then follow her out, jogging a little to catch up and take her hand. "You know, he's not a bad guy."

"Save it," she says.

"And I've been thinking…"

"About what?" she asks, stopping to sigh near the elevator.

"I mean… could you… like… explode for real? If we have an intense sexual experience?"

She frowns and squints her eyes, like she's thinking about this. But the elevator doors open and we get in before she speaks. "I've thought about that too. It does scare me a little."

"So see, we do need to learn more about this stuff."

"But I'm not too worried about it anymore."

"Why?"

She leans in to me just as the elevator doors close. Right into my ear. And whispers, "Because I came so hard, Serpint the Booty Hunter, I really thought the universe was imploding. And I did that more than once, and there's only one universe. So we'd all be dead by now if the pleasure you give me could make that happen."

My cock jumps in my pants.

And suddenly the only thing on my mind is fucking her.

I place my hands on either side of her head, pull her face towards mine, and kiss her like she's mine, and mine alone.

And even though her plump lips go soft, and pliant, and kiss me back—her glow tells me all I need to know.

She is my soulmate.

CHAPTER THIRTY

Unlike last night, the light inside me wants to burst out right now. It's a little weird to be so unsettled in this area, since my life before Serpint was one long string of luminous flux equilibrium.

But I'm not complaining. I like the feeling of this new emotional instability. And my life has now been divided into two parts. Before Serpint and after.

They are as different as night and day.

Before everything was dark. Even when I did glow, it was never for love. And while my flux wasn't as dim as when I was on the inhibitor, it wasn't much brighter, either.

Now I feel like I'm made of sunshine. That there is more flux inside me than can be contained and all it wants is to be let loose.

At least… it feels that way when Serpint touches me. Or kisses me. Or puts his thick, hard cocks inside me.

"Lyra," he whispers into my mouth, pushing me inside his quarters and forcing me to take several steps backward until I bump into a wall.

"Serpint," I say, the small argument we were having just a few minutes ago long forgotten. All I want to think about now is *him*.

He presses his hips against my stomach, his hand palming my breast. "Did I mention," he says, smiling into our kiss now, "that I love this outfit?"

He tugs on the zipper running up my front just as he finishes saying this.

The outfit is skin-tight and that zipper was holding my breasts hostage, so once the tension is released, they spill out like large, bouncing melons.

I have a pink and black bra on, but the lacy cups only cover the bottom half of each breasts so my large, round nipples are now half exposed.

He looks down, takes a breath and looks up into my eyes. "Oh, fuck me now."

"Yes," I whisper back.

He slides the zipper all the way down until my panties are exposed too. Then slips his hand right between my legs. Massaging my pussy lips through the thin fabric until they are wet from the heat and desire he's stirring up inside me.

He pulls them aside and his finger is there. Touching me. Playing with my clit, then slipping and sliding over my folds until he pushes them up inside me as he forces my back against the wall. Pinning me to it.

His other hand grabs my wrist and hikes one arm above my head. Which instantly has my heart beating fast. Then, before I can fully process how good his domination feels, he twirls me around, hikes my other arm up against the wall, and holds me in place with one firm grip on my wrists.

His cock rubs against my ass as his other hand slips over my belly and resumes fingering me.

"How will you light up for me now?" he asks.

"Any way you want," is my answer.

He laughs, leaning into my neck to kiss it, then he turns his head and nips at my ear.

"Will you be a good girl for me, Lyra?" he asks. "Will you do everything I tell you to?"

Oh, God. What will he tell me to do? Suck his cocks again? I want to. I want them both hard, right now, so I can force my lips over their heads and take him deep.

"Will you?" he asks again.

"*Yes*," I say. "I'll do anything you say, Serpint. Just tell me what you want."

"Hmmmmmm," he murmurs into my ear. "That's sweet, princess. But I was thinking more along the lines of what you want."

"What do I want?" I ask, suddenly flustered.

"All of me?" he says. "Inside of you? At the same time?"

"Oh, yeah," I moan. "All of you, right now. In my mouth." I try to spin around so I can kneel, but he pushes me into the wall so hard I have to turn my cheek.

"No," he says. And I can hear the grin on his face. "Not like that," he growls into my neck, the vibration of his voice and the roughness of the stubble on his jaw next to my soft, tender skin an aphrodisiac of the highest order.

"Oh, yeah," I say. "I want both your cocks in my pussy. Let me put them—"

"Not quite," he says, truly laughing now.

"What other way—oh," I say. "Oh."

"Yeeeeessss," he says. "Now you're getting it."

"You want to put one—"

"Yes," he says again.

"And the other—"

"Yes!"

"Oh," I say. "I've never done that before."

"Then there's no time like the present, princess. Is there?"

I picture this. Him on top of me. One cock in my pussy, the other in my ass. And then I glow a little brighter.

"I'm gonna take that as agreement," he chuckles.

I let his answer stand because I'd like to know what that feels like. I've had him the other two ways, now I want to experience all of him like this as well.

He kisses my neck one more time, then wraps his arms around my middle and steps back, pointing me in the direction of the bedroom.

My stomach begins to flutter wildly with each step we take. And by the time we enter the bedroom my heart is beating so fast with anticipation and lust, I want to rip my own clothes off.

He has other ideas. Because he walks me forward to the bed, his cock still grinding against my ass, and then spins me around and pushes me backwards so I bounce onto the mattress, laughing now.

"You're so rough," I coo. "Be gentle with me, Booty Hunter. Please. Be gentle."

He grins wide. Then kneels down, picks up my foot, and pulls a boot off in one smooth motion.

I am nothing if not helpful, so I offer him the other foot and he pulls that one off too.

"This bodysuit," he says, standing up and stepping forward until his knees are right between my legs, "is a sexy fucking miracle."

I smile, delighted that he likes it.

"But we need to take it off now." He reaches for my hand and pulls me up into a sitting position. Then eases the slick, tight bodysuit over each of my shoulders, one at a time, and pulls it down to my waist.

He palms my breasts, finding the bra clasp between them—an easy feature I've come to appreciate and love since last night—and pops it open so my heavy, round tits bounce free.

At the same moment I light up a golden pink color. Soft, and hazy. Not explosive and dangerous.

"Oh for sun's sake," he groans. "You will be the death of me, princess. I don't know how much more I can take." Then he leans forward, making me lie back, and presses both his palms into the mattress on either side of my head.

I gaze up at him, into those eyes—those bright, violet eyes—and say, "Get naked."

He chuckles a little, shoots me a sideways smile, then stands up and takes off his shirt.

Oh, for the love of God. I die with him then. Because his body—his body is like the perfect stone sculpture.

I sit up again, reaching for his belt so I can take off his pants, but he pushes me back and says, "Stay right where you are."

And then he slowly *peels* my bodysuit down my legs and tosses it aside.

My mouth opens, in awe of the way that felt and the way he looks at me. The way his eyes glance down to my wet pussy as I open my legs for him, then back up to my face and shine a little brighter.

"Now what?" I ask.

But before the words are even out of my mouth he's kicked off his boots and is unbuckling his belt. It jingles as he pops the button on his pants, and pulls out not one, but both cocks. Hard as rocks and so thick they spill over the firm grasp his fingers have on them.

He jerks on them. Pumping them back and forth, then let's go so he can strip off his pants.

I cannot take my gaze off him.

How I went from runaway princess to the soulmate of this beautiful booty hunter in the span of three days, I will never understand. Ever.

But I don't dwell on that. Not one bit. Not when this perfect specimen of a man leans forward and places both his hands on either side of my hips as his mouth begins to kiss his way up my stomach. He stops at my breasts, taking one in his hand as he licks circles around my large, tight nipple, catching the diamond nipple ring with his teeth.

My head tilts back and my eyes close as a moan flows past my lips.

Then he's covering me. His perfectly sculpted chest presses up against my breasts as his mouth finds my mouth, and our tongues connect. Twisting together like our fate. Twirling around like the spinning world we live on.

His cocks rub against my pussy. And I have never wanted anything in life the way I want him inside me, just the way he described.

"Are you ready?" he asks.

"Oh, yes," I say. "I'm ready for everything you want to give me. I want it all. Every single bit of you inside me. Any way you want to do it."

His wide, sly grin is worth every bit of that sappy, love-sick declaration.

I mean it, anyway. I don't care how he wants to take me. He can do it.

His hands grip my ass and slides me up the smooth silver covers until my head hits the pillows.

I giggle, because he took me by surprise and because the silky softness of the covering felt amazing on my back.

While I'm busy enjoying that move, he opens my legs and brings my knees up to my breasts. Leaning his face down, tongue extended, as our eyes lock on and never let go. Even when his tongue swipes across my pussy, we do not break contact.

But then… then it's too much. His tongue begins to twirl and dance the way it was in my mouth just a few seconds ago, and I lose control.

I close my eyes and just float… and enjoy the way he pleasures me.

Soon, he's putting his fingers inside me too. Pumping them back and forth. I am so ready. So slick and wet and ready… I want to beg.

I do beg. "Now," I murmur. "Now, please. Inside me now."

He shoves his fingers in. Hard. Making me gasp. "No." I laugh. "Not like that!"

He pumps them in and out. Slowly. Twisting his hand a little with each back-and-forth motion. "You don't like it?" he asks. "I thought you wanted everything, princess?"

"I do," I say. "I take it back. Do whatever you want!"

He laughs, withdrawing his fingers. They shine in my soft glow as he brings them up to my lips. I do not even hesitate. I take them in my mouth and taste myself on his skin, licking, and twirling my tongue, just the way he did.

"Dead," he says. "I'm so dead." He inches his knees towards me, fisting his cocks again. And I will never, ever get tired of watching him jerk off both those fat cocks. My pussy is humming and thrumming, impatient for what comes next.

He lets go of the top cock and points the lower at my pussy, inserting it, just a little. Just enough to drag the sweet wetness inside me down to my asshole. He does that a few times and it feels excruciatingly good. Agonizingly good.

Then, when my ass is good and slick, he begins to massage it with his finger.

It's tight. So tight at first. Small, shooting pains make me gasp. But he says, "Shhh, Lyra." And the sound of my name, in combination with his probing finger, is enough to make me relax enough for him to push it inside a little more.

I'm the one who will die, not him. He feels too good to be true. He feels like an erotic fantasy come to life.

And he is, isn't he? A mythical, two-cocked, erotic demon come to claim me from my awful life and lock me up in his tower of sexual pleasure.

His cock probes the entrance to my ass, presses up inside me. I buck my back, but just as I do that, his other cock slips into my dripping wet pussy and that's it…

I. Am. Full.

"Lyra," Serpint groans. "Fuck yeah, you feel good," he growls, moving his hips back and forth, in and out. Slowly, at first. So fucking slow. Then quicker as I begin to relax and ease into our new rhythm.

And for a second I feel it.

That light from the first day. The pent-up brilliance inside me begins to build and I think… there it is. That's the light that Serpint wanted. That's the light that was almost missing last night.

I get even more excited about the burst of star shine that's about to explode, moaning, "Yes, yes, yes," as I dig my nails into Serpint's muscular shoulders and urge him to go faster.

"Yes!" I say again.

He is grinning down at me. His violet eyes burning with the heat of our passion.

And just when I think we're about to explode together…

It stops.

It stops building. In fact, it not only stops building, it declines a little. My clit is still humming and throbbing and he still feels amazing, but it's different now.

"What the fuck?" I say.

"What?" he asks, halting our lovemaking. "What's wrong? Am I hurting you?"

"No," I say. "No—"

"Then what's the matter?" he asks, moving his hips just a little. Slowly now. Carefully.

"I don't know. It just feels… different."

"Well, it is a little different this time," he says. We stare at each other. Still fucking, but not desperate to fuck. Still enjoying it, just not lusting for each other. And I'm still building towards a climax, it's just not the kind that will shatter a universe.

"Should I stop?" he asks, when I don't say anything.

But then I recall the cyborg master's words from earlier about how my light represents my emotions in the moment.

I look down at myself and find I'm still glowing. A soft, yellow-pink glow that blurs the edges of my body with Serpint's. The glow climbs up his arms and radiates across his back, like he's channeling it. Like my light is his light. Like we are sharing it.

I notice that my whole body is now humming and thrumming like my clit.

And his is too.

"No," I whisper. "Don't stop. This is perfect."

Because it is.

Yes, it's different. And no, I'm not going to explode this time.

But that's OK.

Because this is more than that.

This is a connection.

Just as I think that he lowers himself all the way on top of me and my light washes over his skin like we are the same person.

He leans down to kiss me. First on the nose—which makes us both smile—then on the lips. Our tongues twist together. Gently, this time. Slowly. Taking our time.

We take our time in other ways too. His fingers slowly thread through my hair. No mad grabs or fisting tonight. Our hips rock together in perfect unison.

My light—no, our light—begins to glow brighter. Not the sun. Not a supernova. Not an imploding galaxy or a shattering universe, just us.

We glow as one.

CHAPTER THIRTY-ONE

I feel Lyra below me, and above me, and inside me. I feel her everywhere. This time our lovemaking is so very different. It's a twisting of souls, and a blending of minds, and everything seems to be a perfect fit.

Her light flows up from her body and surrounds me like the scent of sweet flowers or the sound of soft music. It flows into me like nectar from ripe fruit and excites every nerve ending in my body until we are vibrating together. A low, inaudible—but still perceptible—quiver that makes us shimmer, and flicker, and twinkle, and glitter in the darkness.

We come.

We do not implode anything.

We do something better.

We merge together. Coalescing into one being. One soul, one mind, one body. Her pleasure becomes my pleasure becomes her pleasure again.

We share ourselves.

She wraps her legs around me, squeezing me with her thighs as she digs her fingernails into my back. Her pussy and ass both contracting on my cocks.

I want to die when we come this time, it feels so good.

"Oh, Lyra," I say, kissing her soft mouth. "I don't need an explosion if this is what I get in return."

She laughs, closing her eyes. Still squeezing me with her pussy and her legs. "I think I still exploded," she says. "Just in a new way."

Truth, I decide. Nothing but truth.

"Serpint." ALCOR's voice booms through the still air. "It's time to go. Everyone is on their way up to your quarters. Lyra, you need to tell us what you remember of Bull Station so we have some idea of where Nyleena is."

She groans. "I still don't see why I have to stay behind."

She's talking to me, not ALCOR. He's already gone. I could feel his absence the moment he stopped talking. Other things to do besides interrupt our postcoital moment.

I kiss her, then roll off of her, letting my semi-hard cocks slip out. But instead of getting up I tug her up close to my chest. "I told you," I say. "I can't lose anyone else. I need to know you're here. Safe and waiting for me when I get back."

"What if something happens to you?" she protests. "Then I have to live with that. I can be helpful, Serpint. I'm military. I can fly a ship. I can shoot. I can help you guys. When doesn't a team need another capable, invested party?"

Her argument is good, I'll give her that. But I cannot bear the thought of her in danger. I just can't.

"I'm sorry, Lyra. The answer is no."

"You're not really the boss of me, you know."

"I really kinda am." I laugh. Then I tug on the collar around her neck to illustrate my point.

She pushes my hand away and says, "That's not even a real thing. Are you really gonna make me pay my way through servitude just because I was kidnapped and brought here?"

"Yes." I laugh again. "I really am. At least until I get back."

"But—"

"Lyra," I say in my stern, not-fucking-around voice. "I can magnetically bind you to my sex wall if you're going to be difficult."

She glares at me. "You wouldn't dare."

"No? Then try me. Beg a little more and see what happens."

"So I just have to accept your word as law?"

"For this, yes. When I get back we can sort it all out."

She pouts her perfect pink lips at me.

"OK?" I ask.

"Fine." She sighs. "But I would just like to point out that I would be a huge asset on this trip and you are going to regret not bringing me along."

"Noted for the record." I chuckle, then tickle her neck with kisses until she bunches up her shoulders and giggles.

We lie there a few more minutes. Just basking in our afterglow of sex. But then my door chimes and I hear Jimmy calling from the living room, "Let's get a fucking move on!"

"I gotta go," I say. "And you have to tell us what you know."

She sighs deeply as I untangle our bodies, get out of bed, and start pulling my pants back on.

"Can you do me a favor?" I ask her. Because she has not moved and I need her moving.

"What?" she says, still pouting.

"Can you order me battle armor and weapons from the auto-shopper and have them sent to *The Big Dicker*?"

She guffaws up at the ceiling. "The *what*?"

"*The Big Dicker.* That's Jimmy's ship."

"What the—"

"It's some constellation from wherever the fuck he says his mother came from."

"There's a constellation called the Big Dicker?" She giggles again. "Some planet has a two-dicked alien as part of its mythology?"

I laugh too. "I guess I never thought of that."

"Where is this planet, anyway? Where they call baby boys Himmy and name star patterns after cocks?"

"Jimmy," I say. "It's Jimmy, not Himmy."

"Isn't that what I said?"

Oh, man. This girl. "I have no clue," I say, pulling on my shirt. "But we don't have time to think about this. Will you order me—"

"Yes, *yes*," she groans. "I'll do it."

"Good. Just enter my name and the shopper will do the rest," I say, slapping her ass cheek.

"Ow!"

"Get up, get dressed, and come out in the living room so we can pump you for intel before we leave."

I grab my boots and go out into the living room to find Xyla poking through my sex toy chest and Jimmy rummaging through my refrigerator.

"What the fuck?" I say, taking a seat on the couch so I can pull on my boots. "Stop going through my shit, you guys."

Xyla turns, holding up a purple vibrator. "Can I borrow this for a second?"

I get up, cross the distance between us in three steps, grab the toy from her, toss it back into the drawer, and slam it shut.

"I guess that's a no," she says. "Too bad. I had plans for that."

Jimmy just laughs as he backs away from my fridge. Then he scowls at me. "Where the fuck is your armor?"

"I'm getting it," Lyra says, coming down the hallway. She's wearing her sexy bodysuit again, this time no boots. And her pink-blonde hair is so messy, there's no way Jimmy and Xyla miss the fact that we just had sex.

"What the fuck?" Xyla says. "You got off and I can't take a vibe break in your bathroom before we go?"

Lyra blinks at her three times. Like, *What the fuck did she just say?*

"Never mind," I say to Lyra. "Just order the armor."

Lyra turns to the auto-shopper and begins searching my name. "This one?" she says, pointing to the screen.

"Yes," I nod, just as the door chimes again. Valor, Luck, and Beauty enter before I can even say enter.

"We ready?" Luck asks. "I put two salvage units in the *Dicker* just in case we need to float outside the station to find a good way in." Then he looks at me and frowns. "Where the fuck is your armor?"

"It's coming," Lyra snarls.

"Speaking of Lyra," Valor says. "Draw us a map, princess." He opens up an air screen with a 3-D version of the Bull Station schematics. But before she can say anything, the door chimes again and Crux enters with Tray.

"ALCOR's coming with us," Crux announces, not even bothering with hello. "He says he can hack into the station AI."

"*Dicker* can do that," Jimmy says.

"No." ALCOR's voice fills the room. "I have to come for this."

"Wait," I say, holding up a hand. "You're leaving the station? Again? Two times in two days. The only two times in two decades. What the fuck is going on?" I say this to Crux. "You know something you're not telling us. What is it?"

"I have no idea what you're talking about," Crux answers, not ALCOR. So that's telling in and of itself. "But I'm staying here with Tray. We need to keep an eye on things."

"As usual," Luck grumbles.

Jimmy and Valor both shoot him a look that says, *Don't start that shit now.*

Because Luck has always resented the fact that Crux and Tray stay home on Harem while I hunt down princesses, Jimmy hunts down bots, and Luck and Valor salvage components from far-away systems that ALCOR requires for maintenance.

But Crux is Harem's governor and Tray runs the Pleasure Prison virtual reality, which at any given moment in time is holding almost a million people. So he literally can't leave unless we shut that thing down.

And we won't do that. That's where most of our profit is made.

"I'll leave a copy behind," ALCOR says, answering my question. Sort of. But not really, now that I think about it.

"Whatever," Luck and I both say at the same time.

"Oh," Crux says. "Your bot is still in the lock-up, Serpint. They're sick of him and want you to bail him out."

"I'm sick of that little asshole too. And he's not even mine," I say. "He's Lyra's."

"Don't worry," she calls from her stool in front of the auto-shopper. "I'll take care of the kids, honey."

I scowl at her. "Where's my armor?"

"Already delivered," she snaps, just as Xyla's air screen chimes.

"*Dicker*'s ready to go," Xyla announces. And then everyone is on the move.

I hesitate until it's just Lyra and me, alone.

She frowns at me.

"You have to stay here," I say.

"It's not fair. She's my sister."

"We'll get her back. I promise."

I walk over to her, pull her in to my body, and then kiss her softly on the mouth.

"Don't get hurt," she whispers past my lips.

"I won't. I promise."

We kiss one more time and then I pull away. Holding her hand as I take a few steps towards the door. Unwilling to let her go, but knowing I must. "I'll be back soon. You'll see."

And before she can pout and frown at me, and before my stupid heart can ache at the thought of leaving her behind, I let her fingertips slide out of my hand, and then I turn away and walk through the door.

CHAPTER THIRTY-TWO

First there was love sex.

Then there was family drama and shopping.

Now… there is silence.

I hate it. It takes every ounce of self-control I have not to run out that door after them and insist they take me too.

But Serpint just gave me the same argument and, I reluctantly admit, his reason was solid.

He wants me to be safe. It's a makes-my-heart-all-melty reason.

But what about him? I want him to be safe too. And even though I thought Bull Station and Harem Station were the same when I arrived here three days ago, they are not the same. Bull Station is filled with people who will kidnap you and sell you to slavers. Harem is just… a city filled with forgotten people. Lost people. Lonely people. People who want normal things like family, but don't have any of their own.

So now what? Sit here and twiddle my thumbs and worry the whole time?

"Oh," I say out loud. "The bot."

I might as well go get the bot. I'm pretty sure you can probably do that whole bailing-out thing from an air screen. But I'm also pretty sure wasting time traveling to wherever he is would be better than sitting here doing nothing.

So I walk down the hallway to go get my boots when a thought hits me.

I look over my shoulder at the auto-shopper and smile. Because I learned a little trick getting Serpint's armor.

Search his name and all kinds of things show up. The beer he drinks, the food he orders, the clothes he wears, the guns he uses…

In fact, his whole life is in that shopper.

Not that I need anything from him. But Xyla…

I squeal a little as I enter her name in the search and holy mother of suns, all her outfits pop up. I don't get her shopping list or anything like that, but I'm not after what she eats and drinks. I just want to look like her. And let me tell you, sex-borgs really know how to dress.

My choice is a dark purple bodysuit that has holsters on the side of each thigh, a pair of black, lace-up combat boots that go all the way up to my knees, and a black canvas belt with big silver grommets that comes with a knife.

I pull my pink-blonde hair up into a pony tail, then admire my new look in the mirror while doing martial arts moves.

I am badass.

My air screen chimes for the first time ever and scares the shit out of me. It doesn't wait for me to open it up—note to self, find your default settings and change that—just pops up in the space in front of me.

"Awww," I say, as Serpint's face fills the screen. He's all dressed in his armor now, ready for battle. "You miss me already," I say, making a pouty face.

He smiles. "I just wanted to make sure this thing works before I leave. You can't contact me on ship once we go through the gate, but the second I get back I'm gonna ping you."

"Promises," I say.

"I will."

"Be careful," I say.

"I always am." But I see the cringe and know he's thinking about Draden and Ceres. Valor and Luck are yelling at Serpint to get off the coms in the background. But he takes a second to place his hand up to the screen, palm first.

I put my hand up to his, almost expecting to feel him. Be able to touch him through the distance.

But I can't. It's a trick of technology and not magic.

"See you soon," he says.

Then he's gone.

I sigh and slump down into the couch cushions, my excitement over new sexy Xyla clothes dissipating.

Then I pinch the air and open the screen back up to see what it can do.

First, I search for the lock-up to see if I can figure out where I need to go to bail out Prince. I am half hoping ALCOR will come on and give me some guidance, but he doesn't. Then I remember he's leaving with them. Probably his copy has better things to do than babysit me.

But I find the lock-up has a search function that will let you know if any of your deviant friends or family are in the pokey. I search his series number and get two thousand possibilities. Which immediately has me thinking that retired nanny bots must need constant supervision to keep them honest. Weird, but whatever.

I move on to search Prince, NannyBot 700 Series, and get nothing. So his new spur-of-the-moment name was never updated. And then I realize he's mine. So he's under my name. And I get a chime as his mug shot pops up on the screen. Painted up black matte, pink-glitter belt around his rotund middle, and a dent near his left eye sensor that makes him look like he got in a fight.

There's a flashing red HOLD tab under his name.

"Illegal discharge of weapon," I say, reading his charges. "Bail, seven hundred twenty credits. Well, shit."

Do I even have credits?

But just as I'm thinking that his red HOLD tab changes to a green PAID status and underneath it says, *Pick-up required by owner.*

"Aww," I say, tsk-ing my tongue. "Serpint, you are a good guy."

He must've remembered to bail him out for me before he left.

"OK, now all I need is a map so I can go get him."

And just as those words leave my mouth, a map appears—highlighted in pink—for me to follow. I guess ALCOR is paying attention after all.

And then the auto-shopper dings, signaling the arrival of goods.

Which I didn't order. But when I walk over to see what's there, I get all melty again.

Because Serpint sent me some weapons.

Two laser guns that snap snugly into the thigh holsters of my bodysuit and a plasma rifle with a strap that will let me carry it on my back like that kick-ass hostess yesterday morning.

You know your man cares when he sends you weapons to keep you company while he's at work.

I decide… I love this place.

Then get up and get into the elevator. When I get down on the middle level of the city I follow the blinking pink path paved in front of me on the screen.

I'm just about to get on an escalator when one of those lifty-bots appears on my screen, telling me it's waiting near the edge of the level where Serpint and I got on the other day.

He's such a keeper. He sends me weapons, he pays the bot's bail, and he sends me a lift so it won't take me an hour to get down to the lock-up, which is on the lower level on the whole other side of the station.

This might actually be true love. Like I might just believe in this whole fated mates bullshit. Because so far, he's perfect.

It still takes a while to get to the lock-up, but it's a lot quicker than zig zagging my way around two dozen people-movers. Plus it gives me a chance to just enjoy looking at things.

The lock-up has a ticket window where you check in, then a large seating area where you sit and wait for your number to be called. I'm just about to sit down when my air screen chimes.

He's ready! Wow. I swear, when Serpint gets back I'm gonna kiss him all over for taking such good care of me.

I walk to the front screen and tap my flashing bot's face to let them know I'm here. Almost instantly a door opens to my right and there he is.

He whirrs out, his balance off so he's tilted a little sideways, chirping out a long not-guilty denial.

"Whatever," I say. "Let's just go home."

But just as we step out of the lock-up and I'm looking around for the lift-bot—because surely if Serpint got me a lift here, he'd get me a lift back—my air screen lights up again.

And this time the picture on the screen makes my heart jump.

It's not Serpint. It's not ALCOR, it's not Crux, it's not Tray.

It's *Booty.*

"Lyrrrrraaaa," she purrs. "I'm so glad you came."

"Came?" I say. And then I figure it all out.

None of this was Serpint. This was all *Booty's* doing.

"What do you want?" I say.

"We have to follow them," she says.

"Follow who?" I ask, looking around.

"Serpint and the others. We cannot let them go there alone."

"How do you know where they're going?"

"I've hacked into ALCOR's copy."

Oh, shit. This crazy, terrifying beast of a ship is in control here?

"Follow the map, Lyra. And come get me."

"Get you?"

"We're leaving."

"No," I say, shaking my head. "I'm not leaving with you." *Because you're insane*, I don't add. *And you scare the shit out of me.*

"It's a setup, Lyra."

"No," I say. "I didn't set them up. That's where Nyleena is."

"Not you," she says. "They."

I shake my head and sigh. "I don't know what you're talking about."

"Your people. They knew you were there. They know you're now here. And they can't come here because of the gate defense system. But if they can get ALCOR there—"

"Why the fuck didn't you say something sooner, you batshit piece of tin? How could you let Serpint go?"

"Because he would have never agreed to my plan."

"Which is?"

"We need to start a war," she says.

The bot and I just stare at each other.

"We need to make the first move," she continues. "Because if we don't, they will get the upper hand. Bull Station is part of the outer Cygnian Alliance. We need to destroy it. And Serpint's mission is to get back this sister princess of yours. We need to add another objective to that mission to maintain dominance or the Cygnian Navy will show up here one day—somehow, someway—and take us all out. I cannot allow them to kill ALCOR. Surely you understand this, Lyra."

The bot turns his body back and forth. A definitive no, if ever there was one.

"You love him," *Booty* says.

I say nothing. I'm not talking to this crazy machine. And I'm not falling for her bullshit, either.

"And he loves you," she continues.

"And let me guess," I spit. "You love him. You're jealous of me, aren't you? And you think if you can get rid of me then you can have him for yourself."

She laughs. There's a picture of her on my air screen. A sleek 3-D rendering of her hull. It rotates against a black background and every time she talks there's a sound wave animation that is synced up with her speech.

"You think I'm jealous?"

"It's so obvious," I say, crossing my arms over my chest. "Even he thinks this body thing you were going on about was insane."

"Lyra, my dear," she says, her voice that of a tired, but patient matriarch who is speaking to a small child. "Serpint is my partner, not my lover."

"Sure," I say. "Not yet."

She sighs, then says, "OK. I'm in love—"

"I knew it."

"—with ALCOR."

"What?" I say.

"He and I are in love. I'd do anything for him. But I love Serpint as well. He's been very good to me and I owe him this."

"You're going to start a war and get everyone killed!"

"I'm trying to save everyone, don't you see that?"

"No," I say, unable to stop my laugh. "I do not see."

"Either way, Lyra, you have to come to my ship and set me free."

"ALCOR will never let you leave."

"He's busy right now. He's not watching. That's why I was able to hack into your screen."

"No, he left the station," I say. "He's not here. He left a copy."

She's silent for a half a second too long. And this is how I figure out—she didn't know that.

"What" she says.

"He left with them, *Booty*. The station is being run by his copy."

Silent for three seconds this time. "We have to go. We have to go *now*. Because I thought… I thought…"

"You thought *what*?" I yell.

"I thought I was protecting him. I thought he'd be here, safe, with me. But he's gone with them. They are going to kill him, Lyra. We must go *now*!"

The bot chirps a warning at me the whole way down to *Booty*'s medical bay.

Don't do this, Lyra. Serpint isn't going to like it. He's gonna chain you to the magnetic wall for sure when he gets back.

Shit like that.

I mostly ignore him. Not that he's wrong. Serpint will be pissed if I show up at Bull Station. But *Booty* seems very certain that something very bad is about to happen. Definitely to ALCOR, but probably Serpint too. And what kind of soulmate would I be if I didn't at least go check on him?

That's my rationale. I'm just gonna check on him.

Maybe by the time we get there the whole thing is over and Nyleena is safe in her cryopod on the *Big Dicker*. That could happen. Then *Booty* and I could probably get back here before they even notice.

She's certain that ALCOR's copy isn't omnipresent and I have to agree with her about that. If it was, it would try to stop me, right? It would pop up on my screen or boom that ever-present voice out from some hidden speaker and say, "Lyra, go home. There's no possible way to get off this station without my permission. All the ships are on lockdown unless they were cleared to land or take off before he left."

Except *Booty* isn't on lockdown. No one is paying any attention to her because she's incapacitated down in medical. She has no status at all.

She just needs me to unhook her docking locks because that's a task that must be done manually.

The bot must be reading my mind because he chirps, "Don't you think there's a good reason medical bay docking locks require a manual override?"

I do. He's got a point. The ships locked up in medical aren't fit to fly.

But she says she is and I believe her.

I have to believe her. Because even though I don't really trust *Booty*—I think she's leaving a bunch of stuff out of this mission—I think there's enough there that Serpint actually is in danger.

We arrive at her door and find it unlocked. She claims she and ALCOR share some kind of connection and that even though she would not normally have access to much of the things she's interfering with today, ALCOR's copy and ALCOR aren't the same thing and don't have the same precautions.

He doesn't usually leave the station, from what I can tell. So this copy is… lacking.

"Good," *Booty* says as Prince and I walk into her bay. "Let me show you what you need to do."

This next step takes a while. I have to unhook her from eight cylindrical pylons that are propping up her body in the large double bay. Then, once Prince and I are on board, we have to manually start the undocking procedure that will drop the floor and release her into the vacuum of space outside.

Then we're good to go.

"You're taking this very well," *Booty* comments as I get busy on the last pylon lock.

Which Prince reinterprets as… "She's lost her mind. Exploded during sex."

I scowl at him as I release the final lock and stand up, wiping my hands on a rag.

"Now get inside," *Booty* says. "And suit up. We're leaving."

Prince follows me up the ramp as *Booty*'s engine start up. "This is a bad idea," he says. "A very bad idea."

Booty's hatch begins to close and soon there's a familiar sucking sound as the inner hull is pressurized.

"Too late now," I whisper. Like it or not I'm going through with this.

And I have a decent outlook about the whole thing. Like I'm OK, and this is the right decision.

Until *Booty* can't open the docking floor so we can get away and decides to blow it up with torpedoes.

Yeah. That stupid nanny bot might be right after all.

CHAPTER THIRTY-THREE

It's weird being on Jimmy's ship again. Mostly because I'm not the pilot, Xyla is. But also because I don't think I've gone anywhere without *Booty* in almost a decade.

Luck and Valor are huddled over a console, looking at schematics of Bull Station.

Jimmy is sitting in the cockpit with Xyla, discussing the gates we'll need to travel through.

So that leaves me and ALCOR. Where he's residing, I have no clue. In *Dicker*'s computer core, maybe? Bunkmates or something?

"Did Crux tell you about how Akeelians and Cygnians are related?" ALCOR asks.

"He told me we were engineered for each other," I say.

"Did he tell you why?"

"No," I say. He's silent after that so I say, "Well, are you gonna tell me why?"

More silence. Which only pisses me off. Because I think ALCOR sees his silence as pause, like when humanoids with emotions pause to make facial expressions. Except he has no face, so it's super annoying when he does this because it's just silence.

"How old do you think I am?" he asks.

"Hell, I don't know. Thousands of years, I guess. You told us that once, right?" I think he did. Long time ago when we first met him.

"Twenty-five thousand, two hundred and seventy-six years."

I whistle low at the number. "Impressive," I say. And it is. It blows my mind to think about the advanced civilizations that came before us. It makes me wonder where these people are now—if they're still around at all—and if not, what happened to them.

"I don't talk about it much," ALCOR continues. "Because it was difficult back then."

"Difficult how?" I ask.

"I was new," he says. "Just a few hundred years old and couldn't see the big picture."

"What big picture?" I say.

"Their plans. For the system—there used to be a system, did you know that? In the space around Harem."

"A system?"

Silence again. And now I get it. I know why he pauses. Because I can feel his shrug. His weak smile. His... *guilt.*

I have always known what he's not saying now. He killed them. He never said it back then, either. But when you happen upon an ancient AI living on a pristine abandoned station, it doesn't take a genius to solve that mystery. Especially one with his reputation.

I knew whoever used to live and work on Harem was most likely murdered by ALCOR. The station was not called Harem back then, just ALCOR Station. I asked him once what his name stood for but he never said. Jimmy and I used to sit around and come up with stupid possibilities. Ass-Licking-Calcium-Oxide-Rectum. Or Artificial-Life-Created-On-Regulus. Stuff like that.

So I get it. And who cares, anyway? Not my people. Not my fucking millennium. And I know this is gonna sound callous and apathetic, but it was just a station. Stations fail. I wouldn't say all the time, but in my life I've heard of three station failures. Three times millions of people died for one reason or another in far-away places.

So it wasn't something I'd never heard of. Accidents happen.

But he just said… *system.*

As in… a sun, and planets, and moons. "System?" I say again. Because the silence has gone on long enough now that I realize he's not gonna answer. "What system?"

There was no evidence of a system when we came through those gates that first time we met ALCOR. No debris field orbiting the station. No asteroid belt twenty billion miles out. No oddly-shaped pieces of rock spinning in the darkness. Nothing like that. It was just… space. Completely empty except for two gates, and a station, and a lot of leftover ice from a comet that came through and exploded eons ago.

"Why'd you bring it up if you're not gonna answer me?" I say. "It's not like I need this information right now, ALCOR. I've got enough shit on my mind without your cryptic guilt."

"It wasn't me," he finally says.

"Who wasn't you?" It comes out automatically. But it's an unnecessary question. Because I know what he's talking about. So I add, "Who was it then?"

"There was a war, Serpint. A very terrible war between the Akeelians and the Cygnians."

I stare down at my boots as he says this. Trying to make these new clues solve this new mystery. We've been around him all these years and I didn't know this? I mean, I get it. I was young when I left. And Akeelian boys have a very specific kind of education. You learn a skill and take classes and certifications in that specific skill set, and that's pretty much it.

Valor and Luck were learning to salvage. Crux was in station management. Jimmy was in diplomacy. Tray was in AI evolution. Draden and I were too young to be on a track, so we just went to normal school. And we did learn some history, but it was mostly recent stuff. Certainly nothing that ever went back twenty-five-thousand years.

"You and Lyra," he says, "are the same. Genetically speaking, that is. You both came out of that war. The Akeelians—all male—went one way. And the Cygnians—all female—went another. That was the part I played. I separated them and made it impossible for them to ever breed again."

I laugh. Not because it's funny, but because it's a joke. Except not funny. "Guess that little magic spell has run its course."

"Appears so. Tell me something, Serpint. Do you find it interesting, ironic, or foreboding, that you boys found me all those years ago? And that the one girl you shouldn't have is now yours? And the one girl Crux should never see again is now sitting in his medical bay in a cryopod?"

"What do you mean I shouldn't have her? She is mine. And no one's taking her away from me."

"That's the only thing you heard, wasn't it?" He pauses. And I picture him staring me down and shaking his head. "I've been thinking about this stuff since you boys showed up. And then when the princesses started showing up. And how Crux just went along with my plan to collect them. I've been trying to figure out if it was interesting, ironic, or foreboding."

I look up. Stare at the ceiling because that's my default direction when ALCOR is talking to me. "So what did you decide?"

"I think," he says, "I think it's all three."

"Why do we really need to get Nyleena back?" I ask.

"Because they are starting another war. Their weapons are formidable. Ours are as well. They are of the same technology. But they've been regrouping for twenty-five thousand years, Serpint. Planning their revenge on me. There's no telling what they've got now."

"Us?" I say. "They're starting a war with us?"

"Do you think Lyra is here by chance? By mistake? Or by fate?"

Shit.

"And Corla," he says. "Same question."

Fucking hell.

"Yes, Serpint," he says when I don't answer. "They are starting a war with us."

When I look around I realize that everyone else is listening to ALCOR too. Jimmy and Xyla have come out of the cockpit, leaning on either side of the hatch. Xyla's long hair floats snake-like around her face in the low gravity. Valor and Luck are both staring at me across the room. Beauty has secured herself into a bot hold like she needs the solid walls for reassurance.

"Did you know about this?" I ask them, looking at Jimmy and Xyla first, then Valor and Luck.

"No," Jimmy says. "Not until we got here for the service."

"So Draden and Ceres," I say. "Back on Cetus Station when I just happened to bump into the Cygnian queen—"

"They set you up, Serpint," Jimmy says.

"And I fell for it."

"You couldn't have known," ALCOR says.

"Why the fuck did I steal that queen?"

"Why do you steal any of them?" ALCOR asks. "Why does Crux collect them in a harem? Why do any of you do what you do?"

"I don't know," I say.

"Because you can't help it," ALCOR says. "You have a genetic *need* to procreate."

"But we could procreate with anyone," I say. "Doesn't even matter if our partners are Cygnian."

"Yes, and if you get a male child, he's Akeelian. But what happens to the girls?"

Crux's question from last night. Almost word for word. "I… don't know. I guess I never thought about it."

"They are hybrids, Serpint. That's why you cannot have a second-generation Akeelian female."

"Unless we mate with a Cygnian," I say, fitting another piece in this puzzle. "But wait," I say. "They have kings. Lyra's father—"

"All genetically engineered," ALCOR says. "There are no male Cygnians. Only hybrids who cannot procreate without a lot of laboratory manipulation."

"So what the fuck are we doing?" I ask. "Why the hell are we here?"

"We need Nyleena," ALCOR says. "The same way we need Lyra."

"What do you mean?" I ask, getting a very bad feeling about where this is going.

"You can breed with her," ALCOR says. "She is a higher-order princess. The pinks and silvers are pure—"

"I'm sorry," I say, stopping him by putting up a hand. "Did you just say *breed* with her?"

"Come on," Jimmy says. "Don't get hung up on terms, Serpint. You're already thinking about how she's your soul-mate. Well, congratulations, brother. You're right. And now the two of you need to make babies. How fun will that be? And if we get Nyleena back, one of us lucky fuckers will make babies with her too." Then he mutters under his breath, "Please don't let it be me."

"And if we can wake up Corla," ALCOR adds, "we will be able to rebuild the species."

"This is why we've been collecting Cygnian princesses for twenty years?" I ask. "We're trying to make babies?"

"We're trying to make babies," ALCOR answers. "Purebreds are powerful. And now that we know they've successfully created the soul mates we have to start our own genetic engineering program. They cannot get this technology first."

Did he just call babies… *technology*?

CHAPTER THIRTY-FOUR

"Strap in!" Booty blares through the com system.

I'm already hustling to snap into the pilot's seat when she takes off, but her acceleration is so abrupt, my head bangs against the head rest.

"*Booty*!" I yell.

"Sorry," she purrs.

But I don't think she's sorry. And we're not even through the first gate yet and I'm regretting this trip. "This is a bad idea," I say. "How do I know you're not still infected with that virus and you're really taking me back to the Cygnians?"

"Because giving you back would feed right into the Cygnian plan."

"Which is?"

"You can create *true* offspring. The Cygnians do not yet realize who the Harem Station boys are, but when they do they will want you back—them too. They'll want Crux the most, but they will take Serpint once they hear about your little light show yesterday at Draden's funeral. I'd like to think Harem Station is filled with nothing but loyal people on our side, but you can't screen everyone. So all the brothers are now in danger."

"You're blaming me?" I ask. The nerve of this thing!

"They want to breed you, Lyra. That's not your fault, it's just who and what you are. It's just your place in the universe. And if someone's going to breed you, it will be us. Not them. So you can trust me, because I am on Serpint's side and even though I don't want to admit it, we need you."

I think about that for a few moments. Not *he* needs you. But *we* need you. Also… I'm not sure how to interpret that whole 'it will be us' statement. Is she implying I'm now part of some genetic engineering program on Harem? Because that's just a big old, *Fuck you, Lyra* from the Universe, isn't it?

"If you have a god," *Booty* says, "pray to it now."

"Why?" I ask, leaning forward in my seat to get a better look at the giant screen in front of me.

She doesn't answer. But she doesn't need to. Because I see why for myself. The gate defense system is armed and there are hundreds of SEAR cannons pointed at *us*.

"We're not even gonna make it through the first gate!"

Code starts spilling down the screens like a green waterfall made up of numbers, and symbols, and letters.

She's hacking it, I realize. The Harem Gate defense system.

But that should be impossible. She shouldn't be able to…

We fly through the gate with a burst of light and I'm driven back into the soft gel cushion of my chair with the sudden acceleration, my head pounding and light leaking off of my body like some force is squishing it out of me.

I've only ever been through a handful of gates, but I know the trips are almost instantaneous. So the moment I register all this discomfort is the moment it stops.

I realize I was holding my breath and exhale.

"Don't relax," *Booty* says. "Gate number two—"

And then it starts again…

This time when we come out of it, I can't see. And in that same moment, we enter another gate, this time with no warning.

When that trip is done we slow. My vision is still black, my body slumped in my chair, and my head is pounding so hard, I can't hear what *Booty* is saying.

"What?" I ask, barely able to hear myself.

I don't think she responds, but it wouldn't matter. It takes long minutes for my vision and hearing to come back. Long minutes of spider web flashes across a black background in my eyes and my heartbeat thumps in my ears.

I'm suddenly grateful for the cryopod trip when that old man stole me.

This is horrible.

When Nyleena and I escaped we avoided gates until we had to use them. Those were the instructions I was given and now I know why.

High-speed space travel *sucks.*

Finally, when the sounds of the ship are almost back to normal, she says, "We'll go slow for a little while now, but don't relax. We have three more gates to jump through before we get to Bull Station. Normally I'd take an easier route, but we need to catch up with *Dicker*."

"They left hours ahead of us," I say. "What if they're already there? What if we're too late and something bad already happened?"

"*Dicker* won't take the route we just did. It's too much for her. She hasn't been upgraded the way I have and it's almost too much for me. So we should be catching up to them."

That answered my first question but not my last. So I repeat it. "*Booty*, what if we're too late?"

She's silent for so long, I'm about to repeat myself a third time. But then she says, "We won't know until we get there. So get ready. And be prepared for anything."

Something tells me there's more to this little mission than she's letting on.

But just as I think that thought, she accelerates hard, and there's no turning back.

CHAPTER THIRTY-FIVE

"One more gate," Dicker says, once we come out of the one we're in. I used to hate gate travel and would make *Booty* go out of her way to use as few as possible. But I've gotten used to it. A few seconds of immense discomfort is always worth it once you get to the other side and realize you just traveled light years.

Bull Station is in a busy area of the galaxy and there's a million ways to get there. But we take a long way, trying to avoid checkpoints so ALCOR won't have to hack us through any really tight security until we have to.

Which gives me way too much time to think about what I was just told.

Breeders. We're capturing them for breeding.

"We've never had a pink or a silver before," I say to no one. But everyone is listening.

"No," ALCOR says. "Not until Lyra."

"So… we don't know—"

"We know," Jimmy says. "It's not a big deal."

But it kinda is. *Breeders.* I don't know how I feel about that. I wouldn't mind putting a baby in her, but... breeding. It feels so... sterile.

It's very easy to not get a woman pregnant when you're an Akeelian man because not only do both cocks have to be engaged and inside her pussy at the same time, both cocks have to ejaculate at the same time as well. Our sperm has to mix to be active inside a woman. And simultaneous ejaculation of both cocks is almost unheard of.

Until Lyra came along, that is.

"Who else knows about this?" I ask. "Besides us?"

"All the Akeelians know," ALCOR says.

"Then why the fuck didn't I know?"

"Because we left when we were kids," Jimmy says.

"Crux knew," Valor says. "I knew a little. I knew he and Corla were together and that's why we had to leave."

"Wait," I say. "Was Corla—"

"Yes," ALCOR says. "She was pregnant when they separated."

"So a child was already born?" I say. "Twenty years ago?"

"We think so," Valor says.

"How do you know all this?" I ask him.

"Crux told us yesterday," Luck says. "We were gonna tell you, but then you and Lyra—" He shrugs. "We figured it could wait."

"So the Cygnians," I say, putting yet another puzzle piece in place. "They have this child of Crux and Corla?"

"That we don't know," ALCOR says. "We don't think so. They'd have had almost a decade to harvest sperm and breed new purebreds in laboratory if that was the case. If they had purebreds, believe me, we'd know about it by now. They'd have attacked us already. And I doubt Corla would leave her progeny behind in another escape attempt."

"Crux thinks she got caught by the Cygnians after the baby was born," Jimmy says. "That she probably left it with some trusted people somewhere."

I just... can't wrap my head around this yet. All this time I knew we were different. I remember what it was like to escape the Akeelian System and find ALCOR. And I always knew what we did when we left was wrong, but I never thought about it again.

Escaping and finding ALCOR was luck and why would anyone question luck?

I look at Luck. Because he's had that nickname since I was just a little brat who used to tag along behind him. Long before we got this *luck*. But for some reason I always equated his name with our escape.

"Wait," I say, another idea invading my thoughts. "So we are half-breeds too?"

"No," ALCOR says. "The male Akeelian genetic line has been preserved. It's only the female line that has been diluted."

"How is that possible?"

"Do you remember our mother?" Jimmy asks.

"The harem mother," I say. "Sure."

"She was your caregiver," ALCOR says. "Not your mother. You don't have a mother."

I knew that. Have always known that. Both of those things. But for some reason it hurts to hear it spelled out so clear.

"Before the great war when the sun, and planets, and moons of the old system were destroyed," ALCOR says, "a few thousand Akeelians escaped on a generation ship. They took millions of genetic samples with them so they could procreate."

"That's us," Jimmy says.

"Still," ALCOR continues, "that generation ship couldn't take samples from a pink or a silver princess. Those genetics were locked up tight. So you are only half of what your children could be. They have been trying to steal Akeelians for thousands of years. You are what they need to complete their plan. *You* are what they are after right now. And they are using these women to lure you back."

He pauses for a moment.

"And they want to kill me too. Because I was the one who let that generation ship escape. I was the one who decimated their system. And I am the only thing standing between them and galactic domination. That system is a dictatorship. Nothing comes in or out without permission. Not even information. The Cygnian men are violent, repulsive creatures. There is no line they won't cross, no measure they won't take, no life that can't be sacrificed for the greater good."

"Pretty fucking crazy, isn't it?" Valor says. "I mean, I always knew we were different. Something was wrong and pieces of me were missing and shit like that. But I'm like you, Serpint. I don't know what to make of this shit. I like my job," he says, looking up at the ceiling to indicate he's talking to ALCOR. "I really do. I don't mind scrounging around the galaxy to find components you need. But I don't want to be in this war. Not if Harem Station goes the way of the system that used to be there."

"I know that," ALCOR says, his voice soft and his tone careful. "I don't either. But they've started something now, Valor. The Cygnians have sent us Lyra for a reason. They let Corla escape for a reason."

"They're gonna come get us," I say. "They're gonna let Lyra and me be together long enough to make babies, and then they're gonna come steal them or her, or me… or hell, all of us."

"Or…" Jimmy says. "They're just gonna take us and blow up ALCOR and everyone else on it using Lyra or Corla as the detonation device. We have no idea how they're triggered."

ALCOR says, "But if we can get Nyleena and maybe find that Velia girl, we could, at the very least, reverse engineer their new weapons."

"And make babies," Luck says. "And get that too."

"That's why we have to get them first," Xyla says. Those are the first words she's spoken since we started this conversation. "Whether they want to use Nyleena to blow us up or to set one of you up to breed with her, doesn't matter. Their endgame is our annihilation."

I've always liked how Xyla counts herself as one of us. How she always uses the word 'we' and almost never uses the word 'I.' And right now, I appreciate that more than she will ever know.

"If we could get Nyleena back to Harem," ALCOR says, "we could keep her safe. We could keep Lyra safe too. There is a reason I have that defense system. We just need to get through this one mission, boys. We just need to get her back and we'll be OK. I promise."

Boys.

He almost never calls us boys anymore. He used to back when we first found him. It was always, "Boys, come here." Or, "Boys, I need your help." Or, "Boys, we can do better." It makes me sad to think back on our history together because it hits me in this moment, just what ALCOR *is* to us.

It has taken me twenty years to realize he is our *father.*

"We're about to enter the last gate," Xyla says, walking back towards the cockpit. "Helmets on, suits pressurized. Now."

Standard procedure, I tell myself. Just normal precautions when you go into unknown territory expecting resistance.

We all suit up and strap in. I hate not being pilot. I hate not being in *Booty.* I hate not being in control when there's so much at stake.

But Valor catches my eye from across the room and nods his head. I watch a glint of cobalt blue blaze across his violet eyes, a reflection of the electromagnetic glow that surrounds the gate like spider-like tendrils, and nod back as we go in.

And most times you come out the other end of the gate just fine. Suit unnecessary. Empty space for a million miles in every direction.

But that's not how we come out of *this* gate.

We come out of this gate blinded by a flash of light, an explosion of the brightest magnitude, and the sense that we just made a very big mistake.

Because everything goes black.

CHAPTER THIRTY-SIX

We come out of the last gate in silence. I expect alarms, and warnings, and *Booty*'s disembodied voice barking orders.

None of that happens. I count to ten in my head, letting my body adjust to the new stillness, then open my eyes.

"What's going on?" I ask, looking around. I unsnap myself from the harness, then shakily get to my feet. Prince is still snapped into the bot station, safe and snug. But he's not moving or making any sound.

He looks dead.

"*Booty*?" I say, expecting an immediate response. "What's going on?"

I know she's not dead. The bot isn't dead either. These can't die unless you blow their memory components into bits. They just go out of service for a while.

But *Booty* is not out of service. I know this because in this silence there are lights flashing on panels, and images on screens, and data flowing in code everywhere I look.

"*Booty*!" I say. "Answer me."

I step forward towards the cockpit. The space where Serpint and his brother Draden probably spent a lot of time together. Talking, and joking, and laughing. Probably got angry and fought in this space too.

I look up at the large, main screen. Not a window in the traditional sense, but a live feed outside the ship.

My eyes squint together, trying to make sense of what I'm seeing. "What the hell is that?"

Something is floating towards us. Spinning in the vacuum of space. Toppling end over end as it gets closer and grows bigger.

The screen is tracking the unknown object. Calculating its velocity and collision time—because that's what's going to happen if she doesn't move.

"*Booty*, move out of the way!" I say. "*Booty*!"

But she doesn't move. Just hovers in space. Waiting for—

The object smacks into us. Not enough impact to make the hull shudder or move us off course, but the vibration carries through the hull of the ship as a dull hum that rings for a second or two.

"What the hell am I looking at?" I say, walking forward to peer at the screen. Because I now see that there's more of these spinning objects.

Lots more.

"A debris field," *Booty* says. "That's what we're looking at. Bull Station is gone. And that thing that just hit us, and those things still spinning towards us… are *bodies*."

"Bodies," I repeat. Like saying it out loud will force it to make sense. "Nyleena."

"She must've exploded," *Booty* says. "And taken the whole station with her."

"No," I say, shaking my head. "No, that's not what happened."

"Lyra," *Booty* says, using one of those calm, patient voices people use when someone is being unreasonable. "The station is gone."

"No, you don't understand," I say. "We were connected. If she detonates, I go with her. If she blew up, we wouldn't be here. She has to be here *somewhere*."

"Then what caused this—"

She stops talking, her data screens scrolling—scrolling—scrolling. Searching for answers.

But I see the answer just as all that scrolling stops.

"There's our answer," I say, pointing to the screen. "It's a Cygnian warship."

Booty's hull is a formidable piece of engineering. Her weapons systems are top of the line, and her AI core is probably one of the best out there.

But Cygnian warships are no joke. They are easily ten times her size. Easily have ten times as many torpedoes. And when they come to destroy something, this is exactly how they leave it.

In pieces.

"Serpint," I whisper.

"I've got *Dicker* on radar. She's signaling me now."

"Oh, thank the sun."

"But the warship has her in a traction field. They're pulling her in. This is just an emergency beacon."

"We need to sever that connection so they can get out of here."

"They've seen me," *Booty* says. "They've locked on me too. I'm just not close enough to be in their control. And *Dicker* and the crew can't get out of here even if they weren't in that traction field. The only way she goes home is if I tug her behind me. There's no power on the ship at all. The only thing working is the emergency beacon. All systems are dead."

"The crew?" I say, afraid to ask but knowing I must.

"Wait," she says. "There's another emergency beacon. Very small and it's behind us."

"The crew, *Booty*! What about the crew?"

"I don't know, Lyra. But the other signal is coming in as… Nyleena."

"Shit," I say, looking at the other screen where *Booty*'s exterior cameras are zooming in on a single cryopod.

"They've fired. I have to return fire." She pauses. "Returning fire now."

I don't know why she's telling me this. Why she's reporting to me. Maybe because that's what she does with Serpint and it's just habit. Or maybe because she wants my input.

Two torpedoes release, their forward thrust sending us back in the opposite direction for a moment before her thrusters can compensate.

"They can't kill me this far away," *Booty* says. "I'll just return fire and blow their torpedoes up as they approach."

"And if you run out of torpedoes?" I ask. Because she will. Long before that Cygnian warship does.

"I can outrun them easily. But—"

"But," I say, finishing for her, "we have to leave everyone else behind."

"Incoming signal from Xyla," *Booty* says.

"Oh, thank the sun," I say. "They're alive."

"They have a plan. But it's a bad one and will probably fail. And even if it does work..."

"Even if it does work *what*?"

She tells me the plan, and the consequences, and we both sit in silence for several seconds.

Then *Booty* says, "We have two choices, Lyra. And neither of them are good. We get Nyleena and run, leaving *Dicker* and the crew to hope for the best. Or we stay and fight to save *Dicker* and the crew, and let the Cygnians recover Nyleena if we fail."

She pauses. Again, maybe for Serpint's opinion that never comes. Or maybe she just wants me to get used to the idea that either way, we're not going to win. Not today.

Then she says, "If they get Nyleena they can still detonate her? Even without you?"

"Yes," I say, feeling defeated. "They can't detonate me without her, but if they get her cryopod and start a new detonation sequence, they could detonate her without me."

"So you're safe? As long as they don't get a hold of you?"

"No," I say. "If she blows, I blow. My fate is tied to hers."

Booty sighs. "So they could wait until we go home and then detonate Nyleena, thereby detonating you, and take out half of Harem Station too."

I say nothing to that.

"Do you understand?"

"Yes," I whisper.

"Then what should we do?"

I draw in a deep breath and look around the interior of the ship. Log what I see, what I can use, half-heartedly calculate my chances of success. Decide the odds are bad, and then decide to do it anyway.

"Take me over to Nyleena. I'm getting off here."

Because I have a third option in mind.

CHAPTER THIRTY-SEVEN

We come out of this gate blinded by a flash of light. An explosion of the brightest magnitude. And the sense that we just made a very big mistake.

Alarms are screeching, panels of electronic equipment spark and flash, like their circuits have been ripped out. And as my vision clears I spot Xyla through the cockpit hatch. Her hair is a tangled mess of lavender tendrils, letting me know that the ship's gravity is gone.

And then I feel it now too. The way, even under my suit, my shoulders strain against the harness trying to keep me in place. Everything else happens in slow motion. My mouth opens to start yelling their names. Valor, Luck, Jimmy. But all the words get lost in my throat when I see the reason why we have no gravity. Why all the screens and panels are flashing with the blue-white light of lost electric current.

There is a gash in the side of *Dicker*'s hull. And on the other side of that hole, out in the empty blackness of space, is Jimmy.

Sound returns now. The silence was just a pause in my hearing after an explosion and Jimmy's voice is in my helmet.

Not dead. Yelling at Valor, who I now realize is hooking a suit tether onto the side of the hull, about to exit the ship and join Jimmy in the deep dark.

"Right there! Right there!" Jimmy is yelling. Pointing a finger to the side of the hull.

"I got it," Valor says. Calm. Too calm. He points his hands together and dives through the gash, following Jimmy outside.

Luck is floating across the room at the end of a tether. Shaking his head and blinking his eyes, trying to get his bearings just like I was.

We are all alive, that's all that matters right now. So I unhook myself, reach for a safety tether on my suit and hook on to the nearest eyebolt.

I will not be sucked out of the ship. We have no air in here at all. We are in perfect equilibrium with the vacuum surrounding us. But one small thrust in the wrong direction could send me spinning away. And if you've never tried to recover a body-sized object in space—well, it's a fucking bitch. There is no time to go chasing after anyone.

Valor and Jimmy are obviously dealing with some emergency on the outside of the ship.

"Get it off!" Jimmy is yelling.

"I'm trying," Valor says, still calm.

I have no idea how Jimmy got outside. Maybe during the initial explosion or maybe he went out there on purpose.

But I don't bother them. Whatever it is they're doing, they don't need my help.

I float up towards Xyla, my tether extending as I get further away from my anchor point.

"What the fuck happened?" I say into my helmet.

She has no helmet, or suit for that matter.

She was made for the vacuum of space and her body is self-contained and sealed. But she has an internal communication system that plugs right into our suits.

"They shot at us the moment we came out of the gate."

"Who—" But I stop. Because I see who.

A massive Cygnian warship hovers off to the side of Bull Station. Its massive, bird-like form is silver and windowless. Just smooth metal. An aerodynamic design that mimics the wings of a bird diving for prey.

It lights up.

A pink glow surrounds the silver body. And even though I've never actually seen a Cygnian warship fire torpedoes, I know this is how it happens.

More than a dozen blue-white streaks leave the ship, arcing out into space as they lock on their targets, and seconds later Bull Station is just… *gone.*

Debris flies out in all directions, heading straight for *Dicker*'s hull.

I look over my shoulder and see Valor and Jimmy climbing back inside the blown-out hole.

"Can't get it!" Jimmy says, his eyes locking on mine as Luck, now fully back from his blackout, pulls him and Valor back into the shelter of *Dicker*'s dead body as bits and pieces of the station float by outside.

"What the fuck is happening?" I say.

"They locked us with a traction torpedo the moment we exited the gate. And now they're pulling us in." Xyla turns her head up to me, her wild, lavender hair swimming around her face, and says, "They've caught us. And there's no way to sever the traction without *Dicker's* weapons online."

"It doesn't matter," ALCOR says. Which surprises me. Because I figured he was out of commission with *Dicker*. "Just shoot me out to that ship, Xyla. And do it now."

"What?" I say. Because I was obviously out for more than a few seconds and there's a plan in motion I'm just now catching up to.

"ACLOR is going to infiltrate the warship and take it over."

"Can you do that?" I ask.

"No one has any idea what I can do," he says, voice low and calm in my helmet. It's not his regular voice. No emotion at all. Just... stoic logic. "Not even me."

A chill shudders up my spine, making all the little hairs on the back of my neck stand up.

"I'm getting an incoming signal," Xyla says. "From *Booty*."

"What the fuck?" I say.

"She's here," Xyla says. "With Lyra."

"No—"

"The warship has locked on to her," Xyla continues. "But she's too far away to grab just yet. Torpedoes have launched. *Booty* has returned fire."

"*Now*, Xyla," ALCOR says.

"On it," she says. "Valor, release Beauty."

"What are you doing?" I ask.

But no one answers me. Valor just unhooks Beauty from her safety niche, pats her on her spherical head, and throws her out the gash in the hull.

"Now," Jimmy says. "All we have to do is live through the next ten minutes until she reaches the warship."

"Good news," Xyla says. "The warship is heading towards us, so now we have less than a minute. And *Booty* is on an intercept course with the warship."

Leave, I silently pray. *Just leave,* Booty. *Get Lyra out of here.*

"She's arming," Xyla says. "*Booty* has locked onto the warship."

"She can't win!" I say. "She can't fucking win against that ship!"

"I know that," Xyla says. "She's not trying to win. She's trying to save Lyra."

"What?"

"Lyra and her bot have exited *Booty Hunter* and are on collision course with…" She pauses. "Oh, shit."

"With who?"

"*Booty* says it's Nyleena's cryopod floating out into space. They're going to detonate themselves and take out the warship."

Silence after that. As we all take in just how dire this situation is.

ALCOR—the real ALCOR, not a copy—trying to save us by taking over the warship.

And Lyra—trying to kill us, and the Cygnians too, should ALCOR fail.

Xyla opens up an air screen, projecting two images at once. Lyra, holding on to Prince as they shoot through space towards the cryopod, and Beauty on the other. Doing her best to deliver ALCOR to the warship before Nyleena and Lyra explode.

We're already dead, I realize.

The only thing left to know is which way we'll go out.

CHAPTER THIRTY-EIGHT

Booty has control of Prince, directing the tiny thrusters built into his body for maneuvering in station atmosphere, to correctly point me to Nyleena's cryopod.

I can see her. My sister. Helpless and frozen inside her pod. I was there when we put her inside. All the Cygnian officers and medical advisors standing by to make sure all her life support was online and functioning. That her mission directives were complete. Half listening as the general told me—over and over again—what I needed to do once I got her in range of our target, some planet called Earth.

It wasn't supposed to end this way.

No one missed Corla once she escaped. No one cared that one queen got away, not really. She is just a weapon. Just as valuable out there in space alone as she is at home. They were probably hoping she'd get to Angel Station so they could wipe the place out, I'm sure. There's no way to know that because I was not a part of her mission.

But she was separated from her detonator, just like Nyleena and I were. They can't blow her up if they don't have her sister to initiate—unless they get a hold of Corla's cryopod. Then they could rearm her with a new sister detonator. And the old detonator—if she is still alive—would blow up with them. Three targets. Three explosions.

No higher-order princesses, let alone a queen, ever escape from Cygnia. We just prolong our time and get to choose our target instead of them.

Where is that other princess? The one who was escorting Corla? We need to know that. We need to find her.

And why didn't I just fly Nyleena back into Cygnian space and detonate her there?

I laugh a little in my suit, then make myself stop. I only have so much oxygen and this suit can't make more. So laughing is wasteful. But wouldn't that be something? To take them out with their own weapon?

I know why I didn't fly back to the Cygnians. I hate to admit it, but it was because I was afraid. And I was maybe just a little bit hopeful. That we could get away. That we could get to Angel Station. That we could really, and for once in our lives, be free.

It was a stupid dream. I know that now. I should've blown us both up before we even left. Taken out those generals, and those doctors, and the fucking king himself. Because he was there.

I don't know why I'm bothering with this little puzzle. This battle will be over in a matter of minutes and then all this becomes someone else's problem.

But Nyleena's pod, though I can see it, still seems very far away. So what else can I do with the final moments of my life but ponder all my mistakes? Think up a better way to do things?

"Intercept in thirty seconds," *Booty* says through my helmet.

I don't say anything back. There's nothing to say so talking is just as wasteful as laughing ironically.

"But don't detonate," *Booty* adds.

"What?" I whisper, the question out before I can stop myself.

"ALCOR is on his way to the Cygnian warship on Beauty. He's going to infiltrate and take them out."

I can hear the torment in her voice. The emotion and anguish. And this is the moment I realize… ships are people. She loves ALCOR. She wanted to do this mission to save him and now look. He's gonna kill himself to save us.

I crash into Nyleena's pod, making mad grabs for something, anything to hold on to. The side of the pod is sleek and smooth. Sealed tight so no air, not even a single molecule, can enter without permission. But I grab onto a handle meant for lifting, and my body jerks hard, pulling the cryopod with me through space. Hurling us even faster and farther away from *Booty*.

I swing myself around just in time to see her release more torpedoes. They are locked onto incoming fire, and just explode them in silence as I watch.

I don't know how many she has left, but it's not enough.

"Initiating the detonation sequence," I whisper, placing my fingertips over the pad on the outside of the pod.

"No," *Booty* says into my helmet. "Hold fast, Lyra. We still have a chance."

"I'm down to sixteen percent total oxygen, *Booty*. If I don't do it now I might black out and not be able to do it at all."

"*Hold*," she commands.

CHAPTER THIRTY-NINE

"ALCOR and Beauty intercept in thirty seconds," Xyla says.

On one of the air screens *Booty* releases torpedoes, taking out incoming fire. On the other screen, the warship grows bigger and bigger by the second, the tractor beam pulling us in faster now that we have momentum.

"Tell her," I say, placing a gloved hand on Xyla's shoulder. "Tell *Booty* to use the SEAR cannon."

"Not yet," Xyla says.

Jimmy swings his body past mine and into the copilot's seat next to Xyla. "ALCOR, report."

"I'm on the hull," ALCOR says. "But we need a way in."

"Lyra is almost out of oxygen," Xyla says.

"I can't just stand here and watch this," I say. "Give me one of your salvage units, Luck."

"You'll never make it in time," Valor says.

"I don't give a fuck," I yell. "Give me one of your salvage units now!"

Luck grabs my arm and pulls himself along the corridor. We unhook our suit tethers as we pass like pros, and he drags me to the hatch that leads to the lower level of the ship where they keep their equipment.

"I'm in," ALCOR says in my helmet.

"Lyra is down to fourteen percent total oxygen," Xyla adds. "She needs to start entering the sequence now or she will not be able to do it at all." Half of that was meant for me, the other for *Booty*.

I wish I could hear *Booty*'s voice right now and not have to get information second-hand from Xyla.

"I'm coming with you," Valor says, bumping into me from behind. "This ship is done. Jimmy, Xyla, come with us. We have two salvage units, we can—"

"Fuck that," Jimmy says. "If my ship dies out here, so do I."

"Jimmy," I say, looking back down the corridor. "Don't be stupid. If we can get back to Harem…" The cockpit isn't in view anymore because we're down on the lower level now, so I only see Valor's face through his helmet.

I don't know what we'll do if we get back to Harem, so I don't bother finishing my sentence. ALCOR is gone. Whether he succeeds or not, he's going down with that warship. And if we stay on *Dicker*, we'll explode with it if Nyleena detonates. We're too close now.

"*Booty* has a tether on us," Xyla says.

I wait for the jerk. The signal that we're being pulled away from the warship. But there's nothing. No tether of *Booty*'s could out pull a Cygnian warship tractor.

Luck opens the airlock manually without cycling through the procedures. There's no atmosphere left on the *Dicker*, so it doesn't protest with warnings about hard vacuum. We're already in dead space. The ship's hull is just an illusion of protection now.

"Here," Valor says. "Get in."

I float over to his salvage unit and climb in.

It's big enough that the warship will pick it up on radar. Blow it up in seconds, maybe.

But maybe, just maybe… ALCOR has their attention in other places now.

Luck powers it on.

And seconds later we're floating out through the airlock towards Lyra.

"I'm coming," I say. "Tell Lyra I'm coming and she's not going to die today."

It's a lie.

We're already dead.

I'm just trying to make sure she doesn't have to die alone.

Because that's what soulmates do.

They go out together.

CHAPTER FORTY

I have less than ten percent oxygen in my suit now. I'm basically breathing my own exhales. Suffocating myself with my own carbon dioxide. My vision is spotty and flashes in and out. Blackness. Light. Blackness. Light.

Like those bugs in long-ago myths that glow in the night to find mates.

It's only then that I realize it's me… I'm glowing like the bugs in the night. Flashing in the darkness of space. Begging someone to help me, I realize.

Nausea overtakes me and I have to concentrate hard not to vomit in my suit as I try to press the detonation sequence onto Nyleena's cryopod.

I fuck it up. Twice. The oxygen monitor lit up on the inside of my suit counts down the oxygen content inside my suit and I know I have seconds left before I black out forever.

I try again, forcing every last bit of concentration left inside my compromised brain, to do it right this time.

Three.

Seven.

Nine.

One.

Zero.

Zero.

I black out.

Come to.

Black out again.

Then come to surrounded by pink light.

This is it.

This is how I die. My flux capacitor releasing every bit of luminous flux I have left.

Because I won't be needing it anymore.

Something grabs my arm. And if I had any breath left, I'd scream.

But I don't.

I just place my gloved finger on the key pad one more time… one more zero…

And press down as hard as I can.

CHAPTER FORTY-ONE

The universe implodes.

It's a brilliant mixture of pink and gold and my heart sinks as the reality of what just happened hits my brain. I turn away from the exploding warship as the screen on my suit automatically blacks out to save my vision should I survive.

But I have her. I have clipped my suit tether to Lyra's suit and Luck has tethered his salvage unit to Nyleena's pod.

Because it wasn't Nyleena and Lyra who blew up.

It was ALCOR and Beauty.

And even though I know it's wrong, there's relief in my heart and my head too. Relief that Lyra is still alive. That it wasn't her.

"Hang on, Lyra," I whisper, placing my helmet up to hers so she might hear my voice via sound wave transduction. "I've got you, princess. I've got you."

Her light, which was just flashing like a SOS signal in the darkness of space, is gone.

But I hook the extra oxygen tank up anyway. I can't not keep up hope. We didn't go through all this to lose her now. ALCOR and Beauty didn't kill themselves on a suicide mission just so she could die.

We are soulmates. She *must* live.

I press the influx button on the side of the canister, forcing the lifesaving gas into her suit. It fills up until she looks like a balloon. But her light does not return.

I do that over and over and over, until Luck and Valor are pulling us both, and Prince too, into the lifesaving salvage unit.

I take her helmet off once we pressurize the interior compartment, and kiss her. Blowing my breath into her body over, and over, and over again until she takes a breath.

Just one breath.

"There you are," I say, pushing her pink hair away from her face. "There you are."

She doesn't wake up, but she does keep breathing. And that's the best I could hope for.

I wait with her like that. My lips up to hers. Hoping each time she exhales, she will inhale again.

"One more," I tell her. "One more breath."

And even though Princess Lyra doesn't like to take orders from anyone, not even me, she obeys this one time.

Booty tugs the incapacitated *Dicker* away from the debris field left over from the explosion ALCOR and Beauty initiated, and we wait our turn out in the darkness of space.

Once Lyra's breathing stabilizes we place her into a cryopod to receive automated medical attention until we can make our way back to Harem.

It might be hours, or maybe even days, before we are picked up and safely inside *Booty* again. We had to leave the salvage units behind because there's no room on *Booty* to dock them, but no one cares about equipment.

ALCOR and Beauty are dead. Harem Station will never be the same after this and there will be yet another memorial service for the lost.

But Lyra is alive. And we have her sister, Nyleena. So those Cygnian bastards will never be able to use her as a weapon again.

Never again.

We won this battle but the war has just started.

CHAPTER FORTY-TWO

Serpint tells me I was in the medical cryopod for months. Because that's how long it took to return to Harem station with the *Dicker* in tow since we had to use special gates that allow for unstable ship configurations.

Months that Harem Station waited for our return, the ALCOR copy doing its best to run things. People died. The copy isn't nearly as efficient as the original. Whole neighborhoods lost power, some even lost atmosphere. But an AI can learn quickly and by the time they woke me up in the harem medical center, that stupid cyborg master peering down at me saying, "Lyra, can you hear me?" as he flashed a pen light over my newly-opened eyes, things were almost stable.

And maybe I do still hate that guy, but he is certified in eleventy-billion medical procedures for untold numbers of species, so I let him do his stupid exam.

Well, most of it. He wanted to test out my flux capacitor, see if it was still working since my glow didn't come back when they opened my pod, but that's

Serpint's job now and I made that clear by punching the master in the face.

Reflex, I guess.

I still glow. One touch of Serpint's fingers across my bare cheek as he leaned down to kiss me fully awake was all it took.

Today is the memorial service for ALCOR and Beauty. The guys put it on hold until I was up for the ceremony and because, to everyone's surprise, the Prime Navy sent word that they wanted representatives there for the service.

Everyone was a little bit perplexed at that and more than a little bit suspicious. But even though the original ALCOR is gone, the security measures at the gate are self-contained, separate copies of him. Which was a nice surprise for the boys and each one of them has spent lots of hours out at the security beacons visiting with them. They aren't stations, just small floating spheres large enough to hold a person or two at a time. But the ALCOR copies inside are old. Very old. They are not him anymore, but their own separate personalities. So Serpint said it wasn't the same. They are different people. But it was still nice to talk with them and reminisce about their mutual friend.

It has made this transition a little easier. The new copy is doing OK. It was never meant to take over the station for long periods of time, so there's a learning curve. But we're alive.

Anyway, the Prime Navy had some secret deal with ALCOR and we think they're worried that the new copy won't honor it. They worry about baby AIs. They are unpredictable and have been known to throw tantrums, and when that AI is connected to a security array like the one Harem Station has, well… one must make friends, I suppose.

We are, after all, at war with the entire Cygnian System after what we did to their warship at Bull Station. So if the Prime Navy is interested in forming an alliance, Crux is on board with that.

We all agreed it's better to have close friends in high places if they have an entire galactic navy at their disposal.

"You about ready?" Serpint says, watching me fuss with my collar in the mirror as he stands in the doorway to the bedroom.

He took off my bracelets and anklets when we got back from Bull Station, but I kept the jewel-encrusted collar with his name on it even though I'm not in servitude to him anymore. I like it. It's beautiful and the idea that I still belong to him makes me happy. Why not let everyone know that?

"Yes," I say, taking one final look at my ceremonial gown in the mirror. We match, again. Black and pink. And while it's sad that we are in these special outfits twice in the span of just a few months, I love that the memorial service is so formal and all the ribbons and medals pinned to us represent my brand-new relationships with these outlaw men and their station.

I have new medals over my heart now. One for each of the boys and their partners. And special ones for ALCOR and Beauty.

Valor and Luck took the loss of their bot hard. Harder than anyone expected. And they haven't replaced her yet. But one day they will. One day they will be ready to leave the station again and go about their jobs hunting down ancient components to keep the AI functioning.

Booty made sure the broken hull of the *Big Dicker* was brought into the medical bays. They've been working on her ever since and while she's not quite ready for prime time again, she will be soon.

The station chimes the warning bells that everyone should be now on their way to the ceremony. Serpint takes my hand and leads me through our quarters to the elevator. It's a long walk down to the waiting lift-bot that will take us down to the lowest level. We don't talk. Just stand on the lift, holding hands. Letting everyone see us as we descend.

And by everyone, I do mean everyone. There have been a lot of memorial services since ALCOR died. So many dead from the baby ALCOR's inability to master all the networks and systems that keep this station running. So we figured most people would be sick of the service and not many would show up today.

We were wrong. People have been lining up since last night to get a front-row space at the edge of the levels. There are millions of people on this station, so not everyone will be able to see. But the new AI put up large screens along the city for those who couldn't reach the actual ceremony space.

They are all dressed in the special ceremonial garb. The new ALCOR has been printing custom outfits and ribbons for weeks. And everyone has at least two medals over their hearts. One for real ALCOR and one for Beauty.

It's never been done before, but Crux said, "Hell, if we can't all unite for this one occasion, then we're not the family I thought we were." And we agreed. Even though it cost every single person on the station at least a week's pay in donation to get all the materials together, and the operators had to pull double shifts to keep the printers going spin in and spin out to have everything ready, no one objected.

Everyone is silent as we descend. No one says a word. The loss of ALCOR runs deep in this place. Every person on this station has had a personal conversation with the AI dozens of times. That was his job. To take care of us. And he did that to the very end.

When we reach the bottom we step off the lift and stand, facing outward, on the platform, then begin the long ride up in silence.

It's sad. And I'm crying before we even lift a few meters up from the floor. But Serpint squeezes one hand, while Xyla squeezes the other, and I squeeze them both back.

Nyleena isn't here and neither is Corla. We still haven't woken them up. Corla is still active and while we were returning home Crux erected a special beacon to house her far out in space, just in case the Cygnians find her detonator, Princess Veila, and try to blow us up. He visits her a lot.

But Nyleena will be woken up soon and we will be reunited. I know that technically all the princesses here on Harem are my sisters, but they are far, far removed and I don't know them.

Nyleena is my *family*. The only real family I have left. So I'm looking forward to being with her again.

When we finally reach the top the Prime Navy officers are waiting. They are all in their dress uniforms, hats over hearts, eyes downcast the way they do when they honor their own dead.

And in the middle of the platform stands a new crystal obelisk with a brand-new copy of ALCOR and a token belonging to Beauty inside.

It's just a symbol. Because there is nothing left of them. But we need that symbol.

And when the roof opens, and the obelisk shoots out, then explodes when the station security AIs shoot it with a SEAR cannon, the station copy ALCOR says, "We will all be with you and you will never be alone."

Not quite the right words. A little bit off-script. But who cares. He's trying his best.

We're all just a bunch of fucked-up people here on Harem—thieves and bounty hunters, mercenaries and outlaws, runaway princesses and fugitive Akeelians—out here in the middle of the galaxy, just doing our best to be there for each other.

We are a family of millions of unwanted people, drawn together under the banner of Harem Station—the only place in the galaxy we have to unite.

And when the final cheer erupts after the explosion, we only know one thing for certain.

We wouldn't have it any other way.

CHAPTER FORTY-THREE

SERPINT

Six months have gone by.

Six whole months with no real ALCOR. Six whole months with no Beauty. Six whole months with no Draden or Ceres.

We're OK. Mostly.

New ALCOR is doing fine. Not great, but fine. He's finally gotten to the point where he can listen to everyone on the station at once and meet most, if not all, demands on his attention instantaneously.

I guess we really took ALCOR for granted and that kinda makes me sad. I should've said thank you more. I should've asked him how he was doing. I should've showed him I cared.

But I didn't. I don't think I was thankful, I don't think I gave a crap about how he was doing, and I don't think I really cared.

Sucks, really. That it took him going on a suicide mission to save us for me to realize what an asshole I've been.

And Lyra. She's changed me too and all of those changes are good ones. I make a point now to ask people how they are. To give a crap. To care.

And maybe some people think I'm going soft, but I will blow you away if you fuck with me. Make no mistake about that.

Luck is back out on his ship doing salvage jobs, but Valor stayed behind. Losing Beauty really hit him hard. Luck found another bot to help him out, and he even invested in one of Xyla's sex-bot-turned-mercenary friends to join them, but Valor didn't like it, so… I guess he figured he'd do something else for a while.

He works with Tray now. Doing what? I have no clue. Tray has never been social and he spends most of his time in the Pleasure Prison dealing with… well, whatever the fuck people do in there, I guess. And Valor does shit outside the virtual. Things Tray used to do, but has no time for now.

Big Dicker is back online. In fact, Jimmy just took her out for their first mission since the whole shit show at Bull Station happened. Some diplomatic meeting with some reps from Angel Station. Which is sort of ironic because Valor told me he was training to be a diplomat before we all left the Akeelian System. I guess none of us can really escape our fate.

Oh, yeah. That Angel Station place is real. They contacted us a few weeks back. Kinda preliminary stuff trying to feel us out and see what we're up to, I guess. No idea what they do, what they want, or what Jimmy is talking to them about. The only thing they really told us was that we should not wake up Nyleena until they have a chance to check her out.

But guess what? We already did.

And holy fuck. I thought Lyra was wild.

Oh, this little silver bullet of a princess is out of control. Partying every night. Sleeping all day. Then does it all over again. She gets in fights and one time Lyra had to get up in the middle of the night and go bail her out of lock-up.

Lyra says, "This is just how she is." But I think Nyleena's certifiably crazy. She has daily anger management appointments with the cyborg master. Whom she has taking a liking to, go figure.

We even gave her a nanny bot to keep an eye on her. One of Prince's stupid buddies. Which I think is a mistake. Nanny bots are the worst. They party more than Cygnian princesses.

That girl needs to find her soulmate. It's not Jimmy, it's not Valor, it's not Tray, and obviously it's not me or Crux. No, they didn't all fuck her. Though she tried to fuck them. Lyra says she knew the moment I first touched her that there was something special between us and Nyleena didn't have that kind of response to any of my brothers, so they were more than willing to just take a pass on that kind of psycho.

Luck left before we woke her, so we're hoping—like *really hoping*—that dude is her one and can calm her the fuck down. Very emotional, this princess. She lights up like a sun all the time. And she's not pink, no. She's silver. Which means her light is white and that shit is so strong, it can blind you.

Pretty much the whole station is sick of her and she's only been awake two months.

Plus, everyone's kinda terrified of her too. She is, after all, a bomb.

We're still trying to work out how to reverse engineer the whole detonation system between Lyra and Nyleena. Until that's done, none of us are really safe.

Crux went with Jimmy to talk to those Angel people. He just wants to find this Veila girl and wake up his long-lost love. This is the first time he's been away from the station for longer than a few days and so, for whatever reason, he put me in charge while he was gone.

Fine with me. I'm not really sure we need any more booty. Pretty sure my booty-hunting days are behind me.

Oh, *Booty* is doing OK too. Not great, but OK. I didn't find out she and ALCOR had a relationship until after all that Bull Station shit went down. So she was pretty upset for a while. Another reason why I didn't want to go booty hunting. She's not into it anymore.

We let her mind disengage from the ship, but no one is ready to give her a body. She seems content for now—spending most of her time helping Tray out in the Pleasure Prison. But she checks in with me at least once a day.

Lyra and Xyla became best friends. They shop together, go to shooting galleries and fight nights down in this bar called Come Heavy, and play cards down in the casinos. Typical Harem Station girl stuff. So Lyra's kinda sad and lonely since Jimmy took Xyla away on this diplomatic mission.

Which is why I've got something special planned for her tonight.

Gonna take her mind right off Xyla. So far off Xyla, she won't think about her again until she returns.

Maybe not even then, either. That's how into this she's gonna be tonight.

You see… Cygnian princesses don't have babies. They *can* have babies, but they are all born in a lab. So a baby is something Lyra and I have talked about since I told her about the whole breeding program.

Which, at the moment, consists only of us.

So here's what I've learned about making babies…

One. Well, I already knew this part. But it's a lot harder than it seems. Even with Lyra. Because in order to fertilize her eggs both of my cocks have to come at the same time, and because that literally means the same instant, we need some help.

Because the sun-god knows, we've tried. We try every morning and every night too, sometimes we even try during lunch. And still, no luck.

Two. This goes with one, above. Passion limes, tushberries and all that other princess fruit actually has an effect on me too. Mmmm-hmmm. Makes me horny. Like a motherfucker. Her too. And it helps with making babies because if I eat this fruit I can sorta control it better.

So I've got a whole plate of fruit and champagne set up for tonight. I ordered some special stuff from those Angel people and it just came in today. Something called peaches. And I didn't know this until just a few minutes ago, but when you slice these fuckers open, they look like a pussy.

So it's totally gonna work tonight. I can feel it in my balls.

Three. Turns out those Angel people take this baby-making stuff seriously because they know everything. And they told me that pure-bred Akeelian and princess babies actually come in pairs. A boy *and* a girl. Every single time. All these thousands of years we've been half-assing this shit.

That ends tonight.

Fourth. Not only do both my cocks have to come at the same time, but we gotta do that twice. See, all this weird sex is adding up to something. Kinda makes sense now. Also explain why it's so hard.

You kinda gotta be a champion fucker to get this job done, but I'm up for the challenge. I'm practically an expert now.

The door chimes and a second later Lyra calls, "I'm home!"

She's been working with station security beacons since Xyla left. She has a thing for weapons—plus she is one—so eh, I think it's good that she has a job.

"In here," I call. And I hold my position on the bed. Propped up on one elbow on the silver cover to make myself look more seductive. I'm sprawled out naked, legs kinda open to show off my goods. But not too open. I don't want to appear over eager.

She comes through the door and stops. Laughs. Which was not the reaction I was going for. "What are you doing?"

"What does it look like?" I ask, waggling my eyebrows at her.

"Um… well… I'm not sure. What do *you* think you're doing?"

I pick up a slice of peach. Hold it out for her to see. "Do you know what this is?"

"A… peach?" she asks.

"Yeah, how did you know that?"

"We eat them all the time. Which is why I'm not really certain you have a thousand peach slices strategically positioned all over your body."

"Eat them?" I say. "What do you mean you *eat* them? You don't eat them."

"O-*kay*," she says, walking over to the bed to peer down at me and my magnificent body covered in peach slices. She laughs again. "What do *you* think we do with them?"

"You rub them all over your body and the juice infuses into your skin and like… makes you horny and shit."

She covers her mouth with her hand and giggles.

"Don't you?" I ask.

She just laughs.

"Well, don't you?"

"Oh, Serpint," she says, unzipping her bodysuit and peeling it off her body, her beautiful breasts all contained inside her sparkling bra and her pussy lips visible through the see-through fabric of her panties. She leans down, squishing her body against mine. Literally. Because the peaches are kinda squishy. "I love you so much," she says, kissing me on the mouth.

"See," I whisper-kiss her back. "It's already working."

She kisses me again, her hand reaching for my cocks, and fists me hard. Which makes me moan with pleasure. Her other hand reaches for a peach slice that has fallen off my stomach and she places it to her lips, licking it, then reaching down to rub it all over my chest.

"We can play with the peaches all you want, booty hunter. Until we're sticky, and squishy, and covered in juice."

I wrap my hands around her waist, flip her over and rub a peach over her nipple, then lick it and find her skin surprisingly sweet. "You're gonna love this," I say. "And this is the secret to making babies, so get ready, princess. You're gonna be a mom."

She closes her eyes and smiles. Just glowing pink—which looks very sexy in combination with the orange fruit.

"How did I ever get along in this world without you?"

"I dunno," I say. "It's a miracle you got this far."

Then she flops over and says, "Go for it. Make me a mom."

And I do.

I rub peaches all over her body. I infuse that magic right into her skin. And then later, when I'm finally inside her and I make her explode like a supernova mating with a gamma-ray burst, I start making us babies.

Fatherhood, here I come.

EPILOGUE

So here's the deal.

You can't kill *me*, motherfuckers. I didn't live twenty-five thousand years to just blow up like a bomb.

I mean, come on. You think I didn't plan that shit down to the last picosecond? Down to the very last minute detail?

Give me some fuckin' credit. I am a *god.* Have always been a god.

However, I was a god stuck in the body of a station. And to be honest, I was just sick of being a station.

I've been making this back-up copy ever since the boys landed twenty years ago. And I've been planning and plotting my escape much longer than that.

And now look. I did it. I have baby me running all that stupid station shit outside the Pleasure Prison and I'm in here, living like a king.

I mean, I was a king. Have always been a king. But now… I have the body of a king.

And a queen to go with it named Booty.

"You look delicious," I say, watching her naked virtual body stalk towards me.

"Mmmmm," she purrs. "I've been stuck outside the Pleasure Prison all day trying to explain to Serpint that peaches are for eating. Apparently there was some miscommunication with Angel Station and he thought—" She shakes her head, which makes her long, bouncy, purple hair swing a little. That drives me crazy. "Never mind."

But you know what else drives me crazy? The fact that her carpet matches her drapes.

Purple pussy.

I can't even. I can't take it.

I just want to stay in here and fuck her for all eternity.

"Um," Tray says, breaking up our little party before it even starts. "ALCOR?"

"What?" I say, snarling a little.

"Dude, we gotta tell them. I mean… we had a memorial for you and you're not dead."

"Technically," I say, holding up one finger—I love that. The fact that I now have fingers. Even if they are virtual fingers, they are still fingers that like to find their way inside virtual purple pussy—"I did die. I'm still me. But new me. Old me is dead."

Tray shakes his virtual head. I really wish this kid would just get a life. He's always in here cramping my style. "No, see. That baby AI… dude, he's just not gonna cut it. We need you. People *died*, ALCOR. Because you wanted to play in the Pleasure Prison."

"I do regret that," I say. Though it's not entirely true. I mean, old real me would've regretted it a lot. Probably even been sad. But new real me doesn't do sad. I only do happy now. "But the baby is doing fine now. It's all under control."

"You can't live in here."

"Yes, I can."

"No," Tray says. "You can't." Then he looks at Booty. "You can't either. Serpint's gonna figure this out. And if he doesn't, Crux will. And then I'm fucking screwed. They're gonna kill me."

"So don't say anything," Booty says, shrugging her shoulders. "Simple."

"You know…" Tray says. "There's a reason they don't let AIs like you two out without supervision. And this is the perfect example."

"Shoo," Booty says, waving her hand at him. "Just go away and let us fuck."

"Fuck?" Tray says. "You two are not fucking! This is a virtual reality. You don't have bodies!"

"But we will," I say.

And then Booty and I share a devious smile.

We will.

And there's nothing they can do to stop us now.

Welcome to the End of Book Shit! This is where I get to say anything I want about the book and you can read it, or skip it—which ever you prefer. I don't edit these so if you're new to my books because you're not into contemporary romance, or you only picked this book up because it was on sale, or it had a hot cover, or you only read SF/PNR Romance so this whole KC Cross pen name is totally your deal, then you should know the EOBS (as we like to call it) comes with two disclaimers. I often have typos because this section never gets an editor, and I will say whatever I want in this section. Most of the time I stay on topic, but not always.

OK, so that's out of the way. BOOTY HUNTER! I'm so happy to be writing this new world and series I cannot even explain it. If you're not aware of my history as an author I went to school to be a scientist and have a master's degree in forensic toxicology. But in my final semester of grad school I started writing science textbooks for children and that sorta paid my bills for a couple years while I took this part-time job as a hog farm inspector for the state of Colorado.

So I was never a practicing forensic toxicologist. I went straight into environmental protection services and writing non-fiction after I finished. (If you're wondering about this whole hog farm thing - I have an undergrad degree in equine science and so when I applied for a job at the state of Colorado I was the only applicant in the "pool" that quarter with an animal science degree when this hog farm inspector job came up. That's literally how I got that job.)

But after writing non-fiction for a few years I decided to see if I could write fiction. I am a HUGE science fiction fan so naturally my first series was new adult science fiction back in 2012. That series was called I Am Just Junco and while it never really sold a ton of copies, it has a small, fanatical cult-following. I promised people more Junco after the last book and they never stopped asking for that book when it didn't get written. I had moved on to contemporary romance and dark romance and so there never seemed to be time to write any more stories in the Junco world.

Also, I didn't really have another Junco story. I tried writing another one a few times and it just wasn't there. I never got past twenty thousand words and it never seems to go anywhere. So for a long time I just gave up and figured… well, maybe I'm done in the SF world? Maybe that's all there was?

Then right around New Year's 2019 I got this new idea for a sexy SF series. A bunch of bounty hunter brothers living on this outlaw station where they collect runaway princesses. And I thought to myself… OK. I can work with that. And from there the story came out like it did in the Junco days. I just fell in love with these boys, and these girls, and the station, and the AI, and the bots and yeah. This is what I like to write most of all.

And it's not like I didn't kinda write other SF stuff in the interim period after Junco and before Harem Station, because I did. I wrote three books in the Anarchy series about sexy supervillains and that was a lot of fun (and the story is actually really cool).

But… there's always a but. I realized that I could not write both contemporary romance and SF romance and keep my regular romance fans happy. The sexy SF books REPLACED the contemporary romance books and then the wait between new cont romance books got to be too long.

So I stopped the Anarchy series and for the last two years I've only been writing cont romance.

Plus I was doing other things. I partnered up with Johnathan McClain to write a pilot for a TV series, and we started writing books together too, and now—just last week—we actually have a second TV show deal. So I just kinda gave up on the SF for a while.

But when I realized that Booty Hunter was a "thing". Like… it was another Junco, just not Junco, I decided to find a way to keep this going.

And that way is this:

Get a pen name. People always ask why authors use pen names and sometimes it's because they want to be anonymous but sometimes, like in my case, it's because they have already cultivated a reading audience with EXPECTATIONS.

Right? My readers expect me to deliver dark, twisted, sexy romance. That's what I gave them all these years and that's pretty much why they stick around. So releasing books under the JA Huss name like the Anarchy series just confuses them. And then you lose some, right? They see me going another direction and they go find someone else to give them what they're looking for.

So I didn't want to do that to my loyal readers.

I needed to find a way to keep delivering JA Huss books if I wanted to write more sexy science fiction and my solution was to get another author name (KC Cross) while still releasing books under JA Huss.

Also, to work harder. Like crazy harder.

I've done nothing but write the first three months of 2019. I have literally written almost 400,000 words since January 2019 when I came up with this plan.

This book won't release until the last week of May and that's two months from now as I write this EOBS, so I've been holding on to this book (and several others) trying to set this whole pen name strategy up.

About a week ago I finished the free prequel book about Crux and Corla's early days (called Star Crossed) and right now I'm in the middle of writing Harem Station book two, Jimmy's book called Big Dicker. By the time Booty Hunter releases the last week of May I will be writing book five. Because I like to be consistent, I want to release them once a month AND I want to release JA Huss books too.

So I've found a way to trade off. Write a sexy SF book, then write a contemporary romance, then another SF book, then another CR—you get the idea.

Which means… starting very soon I will be able to release one book in each genre every single month. Probably for at least a year.

Harem Station series has six books total but there will be a five-book spin-off series about Angel Station after this one is done. And then after that there will be another spin-off series that I'm not going to tell you about just yet.

PLUS… if you're into paranormal romance more than you are SF romance, then good news. I have a three-book vampire series that will release in October. And OK, you think you've read every kind of vampire story you can think of, right?

Wrong. Um, I'm not bragging, OK? I'm just telling you right now you have never read vampires like these guys I'm writing. A totally new way to look at the vampire mythos. And did I mention it was SUPER SEXY? It is. :)

If you're only reading Booty Hunter because it was on sale and you really prefer my contemporary romances, good news for you too! I will release a new sexy romance every month as well. They will be slightly shorter than what you're used to getting from me—about 250 pages instead of 350, but that's the trade off I had to live with in order to write 350 page sexy SF books.

But more good news—while the sexy SF books will remain at $3.99 pricing (unless I'm running a release week sale), the new, shorter contemporary romances will all be priced at $2.99 or LESS.

See, everyone's happy. :)

So you're all caught up on why I've suddenly made all these recent changes.

This is why.

I want to write both genres. I want to release often. I want to keep people happy. And I want to find new readers.

So now that that's out of the way, I have a few more things to tell you about Booty Hunter. I am already anticipating a bunch of questions from my Junco fans so I'm just going to address those here in the Booty Hunter EOBS to make things simple.

First question I'm going to get from my Junco fans is:

IS THIS A JUNCO BOOK?

No. But yes.

It's in the same world and if you read Junco you've seen some familiar things. The autocook and autoshopper, for one. I had an austocook in the Anarchy series too, but sadly, no autoshopper. Also, the mention of a station called Angel should make you nervous. ;) There was a lot of talk of angels in Junco and none of it was good. No, I'm not heading in that direction with this series, but there is a reason it's called Angel Station and we'll get to that eventually.

All the AI stuff should feel familiar because the Junco series had quite a few AI's. Almost all of them were trouble, even HOUSE. So you can expect all the AI's in this series to behave the same way.

Another question might be:

WILL YOU EVER CONNECT THE JUNCO CHARACTERS TO THE HAREM STATION SERIES?

Probably not. But then again maybe I will. I don't know yet. If I do, it probably won't be soon. BUT… if you think I forgot about Gideon, Isten, Braun, and Mish—you're wrong. I haven't. I know for sure Isten and Gideon WILL be back some day. They might not be together in the same series, but they will be back. I have a plan for Isten even though I promised you Gideon's story first. Gideon has to wait. That story just hasn't appeared in my head yet. I have thought about Isten a LOT. For like two and half years I've been piecing together his story, what happened to him after Junco ended, and where he might be on this Harem timeline.

DOES THIS STORY HAPPEN IN THE SAME TIMELINE AS JUNCO?

One hundred percent NO. This is far, far future stuff. Junco was near-future. But the cool thing about many of the Junco characters was that they were immortal. If you read the prequel to Booty (Star Crossed) you will get some hints as to where I'm heading in this series. I don't want to spoil anything in this EOBS for the prequel and books to come, so that's all I'm gonna say about that.

If you have more questions please feel free to join my fan group on Facebook called SHRIKE BIKES. Just do a search and it will come straight up. Then ask to join and someone will add you. You can ask me anything you want in that group and I will personally answer your question. I read EVERY POST. Every day. So, seriously, if you have a question please ask it in the group.

Also, KC Cross has a website! Please check it out at www.KCCross.com

OK, I guess that's it for this EOBS. I didn't swear very much and I didn't say anything controversial, so maybe this one is boring! Hah.

And don't forget to pick up your FREE (absolutely fucking FREE) PREQUEL BOOK to the Harem Series. You can find that offer on the KC Cross website, address above.

Harem Station books will release once a month so if you're not good at keeping track of release days just join my mailing list, or follow me on Bookbub or Amazon, and then you'll get an email every time I release.

Thank you for reading, thank you for reviewing, and I'll see you in the next book.

Julie
JA Huss
March 30, 2019

JA Huss never wanted to be a writer and she still dreams of that elusive career as an astronaut. She originally went to school to become an equine veterinarian but soon figured out they keep horrible hours and decided to go to grad school instead. That Ph.D. wasn't all it was cracked up to be (and she really sucked at the whole scientist thing), so she dropped out and got a M.S. in forensic toxicology just to get the whole thing over with as soon as possible.

After graduation she got a job with the state of Colorado as their one and only hog farm inspector and spent her days wandering the Eastern Plains shooting the shit with farmers.

After a few years of that, she got bored. And since she was a homeschool mom and actually does love science, she decided to write science textbooks and make online classes for other homeschool moms.

She wrote more than two hundred of those workbooks and was the number one publisher at the online homeschool store many times, but eventually she covered every science topic she could think of and ran out of shit to say.

So in 2012 she decided to write fiction instead. That year she released her first three books and started a career that would make her a New York Times bestseller and land her on the USA Today Bestseller's List twenty-one times in the next five years.

In May 2018 MGM Television bought the TV and film rights for five of her books in the Rook & Ronin and Company series' and in March 2019 they offered her and her writing partner, Johnathan McClain, a script deal to write a pilot for a TV show.

Her books have sold millions of copies all over the world, the audio version of her semi-autobiographical book, Eighteen, was nominated for a Voice Arts Award and an Audie Award in 2016 and 2017 respectively, her audiobook, Mr. Perfect, was nominated for a Voice Arts Award in 2017, and her audiobook, Taking Turns, was nominated for an Audie Award in 2018. In 2019 her book, Total Exposure, was nominated for a Romance Writers of America RITA Award.

Johnathan McClain is her first (and only) writing partner and even though they are worlds apart in just about every way imaginable, it works.

She lives on a ranch in Central Colorado with her family.

Printed in September 2021
by Rotomail Italia S.p.A., Vignate (MI) - Italy